MADMAN MAULING

Edmunds raged, "I am goin' to grind your bones to dust and spit on the remains!"

A fist filled Fargo's vision, but he evaded it and delivered a solid uppercut. Edmunds tried to grapple. Skipping out of reach, Fargo circled, determined to bring Edmunds down no matter what it took.

Keltoon and Frank yelled for Edmunds to stop fighting but they might as well have asked a rabid wolf to stop its mad attacks. Edmunds was beyond the point of listening to reason.

Suddenly the giant prospector swept a boot at Fargo's legs, seeking to sweep them out from under him. Springing up, Fargo thwarted him. But while Fargo was still in midair, iron fingers clamped onto his throat and others onto his belt, and the next instant he was raised over Edmunds' head.

Edmunds tensed to dash him to the ground.

"Now you get yours!"

A GIANT
TRAILSMAN
ADVENTURE

ISLAND
DEVILS

by

Jon Sharpe

A SIGNET BOOK

SIGNET
Published by New American Library, a division of
Penguin Group (USA) Inc., 375 Hudson Street,
New York, New York 10014, USA
Penguin Group (Canada), 10 Alcorn Avenue, Toronto,
Ontario M4V 3B2, Canada (a division of Pearson Penguin Canada Inc.)
Penguin Books Ltd., 80 Strand, London WC2R 0RL, England
Penguin Ireland, 25 St. Stephen's Green, Dublin 2,
Ireland (a division of Penguin Books Ltd.)
Penguin Group (Australia), 250 Camberwell Road, Camberwell, Victoria 3124,
Australia (a division of Pearson Australia Group Pty. Ltd.)
Penguin Books India Pvt. Ltd., 11 Community Centre, Panchsheel Park,
New Delhi - 110 017, India
Penguin Group (NZ), Cnr Airborne and Rosedale Roads, Albany,
Auckland 1310, New Zealand (a division of Pearson New Zealand Ltd.)
Penguin Books (South Africa) (Pty.) Ltd., 24 Sturdee Avenue,
Rosebank, Johannesburg 2196, South Africa

Penguin Books Ltd., Registered Offices:
80 Strand, London WC2R 0RL, England

First published by Signet, an imprint of New American Library,
a division of Penguin Group (USA) Inc.

First Printing, February 2005
10 9 8 7 6 5 4 3 2

The Trailsman

Beginnings . . . they bend the tree and they mark
the man. Skye Fargo was born when he was eigh-
teen. Terror was his midwife, vengeance his first
cry. Killing spawned Skye Fargo, ruthless, cold-
blooded murder. Out of the acrid smoke of gun-
powder still hanging in the air, he rose, cried out
a promise never forgotten.

The Trailsman they began to call him all across
the West: searcher, scout, hunter, the man who
could see where others only looked, his skills for
hire but not his soul, the man who lived each
day to the fullest, yet trailed each tomorrow.
Skye Fargo, the Trailsman, and the seeker who
could take the wildness of a land and the wanting
of a woman and make them his own.

1861, the deep woods of the Pacific Northwest—
where death lurked in many forms
to snare the unwary.

Prologue

Henri LeBeau felt uneasy. He could not say why. Maybe it was the unnatural quiet, or the uncommon chill in the morning air, or the slate gray sky that hung low over the ocean.

For days LeBeau had been making his solitary way north along the Canadian coast. At the moment he was wending his canoe through a cluster of islands half a mile from shore. In his previous travels he had never ventured this far, never set eyes on these particular islands. Nor, he imagined, had any other white man. Civilization's last outpost lay many leagues behind him.

A small island drew LeBeau's attention. Overgrown with vegetation, it was just like every other except for a flock of gulls raising a racket over something that lay half out of the water. Squawking and flapping their wings, they pecked one another in a frenzy.

There were so many birds, LeBeau could not see what they were fighting over. He assumed it was a dead seal or possibly a large fish like a sturgeon. Carcasses often washed up on the beach and became a feast for scavengers. Then several gulls took wing. One had something in its beak and the other two were trying to wrest its prize away. They flew directly over him. Glancing up, he saw the morsel fall. It landed in his canoe with a light *thup*.

Bending, LeBeau felt an icy chill sweep through him. He stopped paddling and gaped, thinking he must be mistaken. But no, it was a human finger, pale and pasty and partially stripped of flesh. Stringy strips hung from the fingernail.

LeBeau's stomach churned. He had come across far worse in his travels and was not squeamish by nature, but this took him by surprise.

One of the gulls swooped down to snatch the finger, but he drove the bird off with a jab of his paddle.

His interest piqued, LeBeau made for the small island. At his approach thirty or more gulls took wing. The rest were so intent on feeding, they did not realize he was there until he was among them, striking right and left and bellowing like an angry moose.

The gulls rose in a raucous cloud but did not go far. Hovering beyond his reach, their wings beating the air in staccato rhythm, they registered their displeasure in loud, harsh cries.

A human form lay face down on a rock out-cropping, the arms out-flung, the legs bobbing with the swell. Surprise piled on surprise. Not only was the dead person white, it was a *woman*. A woman as naked as the day she was born.

"Mon Dieu!" LeBeau breathed.

A mop of wet blond hair fell in chaotic disarray below her shoulders. Her back, buttocks and legs were a welter of peck marks. She had a slim waist and long legs, and in life must have been quite pretty.

Old cravings stirred. LeBeau recalled the last time he had been with a woman, nearly five months ago, recalled the soft feel of her skin and her mouth on his, and he frowned to think that it would be four or five more months before he enjoyed another intimate moment.

Carefully maneuvering the canoe near enough to climb out, LeBeau pulled the bow out of the water. His paddle in hand, he squatted and rolled the body over. A gasp escaped him, and he recoiled and almost slipped. Bracing the paddle against the outcropping, he crossed himself.

The woman's eyes had been gouged out. Not by the gulls or some other creature, but by a sharp implement wielded by a human hand. The same human hand had carved strange symbols into the woman's face and chest, symbols unlike any LeBeau had ever beheld. Deep curls and swirls and looping lines, the overall effect like that of a nest of writhing snakes. The woman's nipples were gone, sliced off as cleanly and neatly as if done by a surgeon.

LeBeau sought to make sense of his find. Whoever she was, she could not have wandered to that remote region alone. Yet how had she gotten there? he wondered. Was she with others? If so, where were they?

Then there were the markings and the mutilation. LeBeau had roved the waterways of western Canada for decades. The many islands and inlets were home to scores of tribes. Some were peaceful; some were as unfriendly as the unrelenting land that spawned them. He knew of a dozen instances where whites had been slain. But he had never heard of anything like *this*. It was hideous.

A thought struck LeBeau, and he rose. The woman had not been dead long. Not more than twelve hours. Since the body lay on the west side of the island, it meant she had drifted *in* with the tide, not out, which, in turn, meant she had been killed farther out to sea.

Squinting into the haze, LeBeau saw a much larger island half a mile away, almost due west. To the northwest, barely visible, was another. But when LeBeau took the time and tides into account, the first island was the likeliest.

LeBeau had a decision to make. Should he investigate? Or go on his way and report the woman's death when he returned to Victoria? Common sense warned him to avoid the other island as if it were a leper colony, and yet part of him was keenly desirous of having a closer look.

For the moment, LeBeau put the matter aside. Sliding his hands under the woman's arms, he dragged her a dozen yards inland. It was as far as he could penetrate without using his ax, so dense was the growth. The ground was soft enough that with the aid of a broken branch he soon had dug a shallow grave. Gently lowering the woman in, he folded her arms across her chest then covered her. He recited the Lord's Prayer, one of the few he knew by rote, and added a layer of branches and weeds to discourage scavengers.

"It is the best I can do," LeBeau said to the mound. Once back in his canoe, he pushed off and paddled north. But he had only gone a short distance when he stopped and shifted and stared at the large island to the west with an intensity born of burning curiosity.

"I am a fool," LeBeau addressed the air, and applying his paddle, he turned toward the island.

The paddle cleaved the water in smooth, powerful strokes. LeBeau sat straight, his bearded jaw jutting in grim determination. If there were hostiles in the area, he should find out before they found him. He intended to hunt and trap in that vicinity, and he did not want to end up like the poor woman he had just buried.

The sky grew dark with the threat of rain, transforming the sea into a dusky mirror. LeBeau could no more penetrate its depths than he could the verdant wall of vegetation on the island. He looked down at his Sharps rifle, then at the Beaumont-Adams revolver on his right hip and the Bowie knife on his left. He was not a violent man, but he would kill to defend himself, and had, on more than one occasion.

The gulls had dispersed and the peculiar oppressive silence once again reigned. Nary a ripple disturbed the dark surface except for those created by the bow of his canoe and the splash of his paddle.

At moments like these LeBeau almost wished he had a partner. But it would never work out. He was a solitary by nature. He liked to be alone. Human companionship was not a necessity but a luxury, in which he indulged only three or four times a year. The rest of the time he wandered the vast wilderness that stretched from Vancouver Island to Alaska, sometimes by canoe, sometimes on foot.

For all its loneliness, LeBeau lived a grand life. He had seen sights few men ever witnessed: the verdant mountains on a misty morn; pods of killer whales knifing the Pacific Ocean in graceful precision; great gray whales in their annual migrations, spouting geysers; seals rising out of the waves to stare at him in bemused wonder; and so much more.

LeBeau had seen bull elk in rut clash with a ringing clack of their antlers and grizzlies take salmon with a flick of their massive paws; he'd watched as a pack of ravenous wolves brought down a lame moose. To him, the rich tapestry of life was a heady tonic, as intoxicating in its way as hard liquor, and he could never get enough.

Now, continuing to work his paddle expertly, LeBeau drew near enough to the large island to note how the exceptionally thick undergrowth was mired in perpetual shadow by towering trees. From end to end the island had to be three quarters of a mile long, yet nowhere was there a hint of a break in the vegetation. No smoke rose above the treetops, no evidence of human habitation marked the shore.

LeBeau wondered if he was mistaken. Maybe the woman's body had drifted from somewhere else, perhaps the island to the northwest. He was about to veer in that direction when a sharp cry caused the short hairs at the nape of his neck to prickle. It came from the depths of the island. A savage shriek more bestial than human, a shriek that rose to a fierce pitch and then abruptly died. He had never heard anything like it. No animal of his acquaintance ever uttered so hideous a sound, no mountain lion or wolf or bear. With baited breath he waited for the cry to be repeated, and when it wasn't, he warily paddled to within a hundred yards of the overgrown shore and slowed.

Many of the islands were oases of wildlife. Deer, squirrels and birds were plentiful. Predators were less so, but he had come across cougar, lynx and even bear tracks on islands over a mile from the mainland. How they got there was anyone's guess. A friend was of the opinion that the predators swam to them, although why they would do such a thing when there was plenty of game on the mainland was a mystery.

A narrow gap broke the shoreline. LeBeau did not deem it worth investigating until a hint of blue stood out against the backdrop of green and gray. Changing direction yet again, he paddled to within sixty feet before he recognized it for what it was: the mouth of a wide stream.

On one side the vegetation grew down to the water's edge; on the other was a flat, bare strip where a canoe could be beached.

Loosening the Beaumont-Adams in its holster, Le-Beau made for the strip. He had bought the revolver from a British officer at the fort and considered it money extremely well spent. Manufactured in England by the London Armoury Company, it held five shots, and while not in the same man-stopping class as his Sharps, it had saved his life more than once.

The crunch of the bow sliding onto solid ground was glaringly loud. His hand on the revolver, LeBeau hopped out and hauled the canoe a few feet, then hunkered to tilt his head and listen. Not so much as the chirp of a songbird reached his ears. Not a single leaf fluttered in the breeze. The island seemed as dead as the woman who had lost her life somewhere in its somber fastness.

He spied tracks and furrows in the dirt, leading from the trees to the water. He examined the tracks and received yet another shock. Although they were human in shape, they were much too flat and much too broad, and *the soles were covered with scales.*

"This cannot be," LeBeau whispered aloud. Yet he could not deny the evidence before his eyes. He followed the tracks into the trees and came on a well-defined trail. Sinking onto his left knee, he studied it. Tracks were abundant. Some were big and some were small, but they all had one trait in common: They all had scales. He started to take the trail.

"What am I doing?" LeBeau asked aloud. Whoever, or *whatever*, lived on that island, it was plain they were not partial to whites.

Wheeling, LeBeau retraced his steps. He would do as he had originally planned and report the woman's death to the government.

With the Sharps in the crook of an elbow, LeBeau strode into the open. He saw the bare strip of earth and the blue of the stream. He saw the vegetation on the other side and the ocean beyond. But one thing he did not see. The one thing that meant the difference between life and death, the one thing he could not do without, was missing.

"My canoe!" LeBeau dashed to where he had left it.

Fresh tracks—tracks with scales—told the story. Two of the island's inhabitants had crept out of the underbrush and pushed the canoe into the stream. Since they were nowhere on the ocean, they had taken the canoe inland.

Impulsively, LeBeau ran along the bank after them. He went a short way, then stopped cold. In the wild a man could not afford to be reckless. Those who lived the longest were those who kept a tight rein on their emotions.

It was bad enough, LeBeau reflected, that he had blundered so badly. Bad enough he was stranded afoot on an island crawling with God-knew-what. They might be watching him at that very moment, watching and waiting to pounce when his guard was down.

Whirling, LeBeau darted into the undergrowth and hunkered. He did not see anyone after him. Staying low, he stealthily paralleled the stream. He had to find the canoe. Without it, he stood no chance of escaping.

LeBeau broke out in a cold sweat. Nervously fingering the Sharps, he probed every shadow, every thicket. When a twig snapped with startling clarity, he spun toward the sound, primed to fire at anything that moved. But nothing did. Not a bush, not a branch, not a leaf.

LeBeau's mouth had gone dry. Licking his lips, he swallowed—or tried to. He kept the stream always in sight, eager for a glimpse of his salvation.

Another piercing cry shattered the still air, a cry identical to the one LeBeau had heard earlier. Only this cry came from directly ahead, and so close, he swore he could reach out and touch whatever made it.

LeBeau almost broke and ran for the shore. The conviction that they were waiting to catch him off-guard steadied his frayed nerves. Whoever they were, they wanted him alive. If not, they could easily have slain him by now. And why would they want him alive? The answer was horrifically plain. So they could do to him as they had done to that woman. He must not succumb to panic, or he would pay the ultimate price.

Unexpectedly, God granted LeBeau a miracle. He spotted his canoe drawn up on the bank. It had been abandoned. Elated, he began to run toward it, then drew up, suddenly wary. It made no sense for them to leave it there like that unless it was bait. Cheese for a mouse, and he was the mouse.

But what choice did he have? LeBeau reflected. He had to get off the island and the canoe was the only way. Girding himself, he cocked the Sharps. In a mad burst of speed, he crashed through the intervening brush. He reached the canoe and pushed it into the water. Hopping in, he snatched up the paddle and was raising his arms for the first stroke when the stream spouted skyward, spewing monstrosities.

For a second LeBeau was paralyzed with fear. Then, grabbing the Sharps, he tried to get off a shot but the rifle was swatted from his hands.

Another instant and they were on him, and all Henri LeBeau could do was scream and scream and scream.

1

Skye Fargo was fit to explode. But he did not let on as he stared at the cards in his hand, then at the weasel of a dealer who had just dealt from the bottom of the deck. Instead, he took a swig from the whiskey bottle at his elbow, wiped his mouth with a buckskin sleeve and waited for the betting to start.

Fargo was in a new mining camp called Elkhorn. Situated high in the Rockies west of Denver, it was named after the creek in which gold had been found. From where he sat, at a table at the back of a large tent that served as a saloon, Fargo could hear a thousand and one typical sounds: the babble of voices, the neighing of horses, the creak and rattle of wagons, the peal of a hammer on metal. He had stopped at Elkhorn the evening before to rest the Ovaro, and sat in on a poker game. Now here it was pushing six in the morning, and the eight players had been whittled down to three.

"I raise," said the man on Fargo's left, a portly character in a store-bought suit and an ill-fitting bowler, whose sleeves fell almost to his knuckles.

"Of course you do," Fargo said, smiling. He watched from under his hat brim and wasn't the least surprised when the portly player slid a card under one sleeve and replaced it with a card from up the other one. As he had suspected, the dealer and the porker were working together. Too bad for them.

"I'll call," the dealer said in that high, squeaky voice of his. He had an oily mustache and oily hair that spilled from under his hat. Glancing expectantly at Fargo, he said, "How about you, mister?"

Fargo made a show of studying his chips. "How about if we drop the limit and bet as much as we'd like?"

"I don't know," the dealer said. "It's against house rules. But I can ask for you." He gestured toward the bar, a long board placed on a row of barrels, and the owner of the saloon came over.

"Is there a problem, gentlemen?" Aces Malone considered himself a flashy dresser. He wore a cheap suit as if it were the most expensive money could buy, and kept his shoes polished to a sheen.

"This guy wants to raise the limit," the dealer said, with a jab of his thumb at Fargo. "I told him it's against the rules."

"That it is, Eddy. That it is," Aces said with an air of smug self-importance. "And with good reason. I run an honest establishment. I don't want any hard feelings from my customers."

"There won't be any," Fargo assured him.

Aces sniffed and said, "That's what they all say, mister. But if they lose, they squawk to high heaven, and when that doesn't work, they cuss and yell and go for their hardware. Which is the last mistake they ever make."

Fargo saw one of the three hired oxen at the bar grin in vicious anticipation, but he pretended not to notice. "I'd take it as a favor."

"I don't know," Aces hedged, playing his part. He scratched his chin as if undecided.

Eddy piped in. "Do as the guy wants, boss. He seems decent enough to me. I doubt he'll cause trouble."

"How about you, Mr. Stedman?" Aces addressed the portly player. "Are you agreeable to my suspending the house limit?"

"By all means, please do," Stedman said. "I happen to have a good hand myself, the best I've had all night."

Aces squared his skinny shoulders. "Very well. But be advised I'm doing this against my better judgment. I don't want either of you to hold it against me if the house wins."

"I won't," Stedman assured him.

Fargo merely smiled while shifting slightly so he could draw his Colt when the time came.

"Resume playing," Aces directed Eddy.

"How many cards do you want?"

"I'll play these," Fargo said, and was amused by the puzzled expressions that came over Eddy and Stedman. But then, the cards were marked, and they knew he had three queens. They expected him to discard the other two cards and try for a full house or four of a kind.

Stedman took one card; Eddy helped himself to four, with two of them skinned from the bottom.

Amateurs, Fargo thought. Rank, stupid amateurs. It was an insult. He had played at many of the finest gambling dens West of the Mississippi River with some of the best gamblers alive. Men so skilled they did not need to cheat—or at least were smart enough not to try when they might be caught.

"So how much are you in for?" Eddy asked.

"All of it." Fargo pushed his stack to the middle. Since he had the most, he had the most to lose. Or so they thought.

Stedman smoothed one of his overlong sleeves. "A man after my own heart. I, too, will put all I have at stake." He added his chips to the pile.

The corners of Eddy's mouth were twitching. "Fine by me, gents." He added his chips and sat back, his whole body twitching now, barely able to contain himself. "Four kings," he announced, and slapped down his cards out of turn.

"I'm sorry," Stedman said. "Take a gander at these." He laid down four aces and started to reach for the pile.

"Not so fast," Fargo said. "That's not quite good enough."

Aces Malone, Eddy and Stedman all visibly tensed, and Eddy growled, "What are you talking about? How can you beat four aces?"

"With five sixes." Fargo drew the Colt and placed it in front of him. Flicking his cards down, he began raking in his winnings.

"Hold on there, mister," Aces said. "This is exactly why I was reluctant to raise the limit. Leave those chips right where they are or there will be hell to pay."

"Unleash your dogs," Fargo said.

Eddy was twitching worse than ever and squirming in his chair as if he had red ants up his pants. "You can't do this. It's stealing."

"The same could be said of dealing from the bottom of the deck," Fargo told him. "Or from up a sleeve." He pointed the Colt at Stedman. "Unbutton them and show me the rigs."

Stedman glanced at Aces, who looked as if he had just sat on a pitchfork, then blustered, "I have no idea what you are referring to."

"Sure you do," Fargo said, and cocked the Colt.

"Let's not be hasty," Eddy said, placing his hands flat on the table. "You're making a big mistake, friend."

"Indeed you are," Aces declared. "I'm willing to forgive and forget if you holster your hardware and leave. If not, don't hold me responsible for the consequences." His head bobbed ever so slightly, and the three oxen at the bar spread out and slowly came toward the corner.

"I'm waiting," Fargo said.

Stedman gulped, then unbuttoned his right sleeve and slid it high enough to expose the thin metal device strapped to his forearm. For most tinhorns one was enough, but he had a second rig up his other sleeve.

Aces Malone acted shocked. "Why, Mr. Stedman, this is an outrage! If we had a lawman in Elkhorn I would bring you up on charges. As it is, I'll have you run out on a rail."

"No, you won't," Fargo said. He had all the chips in front of him. From under his hat brim he marked the three snakes gliding toward him. They had their fists balled. He twirled the Colt into his holster but did not take his hand off the butt.

"I'm not sure I follow," Aces Malone said.

"Sure you do. Stedman works for you. He's your decoy, to make players think the game is on the level."

"How dare you!" Malone huffed. "I'll have you know I have a reputation for honesty in all my dealings."

"You should go into politics," Fargo said. "Hand over my winnings, and no one will be hurt."

"The gall," Aces spat, and stepped back. "I don't know who you think you are, but you're about to learn I am not someone to be trifled with. The last fool who did that is pushing up daises across the creek."

"So you're a killer as well as a swindler?" Fargo only had a few more seconds in which to do something. The three bruisers were only a few yards away. They showed no inclination to go for their hardware, which was just as well. He would rather not kill them if he did not need to.

Eddy and Stedman glanced at one another and both started to slide their hands toward the edge of the table. Fargo beat them at their own ruse. Heaving up out of his chair, he upended the table and kicked it, sending it crashing into them. Stedman and Eddy went down, Eddy squawking like an angry chicken, as the other three converged.

Spinning, Fargo met the first ox head-on. A fist the size of a ham streaked at his face, but he ducked and pivoted and planted his boot where it would do the most good. The man collapsed with his big hands pressed protectively to his groin and his tongue jutting from his mouth.

Eddy and Stedman were trying to shove the table aside so they could crawl out from under. Fargo kicked it to keep them pinned as another of Malone's hired toughs rushed him, seeking to enfold him in a bear hug. Nimbly dodging, Fargo landed a solid upper-cut to the jaw that reeled the ox on his boot heels. A cross to the cheek, and the man was down.

Again Eddy and Stedman tried to get the table off

their legs. Again Fargo kicked it. By then the third thug was on him. Iron fingers closed on his left wrist and he was spun around. A fist flashed at his mouth. Sidestepping, Fargo flicked several tight jabs. He connected with a jaw. An eyebrow spurted scarlet.

The ox howled. Blinking to clear the blood from his eyes, he never saw the looping blow that felled him.

Aces Malone's mouth was opening and closing like a fish out of water. Finding his voice, he bawled, "Get him, damn it!" and fumbled under his jacket.

Fargo seized hold of the chair he had been sitting in and hurled it with all his considerable strength. It struck Malone with the impact of a runaway buckboard and slammed him against the wall. A derringer fell from fingers gone numb.

Stedman's legs were still pinned, but Eddy had made it to his knees. From under his vest he produced a dagger, which he wagged as he crouched to spring.

In a blur Fargo drew the Colt, thumbing back the hammer as it cleared leather. With the muzzle mere inches from Eddy's forehead, he asked, "Do you really want to use that?"

Eddy blanched and shriveled and dropped the dagger as if it were a red-hot coal. "Hey, it's just a job. Malone ain't worth dying for."

"I heard that." Aces Malone was untangling himself from the chair. A nasty gash on his temple dripped large red drops. "You don't have a job anymore. You're fired."

Eddy flushed with resentment. "Why take it out on me? I'm not the one who just stomped you and your boys."

"Fired," Malone repeated. He gained his footing

and leaned against the wall, holding his left forearm with his right hand. He snarled at Fargo, "I think a bone is busted, you bastard."

"You got off easy." Covering them, Fargo backed to the bar. "Where do you keep the cash box?" He had seen Malone put money in it earlier.

"I don't have one," Malone hissed.

"Yes, he does," Eddy piped up. "The third barrel has a false bottom. Push with your toe and a drawer slides out."

"Damn you to hell," Aces Malone said.

"I'll teach you to fire me!" Eddy spat back.

Fargo had to tap the barrel with his boot several times before he succeeded. Ingeniously designed, the drawer was ideal for hiding Malone's ill-gotten gains. No one would think to look in an old barrel. He set the money box on the counter, opened the lid and counted out his winnings. No one attempted to stop him. The fight had gone out of them, except for the fiery spite in Malone's beady eyes.

"I'll find you, mister. I'll see that you pay. You won't live to brag about this. No one gets the better of me, ever."

"Do you see me trembling?" It had been Fargo's experience that those who threatened the loudest were those who never carried out their threats. He crammed his winnings into a pocket and slowly backed toward the tent flap. No sense in tempting them with his back.

"Wait," Eddy said. "Now that I'm out of work, how about if you and me partner up?"

Fargo wondered if he had heard correctly. "What?"

"Sure. We'd be great together. With my brains and your quickness, we could be rich. I'm slick as can be with the cards, and you're slick as can be with your fists and that Colt. What could be more natural?"

"I might as well slit my own throat," Fargo said.

The oxen were still sprawled on the ground, one groaning and rolling back and forth. Stedman had his hands in the air. Malone was staring at the derringer as if he desperately yearned to make a stab for it.

"What if I give my word never to lift a finger against you?" Eddy asked. "I might not look like much, but once I promise, I own up."

"No."

"We could go to Denver. New Orleans. Even New York City. I'll play, you watch my back. Imagine. In a year we'll have more money than either of us will know what to do with."

Fargo would as soon partner up with a rattler. "I'm not interested." He bumped into an empty table and skirted it. Only three other people were in the tent: an old man nursing a drink and two men who had been rolling dice all night. They wisely held their hands in plain view. He was only a few yards from the opening when he saw Aces Malone grin, which seemed strange until a hard object gouged the nape of his neck and he heard the distinct *click* of a gun hammer being thumbed back.

"Hold it right there."

2

Skye Fargo figured the man behind him must be in Aces Malone's employ. He instantly froze. But he was set to whirl and snap off a shot, trusting his life to his reflexes, when the revolver gouging his neck was removed.

"What is going on here?"

Expecting another muscular brute, Fargo glanced over his shoulder. Instead, he beheld a U.S. Army officer in full uniform; a captain, by his insignia, although he looked too young to have earned the rank. "Since when does the army butt its nose into a saloon fight?" he asked.

"I'm on official business," the captain declared. He had short sandy hair and big ears. "I was told that the person I've been searching for is here." His brown eyes narrowed. "You certainly fit the description I was given. Would you happen to be a gentleman by the name of Skye Fargo?"

"And if I am?" Fargo could not think of any reason for the army to be looking for him. He sometimes scouted for them, but at the moment he was enjoying some much deserved time to himself.

"Then I am extremely pleased to meet you," the captain said. He had the stamp of West Point about him: in his ramrod bearing, his new uniform, his formal manner. "General Foster sends his compliments and—" Suddenly he took a short step to the left. "I wouldn't, if I were you, sir."

Aces Malone was reaching for the derringer.

Fargo walked over and scooped it up. "Some people just never learn." He dropped it in a pitcher of ale on the bar.

"If it takes the rest of my natural life, I'll find you and kill you, so help me God," Malone vowed.

"Sure you will." Fargo was anxious to hear what the officer had to say, but just then Eddy came toward him. "What do you think you're doing?"

"I want you to hear me out about being partners. A chance like this doesn't come along every day."

"No means no."

The captain was waiting. Shoulder to shoulder they backed out, their pistols trained on the flap. Malone cursed a mean streak, but no one came after them.

"Now then," Fargo said when they had gone far enough that he deemed it safe to holster his Colt, "you mentioned something about a general called Foster. Suppose you tell me what this is all about?"

"Gladly." The officer patted his stomach. "But can we do it over breakfast? I was in the saddle all night and I'm famished."

"I could do with a bite myself," Fargo conceded. "Follow me."

Around the next bend in the creek was a large tent. Attached to a pair of poles out front was a crudely painted sign that read ELKHORN EATS. CHEAP AND HOT. The long tables were packed with early risers eager to eat and get to their claims for another day of hard toil.

A bench near the kitchen area had space for two.

21

Fargo sat with his back to the wall so he could watch the entrance.

A stout matron in a white apron whisked over and set two tin cups in front of them. "We have eggs and ham or eggs and bacon, or if you have money to burn, eggs with a side of beef."

"I was hoping for pancakes," the officer said.

"We have eggs and ham or eggs and bacon or eggs with a side of beef," the waitress parroted. "Toast is extra."

They ordered. Fargo pushed his hat back on his head, then leaned on his elbows. "I haven't caught your name."

"I forgot? Sorry." The officer had removed his gauntlets and was swatting dust from his shirt. "Captain Edgar Pendrake, at your service."

"Where are you stationed?" Fargo asked as they shook hands. The nearest posts were Fort Laramie and Fort Wise, both hundreds of miles to the east.

"Washington, D.C.," Captain Pendrake revealed, "as a special adjutant to General Foster."

There was that name again. Fargo was puzzled. "They sent you all this way to find me?"

Pendrake placed his gauntlets on the table. "You have served the army well in the past, Mr. Fargo. I've seen your file. Every officer you have ever worked with has gone on record as stating that you are an exceptional scout and extremely reliable. High praise, indeed."

"The army keeps a file on me?"

"On everyone and everything of military significance, yes," Captain Pendrake confirmed. "You might be surprised at how detailed yours is. For instance, it establishes that you are, without a doubt, one of the best trackers alive." His lips quirked upward. "It also makes mention of your fondness for cards, whiskey and the fairer sex, and not necessarily in that order."

"A whole file?" To Fargo, it did not sit well. Sure, he scouted for the army, but on a job-by-job basis. Part of the reason he did not sign on full-time was his need to keep his personal life private and to be free to do as he wanted, when he wanted, without hindrance.

"Routine paperwork, nothing more," Captain Pendrake said, smoothing his sleeves. "Now then, shall we get down to business?"

Just then the waitress returned with a pot of steaming coffee. She filled their cups, asked if they wanted cream and sugar and bustled off.

"General Foster heads his own department," Pendrake explained. "He handles situations that require more care and delicacy than usual, and is answerable only to the President."

"Care and delicacy?" Fargo repeated. He didn't like the sound of that.

"It merely means there are certain matters the President deems best to keep from the public. Matters of national interest, if you will. But all that is neither here nor there. What concerns us at the moment is the assignment General Foster has given us."

"Not so fast," Fargo said. "I haven't agreed to anything." And he wouldn't until he knew a lot more.

"Understood." Pendrake noticed a spot of dust on a shirt button and wiped it off. "When was the last time you were in Seattle?"

"It's been a while. I'm familiar with the area, though."

"Then you must also be aware of the difficulties with the local Indians. A few years ago an uprising occurred, and the situation hasn't improved much since, despite the presence of our troops."

Not much of a presence, as Fargo recollected. During the height of the bloodshed, the settlers were forced to erect their own fortifications until the army got around to converting a blockhouse into Fort Bellingham. But as soon as hostilities ceased, the army abandoned it. The garrison hadn't been gone a month when bloodshed flared anew, so the army set up a new post, Fort Townsend, on the west side of Port Townsend Bay.

"The coastal region is a powder keg," Pendrake was relating. "Several tribes have made no secret of their hatred and want to drive every last white out. They could do it, too, if they banded together, but they hate one another as much as they hate us. All it would take is for a leader to rise up able to unite them in a common purpose, and they could sweep the territory clean of whites clear down to the Columbia River."

"That's not likely to happen," Fargo commented. It was a story as old as the mountains. The Sioux against the Shoshones, the Cheyenne against the Comanches, the Apaches against the Pimas, the Blackfeet against nearly everyone. Indian warfare was a way of life long before the coming of the white man.

Captain Pendrake started to say something, then changed his mind and sipped his coffee. "Our government is doing all in its power to avoid inciting the Indians more than they already have been. Washington sent an envoy to offer peace terms and the message was relayed to the tribes causing the most trouble. Why they resist us, I will never know."

Fargo understood why. Slowly but inevitably Indians everywhere were seeing their land taken away under peace treaty terms that always favored the white man.

"For several months now, things have been fairly quiet," Pendrake related. "An uneasy truce is in effect. But it wouldn't take much to ignite the flames of violence all over again."

"You're taking the long way around the barn," Fargo pointed out.

"I need to impress on you the gravity of the situation," Captain Pendrake said. "Thousands of lives are at stake on both sides. We would like to defuse the situation entirely, but now it has taken a turn for the worse instead of the better."

"How so?"

The waitress arrived, delaying things. She set down their plates, heaped with eggs and beef, and gave each of them a fork and a knife. "If there's anything else you gents want, give a holler."

"They certainly give you your money's worth." Pendrake poked at the meat. "Rather overdone, though, don't you think?"

"Next time ask for it raw," Fargo said, forking eggs into his mouth with relish. He was content to wait until they were finished eating to hear the rest of what the good captain had to say, but Pendrake liked to chatter.

"Where was I? Oh, yes. A turn for the worse. You see, it seems people have been disappearing. Fourteen in the past year alone. General Foster would like to get to the bottom of it before the unfriendly tribes use it as an excuse to start an all-out war."

"They were killed by hostiles," Fargo guessed. "What's so mysterious about that?" In the deserts and mountains of the arid Southwest, whites disappeared without a trace all the time. It was the price they paid for daring to live in Apache country.

Slicing off a small piece of beef, the officer sniffed it. "Definitely overdone. The edges are burnt, too." He took a bite and slowly chewed. "I'm rather finicky about how I like my food."

"Do tell." Fargo dipped his toast into egg yolk and crammed the whole thing in his mouth.

"You probably think it silly of me," Pendrake said. "But we are all creatures of habit, are we not? I happen to like my food a certain way."

Fargo would rather hear about the people who had gone missing, and said so.

"It's impossible to say with any certainty who is to blame. They all vanished without a trace, and none of the coast tribes has claimed credit."

"The Apaches don't take credit for all those they kill, either," Fargo pointed out.

"True. But when a prospector disappears in Chiricahua Apache country, we can safely assume the Chiricahuas were to blame. Or when an army patrol fails to come out of the White Mountain range, it's a good bet the White Mountain Apaches had something to do with it." Pendrake swallowed, and grimaced. "In this case we simply have no idea. But we would very much like to find out."

"That's where I come in." Fargo stated the obvious.

"Precisely. General Foster wants us to get to the bottom of the mystery as quickly as possible. The settlers are understandably upset, and it wouldn't take much to incite open bloodshed." Pendrake set down his fork. "If we leave at first light and take extra mounts, we can be in Seattle by the end of the month. From there, we'll let the evidence be our guide."

"What's this 'we' stuff?" Fargo preferred to work alone. Especially in the wild, where most whites were out of their element.

"General Foster wants me to go along," Captain Pendrake informed him. "This is a delicate matter and must be handled with the utmost discretion. Those were his very words."

"And he doesn't think I can handle it?" Fargo resented the veiled insult.

"No insult is intended," Pendrake said. "Were it up to me, I would gladly return to Washington. But the settlers have been complaining that the government doesn't do enough on their behalf. I will be living proof that the army is committed to protecting them."

One officer, in Fargo's estimation, wasn't much of a commitment, but he contented himself with saying, "The coast country is rugged as hell. Tracking the culprits will be hard enough without having a greenhorn along."

"I beg your pardon?" Pendrake sat up straight. "I'll have you know that although I was raised in Baltimore, I can hold my own with anyone, anywhere."

Fargo had heard that claim before from well-meaning fools who thought city life could compare to life in the wilds. In a city, all it took for a person to survive was money: money to buy food and clothes, and for a roof over one's head. In the wild, food was on the hoof or on the wing, and a missed shot was the difference between a full belly and slow starvation. Instead of a roof there was the sky, a temperamental mistress who unleashed thunderstorms and frigid blasts without warning.

"How about it?" Captain Pendrake asked. "By all accounts you're the best man for the job. General Foster would take it as a great favor, and your country will be forever in your debt."

"Forever," Fargo had learned long ago, only lasted until the next crisis reared its unwelcome head. Still, there were an awful lot of lives at stake. "I'll agree on one condition."

"Name it."

"I'm in charge."

Pendrake blinked, and coughed, and swallowed some coffee. "General Foster made it clear I should be in command."

"Give me one good reason."

"I'm a commissioned officer, and this is a military operation. Even if it is just the two of us."

"A hungry griz doesn't give a damn about your rank," Fargo said. "In the wilds the only thing that counts is a man's wilderness savvy. I'm in charge or I don't go."

"I must say, you're being rather inflexible," Captain Pendrake objected. He met Fargo's gaze, then fidgeted and looked away. "Very well. Since you leave me no choice, and since this situation is of the utmost gravity, I agree. But I'm doing it under duress, and will mention as much in my report."

"We'll ride out at dawn, then." Fargo hoped to heaven he wasn't making a mistake. They were about to venture into some of the least explored territory on the continent, and there was no guarantee either of them would make it out alive.

3

An hour out of Elkhorn they came to the crest of a high ridge and Skye Fargo drew rein and twisted in the saddle. About a mile back were three riders.

"Trouble, you think?" Captain Pendrake asked, swatting at dust on his sleeve. He was a stickler for keeping his uniform immaculate.

"Too soon to tell," Fargo said. The trail they were following, which linked Elkhorn to the Oregon Trail many miles to the northwest, saw frequent use. The three riders might be bound for the Pacific or any point in between.

Late summer was the driest part of the year in the Rockies. The grass was brown, the trees parched. Even at that altitude, the temperature climbed to near one hundred degrees. A few sparrows flitted amid the pines, and to the south several doe watched them pass. By midday every living creature would be holed up, waiting out the worst of the heat.

Fargo did not have that luxury. In order to reach Seattle quickly, they couldn't squander an hour of daylight. Captain Pendrake had bought two extra horses, a sorrel and a chestnut, and they would switch mounts every few hours so their horses were always fresh.

A flick of Fargo's spurs sent the Ovaro down the

far side of the ridge. His lake-blue eyes roved the timber for any sign of Indians or the humped silhouette of a grizzly.

Pendrake breathed deep of the rarefied air and exclaimed, "Ah! This is the life. I can see why you like it so much. The natural man in his natural element, eh?"

"My natural element is a saloon."

The young officer chuckled. "That was a good one. But I'm serious. You're a frontiersman. You spend most of your time in the wilds. As Professor Dunston would say, you are man at his most primal."

Fargo had no idea what the hell he was talking about. "Who?"

"Professor Xavier Dunston, from Harvard. He's written a book on primitives. Comparing the natives of Africa, the aborigines of Australia, and the Indians of South and Central America and our own country to civilized societies."

"We're no different than they are," Fargo said. Whites who looked down their noses at Indians always rankled him.

"That's not what I'm saying. The professor thinks primitive people exist in a more natural state than we do, and I agree." Pendrake paused. "Anthropology is a pet interest of mine. At one time I thought about becoming an anthropologist, but couldn't see sitting behind a desk most of my life. So I chose the army instead. This way, I'll get to see primitive cultures in the flesh, as it were."

"Aren't you a bundle of surprises."

"I know, I know. It must seem strange. But I've always believed a military man should have more interests than just the military. A colonel I know is quite a scholar on the old Romans. General Foster likes to attend plays, and can quote whole scenes from memory."

"Tell me something. Exactly how many of these primitive cultures have you had any dealings with?"

"This is my first time in the field. I was sent to Washington straight out of the academy. My father is a congressman, you see, and his influence has done wonders to advance my career."

Fargo silently swore. He had assumed Pendrake was more experienced. "You know an awful lot about Apaches for someone who has never been west of the Mississippi River."

"From reports and newspaper accounts, yes," Pendrake said. "I'm a voracious reader. There's nothing I enjoy more than to curl up with a stimulating book and a cup of hot mint tea. It's one of life's supreme delights."

The man was serious, Fargo realized. "How does your wife feel about you gallivanting off to Washington Territory?"

"I'm not married," Pendrake said harshly. "And I would appreciate it if you don't bring up the subject ever again." He swatted at a fly. "How about you?"

"I'm too fond of my freedom to step into a female's noose."

"You say that now but eventually you'll give in. Every man does sooner or later. It's a law of nature."

Fargo changed the subject. "Do you have any idea what you're in store for? This is no church social. People are dying, and whoever is killing them won't think twice about killing us."

"There's no proof the missing people were murdered," Pendrake said. "It's entirely possible they are still alive and being held against their will. Some coast tribes take captives as slaves, I understand."

"Word would leak out," Fargo said. It always did. Someone would tell an acquaintance from a different tribe and that person would tell a trader and the trader would let the army know.

"Maybe, maybe not. I simply refuse to jump to conclusions until I've sifted all the evidence."

Fargo waited a full minute before asking his next question. "Have you ever killed anyone, Captain?"

"I don't see how that is pertinent. I'm a soldier. Killing is my profession. If the need arises, I will do what is required, never fear."

"That's a no, I take it?"

"So?" Pendrake retorted. "Oh, I get what you're implying. That I'm a liability. That if we encounter hostiles I won't be of any use. But I'm no coward, Mr. Fargo. Just because I've never had to shoot anyone in the performance of my duties doesn't mean I can't."

"I hope so, for your sake. I don't want to have to bury you." Fargo had buried too many over the years.

"How considerate. But just wait. I will prove to be equal to every occasion, and then some. General Foster has complete confidence in me, and before we're done, you will, too."

Fargo had doubts but he did not voice them. Confidence was one thing, overconfidence another. Pendrake struck him as a peacock better off pushing pencils than daring the dark heart of the unknown.

Above them the sun slowly climbed to its zenith. High atop a switchback, Fargo reined up. "We'll rest the horses for a spell." Dismounting, he arched his back to relieve a kink, then stepped to where he had a sweeping vista of the country below. He did not see the three riders, but he could not see much of the trail, either. Most of it was lost amid the trees or hidden by outcroppings. He was about to turn when movement half a mile away drew his gaze to three distinct silhouettes.

"They're closer," Captain Pendrake said. He walked to his mount and opened a saddlebag. "Close enough that this should come in handy." He held out a shiny new telescope.

Magnified a dozen times, the riders were as clear as clear could be. "Damn!" Fargo angrily declared.

"Do you recognize them?"

"It's the three men I tangled with at Malone's," Fargo said, handing the spyglass back.

Pendrake took it and observed them a bit, then asked, "Could it be a coincidence? Maybe we shouldn't jump to conclusions."

"Seen any flying buffalo lately?"

"What?" Pendrake lowered the telescope. "Oh, I get it. That's your way of telling me I'm being ridiculous. Very well. Since you insist on being in charge, how do you propose to handle the situation?"

Fargo patted his Colt. "By doing whatever it takes. We can't have them sneaking up on us in the middle of the night, so we deal with them here and now."

"Hold on. You're not suggesting we waylay them? I can't permit that. They are civilians, and it is my responsibility to protect them."

"They're after my hide," Fargo said, "and I don't aim to hand it to them. Whether or not any killing is done is on their shoulders."

"I have your word?"

Fargo stared at Pendrake until the captain shifted his weight from one foot to the other.

"I apologize. That was uncalled for. It says in your file that you are a man of your word. Every officer who has ever worked with you has praised your performance. Your only failings are your fondness for cards and the fairer sex."

"I sure would like to see this file someday," Fargo said. Taking hold of the Ovaro's reins and the sorrel's lead rope, he led them in among a stand of firs and tied them so they wouldn't stray. Then, shucking his .44-caliber Henry rifle from its saddle scabbard, he descended the trail to a boulder the size of a stagecoach and stood in the shadow at its base, waiting.

Pebbles rattled, and Captain Pendrake joined him, carrying his own rifle. "I must confess I'm a bit nervous. Have you ever done this sort of thing before?"

"Only when I've had to." Fargo fed a cartridge into the Henry's chamber. Able to hold fifteen rounds, it had a brass receiver and a tubular magazine under the barrel. It wasn't as powerful as a Sharps or some of the other big-bore rifles used for big game, but it could drop a man with a single shot.

"How can you stand there so calmly?" Pendrake whispered. "I have butterflies in my stomach."

"Let me do the talking and don't show yourself unless I say to," Fargo instructed him.

"I'm not a child; I would appreciate it if you don't treat me as one." Pendrake leaned against the boulder, then caught himself and brushed a hand across his shirt.

Fargo was fixed on the trail. Below was a sharp bend. Malone's gunnies would be close enough to bean with a rock when he showed himself, and unable to reach cover without taking a slug.

Captain Pendrake quietly cleared his throat. "May I ask you a question?"

"So long as it's not personal." Fargo estimated they had five minutes yet before the trio appeared.

"How many people have *you* killed?"

"I don't keep count," Fargo answered. Down Texas way, carving notches into revolver butts was a habit, but he was never proud of taking a life. Sometimes it had to be done, and that was that.

"You must have some idea," Pendrake persisted. "Is it five? Ten? Twenty? A man never forgets something like that."

"I do." Fargo always shut it from his mind the instant it was over. As an old-timer once commented, a man's conscience couldn't gnaw at him if he didn't sharpen its fangs.

Pendrake would not let it drop. "How many were Indians?"

"What difference does that make?" Fargo hoped the officer wouldn't be like this the whole journey. His past was his own and not open to discussion. "Hush up. They'll be here soon."

In the pines a jay squawked. A pair of ravens flew past, their black wings beating the air in cadence. On top of a log on the other side of the trail a chipmunk appeared. It saw them, and sitting up, its tail erect, it chattered noisily.

"Won't that racket give us away?" Pendrake fretted.

Before Fargo could answer, hooves thudded dully down the slope. The chipmunk uttered a last *chirk* and bolted into the brush. Fargo pressed his back to

35

the boulder as the plodding hooves grew steadily louder. Suddenly the first of the riders rounded the bend. Slumped in the saddle, his face mirrored boredom. After him came the second and the third. The last one had his hat off and was running his hand through wispy red hair.

"I hate this, Treach. I hate the heat and I hate the bugs and most of all I hate ridin' until my ass is so sore I can't hardly sit."

"Bitch, bitch, bitch," the first rider said. "That's all you ever do, Henson."

"Can I help it if I like my creature comforts?" Henson responded. "I'd rather be back in Elkhorn nursin' a whiskey than traipsin' through these godforsaken mountains. Malone should have let it drop."

"So long as we're on his payroll, we do as Aces tells us. But if you want to go back, be my guest."

"The boss doesn't take kindly to quitters," the second rider commented. "Mad as he is, Henson, he's liable to take it out on you."

"I'm not scared of Malone," Henson said. But he sounded scared. Very scared, indeed.

Treach was only six yards from the boulder when Fargo strode to the middle of the trail and leveled the Henry. "This is as far are you go, boys."

Their astonishment was comical. Henson was the first to recover his wits, and excitedly blurted, "It's him!"

"Shut up, jackass," Treach hissed, then demanded of Fargo, "Are you tryin' to get yourself shot, poppin' out of nowhere like that?"

"Unbuckle your gun belts and let them drop," Fargo directed while sidling to the right so he had clear shots at all three.

"I'll be damned if we will," Treach said.

"You'll be dead if you don't."

The second rider was smarter than the other two. "What's this all about, mister? If you're fixin' to rob us, we don't have much money. Fact is, we're on our way to Salt Lake City to look for work."

"Sure you are," Fargo said. "The gun belts. Now. One at a time." He centered the Henry on Treach. "Starting with you."

Treach was fuming. His mouth twitched and his fingers twitched and he was poised to stab for a Remington high on his hip. But common sense prevailed, and he pried at his belt buckle. "We'll sic the law on you for this."

"Sure you will." Fargo was watching Treach's hands. Cornered coyotes often turned vicious, whether the coyotes were two-legged or four-legged, and he would not put it past them to slap leather.

Then Captain Pendrake dashed into the open, shouting, "Look out! That one is going for his gun!"

Fargo had figured it would be Treach or Henson but it was the gunman in the middle, and he already had his revolver out.

4

Skye Fargo twisted and fired. He did not take aim. He did not need to. At that range all he had to do was point and fire. The Henry boomed, the stock bucking his shoulder a fraction of an instant before the hired killer's gun belched smoke and lead. The gunman's slug bit into the earth between Fargo's legs; Fargo's slug slammed into the gunman's chest and smashed him head over heels from his saddle.

Both Treach and Henson went for their revolvers. Fargo shot Treach through the head, shifted and shot Henson in the chest. Treach toppled but Henson clung to his saddle horn and banged off an answering shot that clipped a whang on Fargo's buckskins. Fargo fired again.

Henson swayed as if drunk and howled like a stricken wolf, then tried to extend his arm but couldn't. His lips curled from his teeth in a feral snarl. "Damn you to hell, you bastard! You've killed me!" And with that he oozed to the ground and lay quivering a few moments before going limp.

Captain Pendrake gaped at the sprawled forms in disbelief. "You shot them! You shot all three of them!"

"It was them or us." Fargo nudged Henson with a boot, verifying he no longer posed a threat.

"But they're *dead*." Pendrake stood over Treach and stared at the grisly exit wound in the back of his skull. Bits of hair, bone and brain sprinkled the ground, and one eyeball lay in the dirt. "God Almighty." Pendrake put a hand to his stomach. "I feel sick."

"You might be in for more of this before we're through," Fargo said. "Are you sure you can handle it?"

Pendrake did not seem to hear. "It happened so fast. One minute they were alive, the next—" Turning away, he took a few unsteady steps while sucking in deep, ragged breath. "Sorry. My conduct is unbecoming for a military man, but I've never seen anyone shot before."

Fargo had lost count of the number of people he had seen take a bullet. Men, women, even children. Violent death was a daily part of life on the frontier. It was not a life for the squeamish. He began reloading.

"Please accept my apology," Pendrake said.

"Don't make more out of it than there is," Fargo responded. "The best thing is to stop thinking about it and get on with your life."

"Easier said than done. I'm afraid I'll have nightmares for weeks." Pendrake turned. He had composed himself, but his throat bobbed. "Where do you suggest we bury them?"

"We don't," Fargo said. "We'll drag them into the trees and leave them for whatever comes along."

"That's preposterous. We're civilized men, not barbarians. We must do the right thing."

"We'll lose time." Fargo stomped the ground, which was as hard as granite. Digging a hole big enough would take hours, time better spent on the move.

"But they deserve it," Pendrake insisted. "They were fellow human beings, after all."

"They hired out to hurt people," Fargo said in mild disgust. "They don't deserve a damn thing." Stooping, he gripped Treach by the wrist and dragged the body into the forest. "Grab one of the others."

Frowning, Pendrake hesitated, then gingerly grasped the second killer's arms. "I didn't envision this sort of thing when I accepted the assignment."

"You can go back to Washington if you want." Fargo hoped he would. "I can find out who is behind the disappearances on my own."

"General Foster would bust me to corporal," Pendrake said. "He says that good officers always see a job through until it's done; bad officers make excuses."

When they had all three lined up, Fargo went through their pockets. "Twenty-seven dollars and a few cents. How much do you want?"

Pendrake was flabbergasted. "Help ourselves to their money? I refuse to countenance robbery. We'll turn everything over to their next of kin."

"How will you find them? Malone isn't about to tell us." Fargo wagged the bills, but Pendrake shook his head. Shrugging, he pocketed them, then held up a pocket watch on a silver chain, a pair of dice and a bone-handled folding knife he had found in Henson's left boot. "Any interest in these?"

"What you are doing is reprehensible. I refuse to have any part in it.

Fargo carried the items to Treach's horse. He placed

them in Treach's saddlebags, turned the horse so it faced toward Elkhorn and smacked it on the rump. With a snort and a flick of its tail, the horse trotted east. One by one he did the same with the others, then reclaimed his Henry and hiked up the switchback.

"Why didn't you keep the horses and saddles, too? They must be worth hundreds of dollars."

Fargo stopped so suddenly, Pendrake nearly bumped into him. "We need to get a few things clear." Controlling his temper, he swept an arm to encompass the forested mountains and jagged peaks. "You're not in Washington, D.C. The rules and laws you are used to don't apply. Out here, it's kill or be killed, and the only one who gives a damn whether you make it through the day is you."

"Wait just a second—" Pendrake protested, but Fargo did not let him finish.

"No, *you* wait. We haven't been on the trail a day yet, and I regret having you along. You're supposed to be a soldier. Start acting like one, or I swear I will go on alone."

"You don't understand," Pendrake said.

"Like hell I don't. You're a city boy who never went hungry a day in his life. Your army career so far has been spent behind a desk, and you're tired of it. You wanted to get out in the field, so when General Foster said he needed someone, you talked him into sending you to find me." Fargo glanced over his shoulder. "How am I doing so far?"

"You think you're so smart," Pendrake replied sullenly.

Fargo did not mince words. "Ever heard the expression 'in over your head'? Because you're in over yours. Do us both a favor and go back to Washington. I'll send word to the general when it's done."

"Even if I wanted to, I couldn't," Pendrake said. "This affair is more complicated than you imagine."

"I'm listening." Fargo did not see anything complicated about hostiles killing whites. It went on all the time.

"It's near Canada, for one thing, and the general wants to avoid an international incident if we can."

"The tribe we're after might live north of the border?" Lines on a map meant nothing to Fargo. He would chase the culprits to the Arctic Circle if he had to.

"Anything is possible," Pendrake said. "So it's best I'm along to represent our nation's best interests."

"Are those the general's sentiments or yours?" Fargo would not put it past him to concoct an excuse to come along.

"Not only the general's but those of certain individuals at the highest levels of our government. President Buchanan personally asked General Foster to keep him apprised of our progress."

Fargo was supposed to be impressed but he wasn't. He had no interest in politics and the inner workings of government, and would just as soon round up every politician and ship them to Asia or Australia. "The President is involved?"

Pendrake nodded. "Yet another reason why you're stuck with me whether you like it or not."

For the rest of the day Fargo was in a testy mood. Toward sunset he selected a clearing bordered by a creek and made camp. After stripping the horses, he gave the coffeepot to Pendrake and went into the woods to gather wood for a fire. The acrid scent of smoke greeted him on his return.

Pendrake had collected a few limbs on his own and had the coffeepot on to boil. "I'm not completely useless," the officer said, almost as if he could read Fargo's thoughts.

Before leaving Elkhorn that morning, Pendrake had bought a plucked chicken from a man selling them in front of the general store. Given the scarcity of meat, they fetched a high price, but Pendrake forked it over anyway. "Our first night under the stars should be a pleasant one" was how he justified the expense.

From a haversack usually tied to his saddle, Pendrake removed a frying pan and a carving knife. He cut the chicken into strips, except for the drumsticks. Groping in the haversack, he removed a sack of flour and a wedge of butter. He made a batter and covered each strip of meat, front and back, then placed them in the frying pan. The haversack also held a sack of potatoes. He set two on flat rocks and set the rocks beside the fire. The next item to come out of the haversack was a loaf of bread. He cut two thick slices and buttered them. "This bread will last a week if we ration it, the potatoes a month or more."

Soon a tantalizing aroma filled the clearing. Fargo poured himself a cup of coffee and sat back against his saddle. "You missed your calling. You should be a cook."

"I always loved working in the kitchen when I was younger," Pendrake said. "It made my father mad, but he never complained about the food." From the haversack he drew a container of salt and a square tin.

"What *don't* you have in there?" Fargo quipped.

Pendrake misunderstood and shook the tin. "Herbs

43

and spices. I told you I was finicky about my food, remember?"

Finicky was an understatement. The young officer fried the strips until they were well done but not *too* well done, as he put it. He refused to touch his potato until he had smothered it in butter. And he liked his bread toasted so the crust was crunchy.

"How does it taste?" he eagerly asked when Fargo bit into the chicken. "Did I add too much salt?"

"It's fine," Fargo said. More than fine: The food was delicious. Tastier fare than the rabbit and squirrel stew to which he was accustomed. "Maybe you will be of some use, after all." To lesson the sting, he grinned.

After they were done, Pendrake volunteered to clean the tin plates and the frying pan, and went off to the stream. Fargo laced his fingers behind his head and closed his eyes. The meal had made him drowsy. Ordinarily he did not turn in until close to midnight, but tonight he might make an exception.

Then footfalls pattered, and Pendrake came running up with the utensils clasped to his chest. "I heard something!" he exclaimed.

"Oh?" Fargo cracked his eyelids. The Ovaro and the other horses were grazing and showed no alarm.

"Off in the trees," Pendrake said. "An animal of some kind."

Fargo had not heard anything. But night was when the predators were abroad. Mountain lions prowled for deer and mountain sheep. Grizzlies and black bears roamed far and wide to find enough food to satisfy their ravenous appetites. Wolves slunk through the dark like spectral wraiths. Coyotes yipped and hunted. Bobcats sought rabbits and birds and whatever else they could catch. "What did it sound like?"

"It was groaning."

Fargo liked to flatter himself that he was familiar with the sounds most animals made, and groaning wasn't one of them. Snatching the Henry, he stood. "Show me where you heard it."

The creek gurgled in the night, an oval pool reflecting the myriad of stars. Pendrake indicated where he had knelt to wash the dishes, then pointed into the benighted timber on the other side. "In there. Listen and you're bound to hear it."

Fargo did, but all he heard was the rush of water and the rustle of the stiff breeze in the trees.

"I swear I heard something." Pendrake had his hand on the flap of his holster. "It gave me gooseflesh."

"Maybe it was the wind," Fargo speculated. People unfamiliar with the deep woods often mistook commonplace sounds for the cries of wild beasts. He remembered the time he was guiding a wagon train and one night a woman went into a fit of hysterics after she swore she heard a bear growl right beside her wagon. It turned out to be a porcupine.

"Give me more credit than that," Pendrake said. "We have wind in Baltimore, you know."

Fargo turned to go back to the fire. "If you hear it again, tell me." He took a step, but only one, for out of the forest wafted a low, wavering moan, exactly as the officer had described.

"There! What did I tell you?" Pendrake crowed. "I wasn't imagining things! Maybe now you'll treat me with more respect."

Crouching, Fargo probed the vegetation. "Stay here and keep watch over the horses." Without waiting for a reply, he waded into the pool. The water only came as high as his knees, but it was cold enough to send a shiver rippling up his spine.

"Wait!" Pendrake splashed in. "I want to go with you."

Fargo came close to slugging him. "Do as I tell you, damn it." He did not care to be stranded afoot. It might be that the moans were intended to lure them out of camp for just that purpose. Outlaws and Indians could be devious as hell. "Or have you forgotten I'm in charge?"

"I haven't forgotten," Pendrake spat, "and I'll thank you not to use that tone with me." But he clambered onto the bank, and hunkering, he drew his revolver.

The moan was repeated, enabling Fargo to pinpoint the direction and the distance: northeast, about thirty feet. Avoiding a boulder, he crept through high weeds to a thicket. The moans came from the other side. Stealthily circling to the right, he came to a pine tree and crouched next to the trunk.

The loudest moan yet sounded.

Fargo edged forward, bending at the knees to duck under a low branch. He glimpsed bushes and a vague shape, and snapped the Henry to his shoulder. "Come out where I can see you."

The crunch of a twig behind him warned Fargo there was more than one. He tried to whirl and felt an arm hook around his neck and clamp hold.

The next instant a knife glimmered in the starlight, the point inches from his throat.

5

Skye Fargo reacted instinctively. Dropping the Henry, he grabbed the wrist of his attacker's knife arm while simultaneously grabbing the forearm clamped to his throat. Then, whipping his body in an arc, he flipped his assailant over his shoulder. He had a fleeting glimpse of a lithesome form and a mane of hair, and dropping onto his knees on his attacker's chest, he tore the long-bladed knife from slender fingers.

"Let go, damn you!"

She had long sandy hair and wore a homespun dress, and had eyes that sparkled in the starlight. Fargo could not tell much more except that she had an hourglass figure and a more than ample bosom. She lunged for the knife, but he jerked his arm back, saying, "Calm down."

"Don't you tell me what to do!" She tried to rise but his weight was too much. Hissing like a riled cat, she clawed at his face.

Fargo seized her other wrist and did not let go. "I won't tell you twice," he warned. "I don't take kindly to people trying to slit my throat."

"Who are you?" she demanded. "Were you sent to fetch us back? You might as well kill me now because I'll die before I let that happen."

47

"Lady, I don't know what the hell you're talking about." Fargo slid one of his knees off her to ease the pressure.

"So you say. But it could be a trick. He sent you to get us, didn't he?"

Fargo scanned the vegetation. "Who else is with you?" Another moan came from the tall grass a few yards away. He started to rise, but the woman clutched at his leg and would not let go.

"I won't let you touch her! You can't do this! What sort of animal are you?"

"The kind with no patience," Fargo said, and slammed her back down. "Now listen." He wagged her knife in front of her eyes. "I'm not here to hurt you or anyone else. Behave, and I'll let you up." He nodded toward the grass. "Who are you protecting?"

Tears glistened, but whether from relief or frustration, Fargo couldn't say.

"My daughter, Ruthie. She's only twelve. She has a bellyache and there's nothing I can do."

Fargo rose, reversed his grip on the knife and offered it to her, hilt first. "Let's get her over to the fire. I might be able to help."

The sandy-haired beauty did not hide her amazement. "You're not after us? I thought—" She stopped and warily rose, still not entirely convinced. "I'm Claresta Landers."

Fargo introduced himself and stepped toward the tall grass, only to have her spring in front of him and brandish the knife. "I thought we had this settled."

"No one touches my daughter but me," Claresta said. "Not until I know them better." Stooping, she scooped the child into her arms. The girl did not stir.

"Where are your horses?" Fargo asked.

"We don't have any."

"Did they run off?" Fargo could not conceive of a woman and child trying to cross the mountains alone and on foot.

"Mister, I don't have the money for a meal, let alone a couple of mounts. I spent the last cent I had for stage fare to Elkhorn."

Another moan from Ruthie galvanized Fargo into wheeling and beckoning. "Come on. Tell me about it after we tend to your daughter."

"This is right kind of you," Claresta said. "A lot of folks wouldn't be bothered to lend a helping hand." When Fargo did not say anything, she added, "The cup of human kindness isn't as full as I once thought it was. I've been mighty disillusioned of late, I don't mind admitting."

"When did your daughter come down sick?"

"Shortly before you and your friend showed up. We were wore out and stopped in that clearing late this afternoon. I tried to bean a rabbit with a rock but it ran off, so we ate some bark and grass and—"

Fargo glanced back. "Couldn't you find anything better?"

"We hadn't eaten in three days. We were half-starved and Ruthie was as weak as a kitten. So I scraped some bark from a pine tree and we nibbled on that and chewed a handful of grass." Claresta had tears in her eyes again. "It was the best I could do."

Fargo quickened his steps. When they came to the stream he offered to carry the child across but Claresta refused his help.

Captain Pendrake was waiting on the bank. "What in the world?" he blurted. "Where did you find them?"

"Under a rock." Fargo went straight to his bedroll and unrolled his blankets and had the mother place the girl on top of them. In the dancing glow of the fire he saw them both clearly for the first time. Claresta had green eyes and a button nose and lips that reminded him of ripe cherries. She was worn and haggard, her dress spotted with dirt and grass stains and torn at the hem. Ruthie was the spitting image of her mother, except that her eyes, when they briefly fluttered open, were brown.

"What can you do for her?" Claresta asked anxiously.

Fargo put his hand on the girl's forehead. It was hot but he had felt hotter. He probed her wrist for a pulse. It was strong, the rhythm regular. When he lightly pressed her stomach, it elicited another moan. "You say she got this way shortly after you ate the bark and the grass?"

Claresta nodded, a tear trickling down her cheek.

"They ate what?" Captain Pendrake interjected. "Did I hear correctly?"

"Whip up some food for them," Fargo said to keep him busy. "Tea for the girl, what's left of the chicken for her mother." Removing his bandanna, he opened his canteen and moistened it, then folded it in half and applied it to the girl's forehead.

"Do you know what's wrong with my baby?" Claresta dabbed at her eyes. "I couldn't bear it if anything happened to her. She's all I have left in this world."

Fargo opened his saddlebags and removed a spare buckskin shirt. "What kind of bark did you eat?"

"From a pine. I'd heard somewhere that pine bark

is edible, but we had to chew and chew before we could swallow it." Claresta thought a moment. "It had a bitter, minty taste, if that helps."

"Did she drink a lot of water after she ate?" Fargo found the bundle he sought, wrapped in a square of rawhide.

"We both did, but she drank more," Claresta confirmed. "Why? Is that important?"

"It had the same effect as eating baked beans, only worse. I have something here that will help." Fargo opened the bundle. Inside were various Indian remedies he had collected on his travels. Balsam fir, which was made into a tea for treating colds. Rattle weed, which eased sore throats. Sandwort root, ideal for cleansing and soothing sore eyes. The bee plant, which helped reduce fever. Alum root for sores and boils. And the one he was looking for, blue flax, which the Paiutes used for bloat. He showed it to Claresta and explained its purpose.

"How is it you know so much about Indian ways?" she asked a trifle skeptically. "And are you sure it will work?"

"I've lived with a tribe or two," Fargo said, but he did not go into detail. "If we keep her warm and quiet, by morning she should be as good as store-bought."

Claresta tenderly squeezed her child's shoulder. "God, I hope so. After all I've put her through, I couldn't bear it if my stupidity killed her."

"It's not very smart to be out here by yourselves."

"We didn't have any choice. We couldn't stay in Elkhorn. I thought there might be a settlement out this way, or another mining camp where I could get work doing laundry or mending clothes. Anything to put food on the table." Claresta paused, and bit her lower lip. "*Almost* anything. I won't do *that*, no matter how desperate I am."

Fargo did not ask what she meant. "The next settlement isn't for hundreds of miles. The two of you would die long before you reached it."

Pendrake had rushed to the stream and returned with a pot full of water. He put it on the fire to boil, and commenced cutting the remainder of the chicken into pieces.

"I didn't know," Claresta said softly. "I didn't think to ask. All I wanted was out of Elkhorn. I couldn't take another beating." She hiked up one of her sleeves to show that her arm was covered in long, thin welts and bruises, then did the same with her dress, lifting it midway to her knees.

Fargo had seen marks like those before. Someone had taken a switch or a cane to her.

"My word!" Captain Pendrake declared. "Who would do such a thing?"

Claresta lowered her dress and bowed her head. "His name is Pol Edmunds. He was one of the first to stake a claim along Elkhorn Creek." Her voice broke and she started to cry but stopped herself and said, "No. I refuse to be weak. It's not my fault. I only did what any mother would do."

Fargo wanted to hear more, but she needed food and rest. Pendrake, though, wasn't quite as observant.

"How is that, ma'am?"

"Do you have any notion how hard it is for a woman to make it on her own?" Claresta responded. "Ever since my husband died, I've been at my wit's end. We had a small farm in Ohio. Not ours, really, but the bank's. One day my Charley was out plowing a field and one of the plow horses became tangled in the traces. When he bent down, the horse kicked him and caved in his skull."

"My word!" Pendrake was aghast. "Please don't tell me you witnessed it."

"No, I found him later," Claresta said. "With his head half split and his brains half spilled out." She shuddered and covered her face with a hand, but quickly jerked it down. "I have nightmares about it nearly every night." She took a deep breath. "Anyway, I couldn't keep up the payments and lost the farm a few months later. I moved into town and worked at a millinery. I didn't earn much, but it kept our bellies full." She touched her daughter.

Pendrake was a fount of questions. "How did you end up in a wild place like Elkhorn?"

"Stupidity," Claresta said bitterly. "I figured I should marry again. Find a decent man who would provide for Ruth and me." She fluffed at her sandy hair. "I'm not much to look at, I admit, but I'm fairly young yet."

Fargo disagreed. She would turn most any man's head.

"The only single men in our town were either a lot younger or a lot older, and I wanted someone about my own age," Claresta explained. "So I let a friend talk me into writing to a distant cousin of hers who was about my age. Edmunds."

Ruth groaned. Claresta bent low and patted her hand, saying, "Hang on, sweetheart. We're going to give you something for the pain and you'll be on the mend soon. I promise."

"Go on with your story," Pendrake coaxed.

"There's not a lot more to tell. Edmunds wrote back

and he came across as the perfect gentleman. Claimed he didn't mind my having a child. Promised that if I came West, he would see to it we were well-looked after."

Fargo did not need a gypsy's crystal ball to guess what happened. "That's not how things turned out."

"No. He wasn't anywhere near as nice as in his letters. He had paid to have someone write them. Still, I'd have stuck it out if he treated me decently. But he took to bossing me around and throwing fits if another man so much as looked at me." Claresta gazed sadly into the fire. "When I tried to reason with him, he beat me with a broom handle. Twice in three days. I made up my mind to leave before he dragged me before a preacher, so when he got himself good and drunk, I slipped out with Ruthie in the middle of the night. And here I am."

"He'll come looking for you," Fargo predicted.

"But he'll think we went East, back to Ohio," Claresta said. "It would never occur to him that we struck off across the mountains on our own."

Fargo was not so sure. Men like Edmunds tended to regard women as their personal property and would scour heaven and earth for what they considered theirs. Once Edmunds failed to find her east of Elkhorn, he would put two and two together and come on quick to make up for lost time.

Claresta was watching Pendrake in rapt fascination. They both heard her stomach growl. "I'm sorry," she sheepishly apologized. "I'm so famished, I could eat that meat raw."

"How about some coffee while the chicken is cooking?" Fargo asked.

"Not until Ruthie has her tea. It wouldn't be right."

Claresta tucked her legs under her and raised her daughter's head to her lap. The dress slid up above her ankles, revealing more welts and bruises. For her to have so many, Fargo realized, Edmunds must have beaten her within a yard of crippling her. For some, that would crush their spirit, but not Claresta Landers. She had to be strong inside. Or maybe it was her love for her daughter that compelled her to take risks no sensible person would dare. "Hurry with the tea," Fargo urged.

"I can't make water boil faster," Captain Pendrake muttered, but he added another limb to the fire.

Claresta stroked Ruth's hair. "All I want out of life is a decent husband and a nice home. Is that too much to ask?"

Fargo mustered a grin. "Don't look at me. I don't plan to marry before I'm eighty-four."

Despite herself, Claresta smiled. "Honesty. I admire that in a man. All the more since I let Pol Edmunds dupe me into believing he was a godsend." She placed a hand to her forehead. "What was I thinking?"

"I have to wonder the same thing," Pendrake commented. "You would never catch me offering myself to someone through the mail. The very idea is degrading. The practice should be abolished."

Fargo almost backhanded him. "Easy for you to say. You're not in her shoes."

"Please don't squabble on my account," Claresta said. "I want all of us to get along. Especially since we'll be together quite a while." She beamed at Fargo. "I don't know where you're headed, but wherever it is, we're going with you."

Captain Pendrake shot to his feet. "Over my dead body."

6

As was his habit, Skye Fargo awoke at the crack of daylight. Claresta and Ruth Landers were sleeping peacefully, Ruthie's head on her mother's shoulder. Captain Pendrake liked to sleep with his blankets pulled over his head—a silly and dangerous practice, in Fargo's opinion. From under his blankets came loud snoring.

Fargo had slept sitting up, his back to a tree at the edge of the clearing. Someone had to keep watch, and he did not trust Pendrake enough to put his life in the young officer's hands.

Stretching and yawning, Fargo saw a pink tinge on the eastern horizon. The sun would rise in half an hour. Plenty of time for him to do what needed doing. Rising, he padded across the clearing to the trail east and along it until he came to a tree high enough for his purpose. Propping the Henry against the trunk, he climbed from limb to limb until he was above the surrounding vegetation and could see for miles.

Settling in a convenient fork, Fargo waited. He had a decision to make and he might as well make it now. Last night, Pendrake had argued against letting Claresta and her daughter tag along as far as the next settlement, saying it would slow them down and point-

56

ing out that they must reach Seattle as swiftly as they could. Claresta had listened with a hurt expression on her face, and only mentioned that she would be in their debt if they would help her escape Pol Edmunds.

Fargo had not said anything. Pendrake had acted as if his say was the final say, and had turned in apparently thinking the issue was settled. It wasn't.

The pink tinge became a rosy glow. Presently, a golden crown tipped the rim of the world, and songbirds came alive with their avian welcome.

At the limit of Fargo's vision gray wisps rose from the forest, tendrils from a campfire.

Fargo swung from his perch and rapidly descended. The Henry in hand, he jogged to the clearing. Pendrake was snoring louder than ever and didn't budge when Fargo raised the edge of the blanket. Fargo had to shake him three times before he stirred and smacked his lips and slowly opened his eyes.

"What is it?" he thickly asked.

"Keep your voice down," Fargo whispered. "Let Claresta and Ruth sleep as long as they want. I'll be back in a while."

Pendrake's sleepiness vanished in a heartbeat, and he sat up. "Where are you off to? We should get an early start."

"Make sure nothing happens to the Landers." Fargo moved to the Ovaro and quickly threw on his saddle blanket and saddle. He tied on his saddlebags and shoved the Henry into the saddle scabbard.

"You haven't answered me." Pendrake had the blanket bundled about his shoulders. "Where are you going?"

"I have something to do." Fargo lifted the reins, but the officer stepped in front of the Ovaro.

"You're not fooling anyone. I hope you realize that."

"I'm not trying to." Fargo glanced at Claresta and Ruth, cradled in the heavy slumber of utter exhaustion.

"I saw how you looked at her," Pendrake said, "and I must tell you, I find your lack of decorum deplorable."

"Did you eat a dictionary when you were younger?" Fargo clucked to the pinto. He held to a walk until he was a hundred yards from the clearing so as not to awaken the Landers. Then, bringing the Ovaro to a gallop, he rode into the rising sun until he crested a rise and spied four men hunkered around a fire, sipping coffee.

All four rose at his approach. Only two wore revolvers. Their clothes were well-worn homespun, their boots badly scuffed, their hats in need of mending. The biggest had shoulders as broad as a bull's and a bushy black beard that fell to his waist. He put a brawny hand on the revolver tucked under his wide leather belt and demanded, "What can we do for you, stranger?"

Fargo pushed back his hat and smiled. "I've been riding all night, and that coffee sure smells good."

"Light and rest a spell," the big man offered. "We're not headin' out for a while yet." He raised a battered tin cup to his thick lips and slurped, and coffee spilled onto his bushy beard. "I'm Pol Edmunds."

"I'm obliged." Fargo dismounted and fished his own cup from his saddlebags. "Isn't there a mining camp east of here a ways?"

"Elkhorn," Edmunds confirmed.

"Is that where you're headed?" Fargo made small talk to put them at ease.

"Nope. We're goin' in the other direction. We're after someone."

"Do tell." Fargo filled his cup and blew on the steaming hot coffee. The others sat back down.

"Yep. We're after my woman. Damn her contrary hide."

Fargo feigned innocence. "Your wife ran off on you?"

"She ain't my missus," Edmunds growled, flushing with anger. "Not yet, anyhow. But wife or not, no female skips out on me without my say so."

"What makes you think she came this way?"

"We rode east a full day and didn't see hide nor hair of her or her little girl," the prospector said. "We asked everyone we ran into, but no one had seen them." He snapped his big fingers. "Say, I bet you saw them, though. A fine-lookin' woman with hair like straw? And her brat?"

"Can't say as I have," Fargo lied. "I met a few Mormons a couple of days ago. And yesterday I came on a cavalry patrol."

"Cavalry?" one of the men at the fire bleated, and nearly spilled his cup in his haste to rise. "Pol, did you hear? What if she tells them?"

"We haven't broken any law," Edmunds responded. "She promised to be my wife, and I aim to hold her to her promise whether she likes it or not."

"Promise?" Fargo coaxed.

"I answered one of those ads you see in the newspapers," Edmunds said, "and she wrote back sayin' as how she would be delighted to make my acquaintance."

"Doesn't sound like much of a promise to me,"

Fargo observed, taking a step to his right so he could watch all four at the same time.

"She came, didn't she?" Pol Edmunds snapped. "That's the same as a promise, the way I see things. I figured she would be grateful, me doing her a favor and all, but no."

"Favor?" Fargo casually rested his right hand on his Colt.

"Sure. How many men are willin' to get hitched to a widow with a brat in tow? Not many, I can tell you. She should have dropped to her knees and thanked her Maker I took an interest. But no. Instead she sassed me all the time, and would look at other men when my back was turned."

"If your back was turned, how would you know?"

"Are you tryin' to be funny?" Edmunds bristled like a mad boar. "A man can always tell when a woman is misbehavin'. And there's only one thing to do when that happens."

"Beat her until she begs for mercy," Fargo said.

"Exactly." Edmunds nodded. "Females are like dogs. The only way to keep them in line is by tannin' their hides. My pa used to beat my ma and my five sisters, and they knew better than to complain."

One of the other men, older than the rest, shook his head and said, "I don't go in for beating females and I don't have much respect for them that do. If I had known you beat her, Pol, I wouldn't have agreed to help find her."

"I never took you for a weak sister, Kelton," Edmunds said. "And my personal life is my own affair."

A second man bit his lower lip and swirled the coffee in his cup. "I agree with Kelton, Pol. Beating a woman ain't right."

Edmunds puffed out his cheeks and swelled his broad chest to twice its normal size. "What is this? My woman is missin' and all you can do is nitpick? Besides, I would never really hurt her, Frank. All I did was slap her around some."

"With a broom handle," Fargo said.

"It was handy, so why not?" Edmunds replied. "I didn't hit her on the head or the neck or anywhere like—" He suddenly stopped. "Wait a minute. How in hell did you know that? Who are you, anyhow?"

"Someone who can't wait to stomp you senseless." Fargo drew his Colt as he spoke and slammed the barrel against Edmunds' temple. For most, that would be enough to drop them where they stood, but the prospector was solid muscle. Edmunds staggered but he did not go down.

"That was for the first beating you gave her," Fargo said. "This is for the second." He slammed the Colt against the prospector's head a second time.

Pol Edmunds nearly pitched forward but recovered his balance and stood swaying like an oak in a chinook, blood trickling from his split skin, his dark eyes glittering like those of a mad bear.

Kelton and Frank and the third man were too stunned to do anything.

"Claresta Landers is with me now," Fargo said. "Show your face anywhere near her and I'll blow it off." Twirling the Colt into his holster, Fargo began to back toward the Ovaro.

Pol Edmunds was a beet and growing redder by the moment. "No one pistol-whips me!" he snarled. Baring his teeth, he spread his arms wide, voiced an inarticulate cry of uncontrolled rage and charged.

As much as Fargo wanted to shoot him, he could

not bring himself to gun down an unarmed man. Instead, planting himself, he dropped his cup and met Edmunds' rush with a right uppercut backed by all the strength of his steely sinews and all the weight of his powerful frame.

By rights it should have stretched Edmunds out flat, but the enraged Goliath was merely slowed. Shaking his head to clear it, he roared and pounced.

Fargo tried to skip aside, but Edmunds was quicker than he appeared. Tree-trunk arms encircled Fargo's waist, and he was lifted bodily off the ground.

"Now you'll get yours!" Edmunds gleefully howled. A wild gleam lit his eyes and spittle flecked his lips. "I'll break you like a reed!"

The pressure was tremendous. To Fargo it felt as if his spine was being crushed, his insides squeezed to pulp. He pushed against Edmunds' chest, but it was like trying to move a mountain.

"Go on! Fight, for all the good it will do you!" Edmunds crowed. "I'm fixin' to cripple you for life!"

"Pol, don't!" Kelton shouted, but Edmunds paid him no mind.

Fargo slugged him on the jaw. Once, twice, three times. It was like punching a block of stone. He tried to knee Edmunds in the groin but could not raise his leg high enough. The world spun and bile rose in his gorge. In desperation, he jabbed his thumbs into the prospector's glittering eyes.

Edmunds shrieked and danced backward, nearly stumbling into the fire. But he did not let go.

His teeth clenched against the agony, fighting to stay conscious, Fargo gouged his thumbs in harder. Edmunds' grip slackened, but not enough.

"I'll kill you, mister! Do you hear me?"

Fargo butted his forehead against Edmunds' bulbous nose. At the *crunch,* wet drops spattered his cheeks and chin.

Cursing furiously, Edmunds pressed his hands to his face. "You broke my nose!" he bellowed. "You broke my damn nose!"

Fargo wasn't done. He landed a combination to the ribs, then ducked when Edmunds threw a haymaker. Straightening, Fargo delivered two jabs to the jaw, but all they did was make Edmunds madder.

"I am goin' to grind your bones to dust and spit on the remains!"

A fist filled Fargo's vision but he evaded it and delivered a solid uppercut. Edmunds tried to grapple. Skipping out of reach, Fargo circled, determined to bring Edmunds down, no matter what it took.

The other three had backed to safety. Kelton and Frank yelled for Edmunds to stop fighting, but they might as well have asked a rabid wolf to stop its mad attacks. Edmunds was beyond the point of listening to reason.

Suddenly the prospector swept a boot at Fargo's legs, seeking to sweep them out from under him. Springing over them, Fargo thwarted him. But while Fargo was still in midair, iron fingers clamped onto his throat and others onto his belt, and the next instant he was raised over Edmunds' head and Edmunds tensed to dash him to the ground.

"Now you get yours!"

Fargo pried at Edmunds' fingers, but they were as thick as railroad spikes. He drove a knee into Edmunds' face but he still could not break free. The world began to fade to black.

Snarling and spitting blood, Edmunds cackled.

"When I'm through with you, I'll go get her and the brat. They can't be far."

Unable to breathe, barely conscious, Fargo willed the lower half of his body to move, to twist. He slammed both knees down and in, and Edmunds grunted and teetered. Edmunds' face was a scarlet ruin and two of his teeth were broken.

Fargo's flailing fingers found the bigger man's beard, and with a savage wrench, he yanked with all his might.

A howl rent the clearing. Edmunds fell back, gruffly declaring, "Damn you to hell!" His shoulder muscles bunched and he dashed Fargo to the earth.

Fargo struck on his shoulder and rolled to put distance between them. He heard a lurid oath and the *stomp* of a boot strike near his ear, and rolled faster, his senses flaring with renewed clarity. He was worried he would roll into the fire. Instead, he collided with a log. He got a hand on it, but before he could rise, corded arms were about his waist again and he was being shaken like a marmot in the grip of a grizzly. Shaken until his teeth rattled.

"Say your prayers, mister!"

Fargo could not withstand another bear hug. He pounded on Edmunds' head. He punched Edmunds on the jaw and the cheek. He kicked Edmunds below the belt. But Edmunds laughed the blows off.

Once again the world swam, and Fargo heard his blood roaring in his veins.

"How does it feel to die?" Pol Edmunds asked.

7

Life on the frontier was violent. Skye Fargo had seen more than his share of it, and had been in more fights than most, in large part due to his fondness for saloons. One thing he had learned never to do during a fight was talk. As an old-timer once told him, "Don't be jabberin' when you should be swingin'." Advice he took to heart.

Pol Edmunds had never heard that advice. He loved to hear himself talk. "I can't hear you, mister," he taunted. "What's the matter? Cat got your tongue?" He thought that uproariously hilarious.

It was then, when Edmunds threw back his head and laughed in sadistic delight, that Fargo did the only thing he could to keep from having his spine snapped; he punched the prospector in the throat. Not hard enough to kill, but hard enough that Edmunds gurgled and sputtered and staggered.

Drawing back his right fist, Fargo put everything he had into a punch to the tip of Edmunds' jaw. He thought for sure several of his knuckles burst, but the important thing was that Pol Edmunds finally crumpled to his knees.

His huge arms limp, drool dribbling over his lower

lip, the woman-beater blinked numbly up at him. "Damn you," he said.

"Damn *you*," Fargo replied, and hit him again, twisting as he struck to add more power to the blow.

Pol Edmunds pitched onto his bearded face.

Breathing heavily, his temples still pounding, Fargo spun toward the others and put his hand on his Colt. "How about you?"

Kelton held out both palms and shook his head. "Easy there, mister. I don't agree with what he did any more than you do."

"Same here," Frank piped in. "Fair is fair. He got what he deserved."

"Not quite yet," Fargo said.

Edmunds was trying to rise. He was on his hands and knees and huffing like a boar. Suddenly he reared back and spread his arms.

Fargo never gave him the chance to spring. In a single step he was close enough to plant his boot. Pol Edmunds turned purple, his eyes nearly bulging from their sockets. Fargo kicked him again in the same spot and Edmunds fell flat on his stomach and was as still as a board.

"He won't be sowing any oats for a while," Frank commented.

Fargo walked stiff-legged to the Ovaro and mounted. His back and ribs hurt something awful. Grimacing, he reined around. "When he comes to, tell him that if I hear of him bothering the Landers woman or her daughter ever again, I'll finish what I started."

"I'll gladly pass it on," Kelton said.

The third man had not uttered a word and Fargo did not entirely trust him, so he shifted in the saddle to keep an eye on him to avoid a bullet in the back until he came to a bend. Once out of sight, Fargo spurred the Ovaro to a trot.

First Aces Malone, now this. Fargo was making a lot of enemies of late. But he deemed it unlikely either would care to confront him again. Malone had lost his hired guns, and Edmunds wouldn't walk right for a month of Sundays.

The sun was up. Soon the temperature would climb. A doe crossed the trail ahead, and to the southwest a hawk wheeled high in the sky.

The Landers were still asleep. As Fargo brought the stallion to a stop, Pendrake stood.

"Where did you go off to?"

"No place in particular." Fargo checked the coffeepot, then squatted to rekindle the fire. "After breakfast we'll be on our way."

"What about the woman and her child?"

"What about them? We can't just leave them here. They're going with us. They'll use our spare horses."

Pendrake shook his head. "I thought we settled this last night. They'll slow us down. Need I remind you we are on official government business? We can't afford any delays."

Fargo looked up. "You want to strand them in the middle of nowhere? You can do that?"

"I do what is best for my country," Pendrake said. "They stranded themselves, when you get down to it. If the woman had stayed in Elkhorn, they wouldn't be in this predicament."

"If Claresta had stayed in Elkhorn, Edmunds would have forced her to marry him and then beat her anytime he wanted. And any man who will beat his wife, sooner or later beats his kids."

"Since when did you become the Good Samaritan?" Pendrake asked. "I've read your file, remember? The kind of women you fancy aren't the marrying kind. So why put yourself out for her and the girl?"

"If I have to tell you, you wouldn't understand." Fargo was the first to admit that he led the kind of life a parson wouldn't approve of, but there were certain lines he never crossed, certain things he would never do.

Pendrake would not let it be. "Oh, please. I graduated at the top of my class at West Point. Explain away. I might surprise you."

Fargo exposed an ember and blew on it until it glowed red. He covered the coal with a few twigs and when they ignited he added enough wood to get the fire blazing. Only then did he say, "I'm not in the habit of explaining myself. Claresta and Ruthie are coming with us, and that's that."

The officer said something under his breath, then raised his voice. "Aren't you forgetting something? Our mission is crucial to United States interests. It takes priority over all else."

"The country won't fall apart before we get there." Fargo's temper was close to the snapping point. "If you're in such an all-fired hurry, go on ahead and I'll catch up when I can."

"Causing even more delay," Pendrake said resentfully.

"Then I reckon you have a decision to make." Fargo smirked and added a broken branch to the growing flames.

Claresta Landers was awake, staring at him with a quizzical expression. "Thank you for standing up for us."

"Don't make more of it than there is," Fargo cautioned. "I'm doing it for Ruthie more than anything."

"Sure you are," Claresta said. She stroked her daughter's hair, then carefully eased out from under the blankets. "You puzzle me, Mr. Fargo. I can't make up my mind what to make of you."

Pendrake had his hands on his hips and was glaring like a spiteful ten-year-old. "I know what to make of him. And he has me over the proverbial barrel. We will take you with us, madam, but only as far as the first settlement we come to. Agreed?"

Claresta answered before Fargo could. "I would be ever so grateful, Captain. I'm sorry Ruthie and I are such a burden. We don't mean to be."

"That's quite all right. True, you are a stumbling block, but a temporary one, at best." Pendrake's forehead knit and he glanced at Fargo. "How close is the next settlement, anyhow?"

"Not more than a few hundred miles, I should think," Fargo answered.

"A few hun—?" Pendrake sputtered, and pointed at Ruth. "Wake her up, if you please, Mrs. Landers, so we can be on our way."

"There's no hurry," Fargo said. "She can sleep in." The child had been through hell the past several days and needed her rest.

"If it's not one thing, it's another," Pendrake groused. "You're trying my patience. If you ask me, your reputation for being reliable is greatly exaggerated. General Foster will be most displeased when he hears how you have behaved."

"Glad to disappoint him," Fargo said, and he was equally glad when the captain finally dropped the subject.

A full hour passed before Ruth woke up. By then Pendrake had taken some cornmeal from his haversack, added appropriate amounts of sugar and water, and made a batch of johnnycakes. Whatever other faults he had, the man could cook, and took great pride in it. "Here you go," he said, offering a plate to Claresta. "So tasty they will melt in your mouth."

Claresta gave the plate to Ruth and accepted another. "We thank you for your kindness, Captain."

"Like Fargo said a while ago, don't make more of it than there is, Mrs. Landers. The sooner you're fed, the sooner we can head out."

Ruth was shy. She would not look directly at them, and did not say a word until she was finished, when, smacking her lips, she grinned sheepishly at Pendrake. "Those cakes are the best I ever ate. Even better than my mother's."

"I'm pleased to hear that." The peacock ate up the flattery. "The secret is in the proportion of cornmeal to sugar."

"How is it you're so good at cooking?" Ruthie asked. "My father always said it was woman's work, and he couldn't be bothered."

"My father always said the same thing," Pendrake said, "but my mother died when I was your age, and someone had to do the cooking." He forked a piece of cake into his mouth and chewed with relish.

"Do you like being a soldier?" the girl asked.

"Very much so," Pendrake responded. "I love my country. Patriotism runs strong in my family. The first Pendrake to set foot on American soil was at Bunker Hill."

"I think you're a nice man—" Ruth said, then transformed to stone with her mouth half open. She was gazing past Fargo and saw something that twisted her face in raw fear.

Fargo started to turn, his hand dropping to the Colt. He knew who it would be, and he mentally swore at himself for being so careless.

"God, no!" Claresta Landers exclaimed.

Pol Edmunds held a double-barreled shotgun. Both hammers had been pulled back. He shuffled slowly toward them, his back slightly stooped, his face swollen black and blue. "Anyone so much as twitches and I'll blow them in half."

Fargo imitated a tree. At that range buckshot would rip them apart. He shifted his eyes to Pendrake, worried the captain would try to draw, but Pendrake had frozen with a fork in one hand and his tin plate in the other.

"Didn't count on seeing me again, huh?" Edmunds said to Fargo. "Figured you had stomped me so bad, I would go back to Elkhorn with my tail tucked between my legs. Shows how much you know."

"What's this?" Claresta was confused. "What are you talking about? Mr. Fargo has been with us since yesterday."

"Look at me!" Edmunds growled. "Do you think I'm makin' it up, you stupid cow?" He halted a dozen feet away, the shotgun centered on Fargo. "Kelton and Frank tried to talk me out of comin' after you. As if I give a damn what they think after they stood there and did nothin'."

Claresta took a step but stopped when the shotgun's twin muzzles swung toward her. "Pol, be reasonable. What do you hope to accomplish?"

"What else?" Edmunds rejoined. "I'm takin' you and the brat back with me, and we're huntin' up that reverend who showed up a few days ago so he can hitch us nice and legal."

"I refuse to marry you," Claresta said. "I've already made that clear."

"What you want doesn't count," Edmunds bluntly rasped. "You answered my letters. You got my hopes up by comin' to meet me. Now you'll do what's right and take me for your husband."

"I would rather die."

"Now you're gettin' it," Edmunds said. "And if I do you, I might as well do the brat, too. Without you, she's of no use to me."

"I'm not a brat," Ruth said.

Claresta's hand rose to her throat and she moved to the right, placing herself between the shotgun and her daughter. "Please, Pol. Let's not lose our heads. We're adults. We can reason this out."

"Don't take on airs with me, woman," Edmunds warned. "That's been part of your problem all along. Lookin' down your nose at me. You think you deserve better. As if you're better than I am."

"I never said that."

"You didn't have to. I could see it in your eyes." Edmunds trained the shotgun on Fargo again. "First things first, though. How about if you shuck that gun belt, mister. Nice and slow. Then the soldier boy can do the same with his."

Captain Pendrake set down his plate. "Now see here. I wasn't a party to whatever took place between Fargo and you. And I certainly never wanted to be shackled with these two. I'll thank you to accord me the respect my uniform deserves."

Pol Edmunds laughed. "You're mighty fond of yourself, aren't you? I couldn't care less about your silly uniform, soldier boy. If your friend acts up, he gets one barrel and you get the other. Ever seen what buckshot does to a man? I have. It sure makes a mess of his innards."

"That would be murder."

"You make it sound like a bad thing. In these parts a man has to stand up for himself or he isn't much of a man."

"Kill me, and you'll have the United States Army down on your head," Pendrake said. "There will be no place you can hide, nowhere you can run." His right hand brushed the flap to his holster.

Instantly, Edmunds centered the shotgun on his chest. "Another dumb move like that, soldier boy, and you'll have a hole in you the size of a watermelon. As for the army, how are they goin' to find out? I sure as hell won't tell them, and neither will either of these females after I get done with them."

"Quit calling me soldier boy," Pendrake spat.

Fargo kept hoping the prospector would lower the shotgun an inch or two, enough to give him the edge he needed. But no such luck.

Edmunds once again pointed it at him, a thick finger curled around the twin triggers. "What are you waitin' for, mister? Shuck your hardware or be blown to kingdom come." Edmunds' puffy lips curled in a sadistic sneer. "Personally, I hope you're stupid enough to try me. I've never wanted to kill anyone so much in all my born days."

8

There was a saying common in Texas and elsewhere: Buckshot meant burying. A shotgun at close range was always lethal. It literally blew a person apart. Only a fool would draw on a man holding one, and Fargo was no fool. Moving slowly so as not to provoke Pol Edmunds, Fargo unfastened his belt buckle and let the gun belt fall.

"Smart man," Edmunds congratulated him. "You get to live a little longer yet. Not much, but every minute counts."

"Please, Pol," Claresta said. "Take me if you want but don't harm him. He was only trying to help."

"By doing this to me?" Edmunds demanded, pointing at his battered face. "I'm not the forgivin' sort, woman. You should know that by now."

Ruth Landers surprised all of them by suddenly standing and shaking a fist at him. "You're wicked, and I wish you were dead!"

Edmunds looked fit to slap her, but instead he chuckled and said, "You've got spunk, brat. I'll give you that. But mark my words, I'll soon beat that spunk out of you. You'll learn to treat your betters with respect, or else."

Now it was Claresta who flared with anger. "Don't you dare lay a finger on her! Do you hear me, Pol?"

"Spare me your threats. They won't come to anything, not after I've taught you to mind your tongue."

Captain Pendrake had not unbuckled his belt yet. "Is that your answer to everything, Mr. Edmunds? To hit people? To beat them up? What manner of brute are you?"

"The kind who doesn't cotton to sass." Edmunds aimed the shotgun at him. "Your hardware or your life, soldier boy."

Fargo wondered what the prospector was up to. By rights, Edmunds should kill Pendrake and him then and there. Pendrake apparently had a similar thought.

"What are your intentions, sir? You have yet to make them plain."

"How is it soldiers are so stupid? Squashin' a fly ain't half as much fun as pluckin' the wings first and then squashin' it."

"You will never get away with it."

"Don't start that again," Edmunds said. "After I've had my fun, I'll bury you and this other bastard off in the woods where no one will ever find your bodies."

"Your fun?" said Claresta.

Fargo hoped they could keep Edmunds talking. He still had his Arkansas Toothpick in an ankle sheath, and if he could get to it without Edmunds noticing, the outcome would not be to Edmunds' liking.

Pendrake had shed his revolver.

"All right. I want all of you to sit down facin' away from me and with your hands behind your backs."

"I'll do no such thing," Captain Pendrake refused.

"Then you'll be the first to die." Edmunds raised

the shotgun to his shoulder. "Woman, you and the girl might want to move away from him. Heads tend to splatter when they're blown apart."

Fargo was as startled as the prospector when Claresta boldly stepped in front of Pendrake and folded her arms across her bosom. "I've taken all I'm going to take, Pol. To kill him, you must kill me."

"And me," Ruthie said, scooting to her mother's side.

Edmunds was nearly beside himself. He jerked the shotgun down, then jerked it up again. "Damn you. You're more contrary than mules. All the grief you've caused me, I almost wish you never answered my letters."

"That makes two of us," Claresta said.

His mouth twitching, Edmunds walked up to her and backhanded her across the face. She would have fallen if not for Pendrake, who grabbed her about the waist to steady her, and quickly let go.

Little Ruthie flew into a rage. Suddenly springing at Edmunds, she beat on his legs and hips while shrieking, "Quit hitting my mother! Quit hitting my mother!"

Edmunds seized her by the hair and turned to fling her from him. In doing so, he turned his back to Fargo. It was the moment Fargo had been waiting for. Bending, he hiked his pant leg high enough to slide his hand into his boot and palm the double-edged toothpick. The blade gleamed in the sunlight as he uncoiled and sprang.

Maybe it was the bright flash of steel that warned Edmunds. As fast as a striking rattler, he spun and sought to level the shotgun, but Fargo was on him before he could.

Fargo thrust at Edmunds' ribs, but Pol blocked the knife with the shotgun. Fargo stabbed again, opening one of Edmunds' hands, and he inadvertently let the shotgun fall and frantically backpedaled.

The next moment Edmunds had a hunting knife in his other hand. As usual, he talked when he should have been attacking. "Do you really think you can take me that easy, mister? I've gutted better men than you."

"Prove it," Fargo said, attacking. He thrust low, then high, then feinted low but stabbed high.

Edmunds parried and weaved, proving to be better with a knife than he was with his fists. "Told you!" he crowed. "I'm a hellion with cold steel."

Fargo dropped into a crouch and slashed at the prospector's legs. Edmunds retreated, but only a step, then lanced his longer blade at Fargo's neck. Fargo dodged, but barely.

"Almost got you that time!" Edmunds circled, seeking an opening, then stopped and glowered. "What the hell!"

"That will be quite enough," Captain Pendrake said. He had his revolver centered on the prospector's chest. "Drop your weapon and raise your arms in the air or I will shoot you where you stand."

"I don't think you've got the grit to pull that trigger, soldier boy," Edmunds blustered. He took a step, and when Pendrake didn't shoot, he took another. "I don't think you've ever killed anyone your whole life."

"There's always a first time," the officer said, but he did not sound particularly convincing.

Edmunds took another stride, and instead of squeezing the trigger, Pendrake backed up. "See? You're a gutless worm."

Fargo's Colt lay ten feet away, the shotgun closer. Glancing at Claresta, he said, "Cover Ruthie's eyes." Then, without waiting to see if she complied, he dived for the shotgun. Edmunds saw him and dived for it too, but Fargo had hold of it and was rolling onto his side when Edmunds leaped. Edmunds' face was a whisker's-width from the twin muzzles when Fargo squeezed both triggers.

At the thunderous blast, the shotgun recoiled so hard Fargo nearly lost his grip. A heavy impact on his lower legs caused him to scramble toward the Colt, but he need not have bothered.

Pol Edmunds would never beat anyone. His head was gone except for part of his mouth and lower jaw. A flap of flesh and hair dangled to one side. Half an ear hung by a shred.

Captain Pendrake still had his revolver in his hand. Blood and chunks of hair and bone were spattered over his face and down the front of his shirt.

Claresta, too, was speckled with scarlet drops and tiny pieces of blasted matter. Ruthie, though, had been spared, thanks to her mother, who shielded the girl with her body.

"Dear God," Pendrake breathed. "You blew him to bits." His throat bobbed. Putting a hand to his mouth, he spun and ran into the trees. Sounds of retching explained why.

Claresta stared grimly at the body. She had one hand over Ruth's eyes, the other covering one of her ears. "Why don't I feel anything? Regret? Remorse? Something?"

"Would you regret shooting a snake?" Fargo slowly rose, broke open the shotgun, and extracted the spent shells.

"He was a human being."

"He was a son of a bitch. Don't feel bad if you can't shed tears." Motioning at the spot where Edmunds had emerged from the woods, Fargo suggested, "Why don't Ruth and you go find his horse while I clean up this mess? Take your time. It will be a while."

Claresta nodded. She pressed Ruth's face against her dress until they were at the edge of the clearing, then guided Ruth eastward, walking behind her so if Ruth looked back she would not see the shotgun's handiwork.

A search of Edmunds' pockets revealed a handful of gold nuggets from his claim on Elkhorn Creek, along with a poke that contained mostly coins. Fargo stuck the nuggets in the poke and the poke in his pocket. He dragged the body into the trees, and at a suitable spot dug using a broken tree limb. He had a shallow hole six feet long and three feet wide when the undergrowth crackled and out walked Captain Edgar Pendrake.

"Here you are. I looked all over."

Fargo jabbed the end of the limb into the soil. "You can help if you want. This hole needs to be deeper." Were it up to him he would leave the body lying there, but Ruthie might stumble across it before they left, and he did not want that.

Pendrake averted his gaze. "I don't see how you do it. I've never been so sick."

"Out here you get used to it," Fargo said. Which was not entirely true. No matter how many people he saw shot or killed, a part of him was always affected.

"I could never get used to *that*."

"Then why did you enlist? War is the same only there is more of it. A lot more." Fargo had taken part in more than a few army campaigns against hostiles and banditos along the border with Mexico, and had seen things that would turn Pendrake's hair white. Mule skinners tied upside down to wagon wheels by Apaches, with fires lit under them to bake their brains. A deserter caught by the Sioux, lashed to a pole and roasted alive. The members of a wagon train mutilated beyond any hope of identifying them. And on it went.

"War is different. It's less personal, less gruesome. I would be one man among many."

"Think so, do you?" Fargo scraped dirt from one end of the hole to widen it enough to accommodate Edmunds' broad shoulders. "You have a lot to learn, if you don't mind my saying so."

"Not at all," Pendrake said, but it was plain he did. "I can't expect to know everything, like you apparently do." He stalked off.

Fargo sighed and continued digging. More than ever he regretted letting Pendrake come.

Mother and daughter were waiting by the fire when he was done. Claresta had washed her face and done what she could with the drops of blood on her dress, but not all of them would wash out. She had her arms wrapped tight around her legs and her chin on her knees. Ruthie was smiling and humming to herself, the happiest she had been.

"All taken care of?" Claresta asked.

Fargo nodded and walked to the bay they had brought back. The saddle was in good condition. The saddlebags contained a pair of pants, ammunition for the shotgun and a small pick.

"That's a real nice horse," Ruthie said. "It didn't give us a lick of trouble."

"It's your mother's now." Fargo reached in his

pocket for Edmunds' poke and handed it to Claresta. "This is yours too."

"What is this?" Claresta upended it over her palm and gasped when the nuggets and coins spilled out. "There must be a couple of hundred here."

"Closer to four" was Fargo's guess. "It should tide you over until you find a job you like."

Claresta looked at him, her eyes shimmering with budding tears. "I can't. It wouldn't be right. This should go to his next of kin."

Fargo admired her honest streak, and how her dress outlined the swell of her full breasts. "No one deserves it more than you after what he put you through. I don't need it, and it's against army regulations for Captain Pendrake to help himself."

"Still—" Claresta said, then clutched the poke to her and said softly, "I can't begin to thank you."

"No need," Fargo said.

Claresta bestowed a warm smile that betrayed no hint of anything more than friendliness. "I will find a way, though. Wait and see."

Wondering what she meant, Fargo turned and beheld Captain Pendrake. "How long have you been standing there?"

"Long enough. I think it's wrong to give her Edmunds' poke. We should turn it over to the law."

"What law?" Fargo scoffed. The nearest marshal was in Denver, more than a week's travel in the opposite direction. Salt Lake City had duly appointed law officers, but they had no jurisdiction.

"You make it sound like the rules of proper conduct we've lived by all our lives don't apply. I don't believe that. We're not barbarians, after all. We're civilized, and should act accordingly."

"Tell that to men like Edmunds." Fargo had little patience for those who refused to see the world as it was and not as they imagined it to be. He liked to compare them to horses with blinders on. They went through life seeing only what they wanted to see and ignoring the rest.

"Let's just get under way, can we?" Pendrake said. "We have a long ride ahead of us."

Several times over the next few hours as they wound deeper into the Rockies, Fargo caught Claresta studying him. The next time it happened, he slowed to let her bay come up alongside the Ovaro. She had done something with her hair, and her face was radiant. "How are you holding up?"

"Fine," Claresta said. "I'm so excited to be free of Edmunds, I doubt I'll sleep a wink tonight."

"We can always sit up late playing cards," Fargo proposed. "I have a deck in my saddlebags."

"That would be nice. Ruthie loves to play." Claresta added enigmatically, "But I had something else in mind."

9

A week and a half of hard travel brought them to a lush valley, the last vegetation they would see for a while. Beyond lay arid wasteland. A river meandered down the valley, and it was Fargo's notion to lay up for a couple of days and strike off across the wasteland after their mounts were well rested.

The last time Fargo had been to the valley, it was virgin and pristine. But now, as his small party came to the crown of a hill, he was surprised to see that a small settlement had sprouted in a bend of the river. A backwater hamlet of crudely constructed log and plank buildings.

"What's this place called?" Ruthie Landers asked.

"I have no idea," Fargo admitted, kneeing the Ovaro down the hill.

"I hope there's a general store where I can get clothes. Mine are a mess." Ruthie pointed. "Say, what kind of bird is that?"

The girl had a fount of questions the whole trek. Every new tree or flower had to be identified. The habits of every animal had to be explained. She absorbed knowledge like a sponge absorbed water. Always cheerful, always smiling, her disposition was as sunny as the sun itself.

Fargo had to admit it took some getting used to. He was seldom around children for long periods, and a bundle of energy like Ruthie had him wondering how parents stayed sane. He liked the girl, though, and he wasn't the only one.

Although cold and reserved at first, Captain Pendrake gradually melted under Ruthie's constant praise. At every meal she told him what a great cook he was. She liked to compliment him on how handsome he looked in his uniform. It was plain she was smitten, a girlish fancy that flattered him. She besieged him with questions about army life, and slowly but incredibly, before Fargo's eyes, Pendrake began to treat her more like a younger sister than a nuisance. They would ride side by side for hours, talking away.

Pendrake stopped complaining about delays. He stopped grousing about how upset General Foster would be. He did mention, several times, that it was important they find a place where Ruthie and her mother could settle and start over. It was always "Ruthie and her mother," never "Claresta and her daughter."

Fargo had many a secret laugh.

"Is this where we part company?" Ruthie asked as they wound along the valley floor. She did not sound happy about the prospect.

"Could be," Claresta said. She did not sound particularly happy about it either. "We can't keep imposing on the good graces of Mr. Fargo and Captain Pendrake. It wouldn't be fair."

Fargo glanced under his hat brim at Pendrake, who by rights should be overjoyed to finally be shed of the two inconveniences, but who wore a scowl down to his knees. He smothered a chuckle and commented, "Edgar will be glad it's just the two of us from here on out. We can make better time." He had taken to calling the captain by his first name when Ruthie started doing so, which annoyed the young officer considerably.

"I never said that," Pendrake snapped. "Don't put words in my mouth."

"Too bad we can't go with you all the way," Ruthie said wistfully. "I would like to see Seattle."

"It does sound nice except for the hostiles," Claresta commented. "But they have important business to attend to."

The hamlet lay quiet under the afternoon sun. Horses were tied to hitch rails and a few people were moving about. The place had an air of neglect about it. Dust caked the buildings. Some of the walls were at odd angles. Roofs sagged in the middle. One building looked to be on the verge of collapse. None of the windows had glass panes.

The few people out and about stopped to stare. All were men. Grungy, dirty sorts who apparently never took baths. A skinny one grinned at them as they went by, revealing yellow, half-rotten teeth. Several women appeared in windows and doorways to coldly stare. They were as grungy and dirty as the men.

"I don't think I like this place," Ruthie whispered.

"Hush," Claresta said.

The largest building bore a sign: HECTOR'S DRY GOODS AND HARD LIQUOR. Fargo drew rein and dismounted. He stretched, shucked the Henry, looped the reins around the hitch rail and stepped up onto a narrow porch. A rickety door had been propped open with a rusted rake. From within came a faintly foul odor, like the smell of a hog pen on a hot summer's day.

"Must we go in?" Ruthie asked.

"How else are we to find out where we are?" Claresta rejoined.

Captain Pendrake was unusually quiet. He gazed up and down the short dusty street with disgust written plainly on his features.

Fargo entered first and stopped past the threshold to let his eyes adjust to the gloomy interior. To his right was a counter, to his left tables where three men were playing cards. Straight ahead were shelves piled high with goods. The foul smell was so strong, he tried not to breathe too deeply.

The men at the table did not seem to mind. Their clothes were as dirty as their faces. One had a scar on his left cheek. Another was chewing tobacco.

Behind the counter stood a heavyset man wearing a dirty apron. Smiling, he spread stout arms. "Welcome, stranger! What will it be? Coffin varnish to wash down the dust?" He suddenly stopped and blinked.

Claresta and Ruthie were in the doorway, Claresta with an arm draped protectively over the girl's shoulders.

"Well, I'll be switched!" the man behind the counter declared. "Females! Welcome, ladies! Welcome! Would you care for some water? Or maybe some apple cider?" He took a dirty cloth from a dirty shelf and swiped it at the dirty counter. "Come on over. It's on the house." Then his smile vanished.

Captain Pendrake had strode inside. His hands clasped behind his back, his spine straight, he sniffed and said, "Hasn't anyone here ever heard of soap and water?"

Fargo noticed the three men at the table tense up. The man with the scar started to slide his hand under the table, but the one chewing tobacco shook his head.

"As I live and breathe!" exclaimed their genial host. "An army officer, or I'm a Flathead."

"Captain Edgar Pendrake," Pendrake said with his most pompous air of authority. "What is the name of this godforsaken blight?"

"I decided to call it Lucifer."

Pendrake moved toward the counter, careful to avoid stains on the planks. "Why in God's name would you do that?"

The man shrugged. "It fits how I think about things." He offered a pudgy, dirty hand. "My name is Locan. You could say I'm the leadin' citizen."

Pendrake went to place his hand on the counter but a fly took wing and he lowered the hand to his side. "Are lodgings available? Mrs. Landers and her daughter are looking for a place to stay."

"They are?" Locan lit up like a candle. "Why, we would be plumb honored to have them. Wouldn't we, boys?"

The men at the table nodded or grunted their agreement.

"Mother?" Ruthie said, pressing close to Claresta.

"How many other women live here?" Captain Pendrake inquired.

"Seven at last count," Locan said. "Wives of the menfolk."

Pendrake looked at Ruthie. "How many children?"

"None yet. But it ain' for a lack of tryin'." Locan

chortled. "But don't worry. We would make your friends feel right to home."

Fargo stepped to the counter and laid the Henry on it with a loud *thump*. "How many men in Lucifer?"

"Seventeen," Locan said, eyeing the Henry. "Say, that's a fine rifle you've got there, friend. One of those new ones that folks say you can load on Sunday and shoot all week. I don't suppose you would let me hold it?"

"You suppose right," Fargo said. "Give me a bottle of whiskey and a glass. A clean glass," he amended.

Locan took a bottle from a shelf and a glass from under the counter. "Is this clean enough?"

Fargo held the glass up so the sunlight spilling through the door caught it just right. The glass was speckled with rings and smears. He sniffed it, and frowned. "Just the bottle will do." Opening it, he took a swig.

"I don't know as you should do that with the Landers present," Captain Pendrake commented. "You should set a good example."

Fargo took another swig and winked at Ruthie, who giggled.

Locan cleared his throat. "You were wonderin' about lodgin'? How about if I show you a room I have out back? I could let these fine ladies have it for, say, five dollars a month."

"A room in a saloon?" Captain Pendrake responded. "For a young girl?"

"I sell dry goods too," Locan defended himself. "But if that's not good enough, there's a room across the street. Follow me and I'll show you."

Fargo turned his back to the counter and swallowed more whiskey. A warm burning sensation spread through his belly. He did not follow Locan and the others out. Picking up the Henry, he walked to the table where the three men were playing cards. Instead of coins or chips they were using toothpicks. The man chewing tobacco had the biggest pile. "They should come in handy," he said with a nod.

"What are you talkin' about?" The man spat on the floor and wiped his mouth with his sleeve.

"This is a private game," said the one with the scar. "You should tag along with your friends."

Fargo set the Henry's stock on the table and leaned on the rifle. "Not very hospitable, are you?"

"There's no law that says I have to be," the man with the scar replied. "Mosey along before I show you just how inhospitable I can be."

The player chewing the tobacco stopped chewing to say, "Now, now, Vern. Where are your manners? You wouldn't want this hombre to think poorly of us, would you? With his lady friend thinkin' about stayin', and all?"

Vern's brow puckered, then his mouth creased in a sly smile and he said, "You're right, Wes. I'm sorry, mister. Sometimes I tend to be grumpy."

"Must be the shortage of women," Fargo said to gauge their reaction.

Vern and Wes exchanged sharp glances, and Vern smirked and remarked, "Oh, we manage to get by, don't we, boys?"

"That's enough out of you," Wes said harshly.

"What did I do?" Vern rejoined.

"Pay this lunkhead no mind, mister." Wes addressed Fargo. "We've been drinkin' all day and he's half sloshed."

"I am not." Vern was confused and mad.

They fell silent. Fargo took another sip. "Don't

spend all your toothpicks on red-eye," he said, and ventured onto the porch. A chair at one end was inviting. It had warped slats and a front leg shorter than the rest. Leaning back against the wall, he placed the Henry in his lap and mulled what to do.

More scruffy sorts and several scruffy women were lounging outdoors, pretending not to be interested in the goings-on. The women wore clothes little better than rags, their hair stringy and limp, their faces stripped of life.

"Over my dead body," Fargo said to himself just as Locan emerged from a ramshackle house across the dusty street and came toward the store.

"—can be cleaned up right nice. All it will take is some scrubbin' and a good dustin'. What do you say? Will you take the room?"

Ruthie was clinging to her mother. For her part, Claresta was gnawing on her lip in uncertainty.

Pendrake trailed them, his bearing as military as ever. He, too, appeared unsure, and kept glancing at Lucifer's other inhabitants.

"Well?" Locan prodded when Claresta did not answer him. "What will it be, Mrs. Landers? Five dollars a month is more than fair. And as for findin' work like you mentioned, I can always use help at my place." He noticed Fargo and drew up short. "How about you, mister? Any provisions you need before you and the captain light a shuck?"

Fargo patted the whiskey bottle. "I've got my provisions right here."

Locan laughed, but neither Claresta nor Pendrake found it humorous. Claresta stopped at the hitch rail and gazed at Fargo in appeal. "What do you think? Should we or shouldn't we?"

"It's a nice room," Locan said much too quickly. "With a window with a view of the valley."

"And a bed that stinks and a dead snake in the corner," Ruthie said. "I don't like it here. I don't like it at all."

"Why not?" Locan asked a trifle testily. "Look around you. Lucifer is as quiet and peaceful a place as you're ever likely to find. Why else do you think we settled so far off the beaten path?"

"I just don't know," Claresta said, and again looked to Fargo. "Please. I value your opinion. Would you take the room?"

"Not even if *they* paid *me*."

Both Claresta and Locan said, "What?" at the same instant.

"If you stay here it will be as bad a mistake as Pol Edmunds," Fargo said. "Worse, since he never forced himself on you."

Locan's mouth began to twitch. "What the hell are you on about? Who's this Edmunds? What does he have to do with anything?"

Fargo made him wait. Chugging a third of the bottle, he set it down next to the chair. "Edmunds was a two-legged sidewinder. He would be right at home here if he was still alive."

"I resent that," Locan said.

"Ask me if I give a damn," Fargo responded.

Claresta let out a long breath. "Thank you, Skye. You've helped me make up my mind." She smiled at Locan. "I'm sorry, but we won't be taking the room." She hugged Ruthie and kissed her on the forehead. "I'm glad that's settled."

"Like hell it is," Locan said.

10

Just then Vern and Wes and the other man filed out, and Vern asked, "Somethin' the matter?"

"I don't much like his attitude," Locan said, jerking a thumb at Fargo. "He thinks our town is a dump and he doesn't want the woman and her kid to stay here. The gall of some jackasses," he added with a meaningful glare.

"Is that a fact?" Vern turned toward the chair. Wes and the third man each took a few steps to either side so they were not bunched up. "I don't know as I like that. Not a little bit."

Captain Pendrake came foward. "Now see here. This is the United States of America. A person is free to express their opinion. And to live where they want. Ruthie and her mother are entitled to go on with us if that is their wish. It's not a slight against you."

"Sure it is," Locan said. "We offer you our hospitality and you throw it in our faces."

"You're being ridiculous," Pendrake said.

"Am I?" Locan untied his apron. The butt of a pistol poked from a pocket and he had a knife in a sheath on his right hip. "What if I told you the lady and her kid are stayin' whether they want to or not?

What if I told you that you don't have any say in the matter?"

The street was filling with more of Lucifer's inhabitants, and many of the men were drifting toward the store.

"You're being ridiculous," Captain Pendrake responded. "Interfere with us, and you will have the United States Government down on your heads."

"Mister, by the time anyone shows up askin' about you, you'll be long buried. We'll claim we never saw hide nor hair of you, and they won't be able to prove different." Locan grinned, his pudgy fingers inches from his revolver.

"You're threatening us?" Captain Pendrake was incredulous. He noticed the men in the street, and asked, "What's going on here? What sort of town is this?"

Locan had his eyes on Fargo. "Why don't you ask your friend here? We haven't heard much from him."

Fargo still leaned against the wall, his hands folded in his lap. To Pendrake he said, "This isn't a town so much as a rattlesnake den. Did you see many wagon tracks on the way in?"

"What?" The captain glanced back up the street. "No. Now that I think about it, I can't say as I did. Of what significance is that?"

"These people settled here because they don't want anything to do with the outside world. They keep to themselves and like it that way. They do as they want when they want, and don't give a damn for the law." Fargo grinned at Locan. "How am I doing so far?"

"Not bad." Locan's fingers were practically touching his six-shooter. "But you left out the best part." He chuckled mirthlessly. "We also kill who we want when we want, and right now I'm thinkin' that you and the rooster have reached the end of your string. Any objections?"

"Sounds fine to me," Vern said.

"But not to me," Fargo said, and shot Vern through the stomach as he started to draw. They had not noticed the Henry was already cocked. All he had to do was place one hand on the barrel, his finger around the trigger and shift and squeeze.

Kicking to his feet, Fargo fired at Wes as he cleared leather. The slug smashed into Wes's lower jaw and sent him flying over the hitch rail. Pivoting, Fargo had the Henry trained on Locan before anyone else could so much as twitch. Locan had his revolver half out, but froze. So did everyone else.

"Just hold on there, mister!" Locan jerked his arms in the air. "You wouldn't shoot a defenseless man, would you?"

"Sure I would," Fargo said, and shot him through the thigh. Carefully watching the others, he stepped from the porch and up to the squawking figure flopping about in the dust.

"Damn you to hell!" Locan fumed, his fingers red with blood where they clutched the wound. "I had my hands up, didn't I? Why did you do that?"

"For what you were planning to do to her," Fargo said, indicating Claresta. He raised his right boot and brought it down on Locan's thigh.

Howling and hissing, Lucifer's leading citizen thrashed madly about. He kept it up until Fargo gouged the Henry against his temple.

"Tell your friends to back off."

Several men were drifting menacingly toward them.

Thrusting a bloody hand at them, Locan bawled, "Do as he says! No one is to lift a finger? You hear me?"

Fargo relieved Locan of his revolver. "Mount up and ride," he said to Pendrake and the Landers. "I'll join you after while."

"We're not leaving you here alone," Claresta said. "It wouldn't be right."

"It's not open to debate," Fargo said. They were badly outnumbered. He couldn't protect them if lead started to fly. Swinging the Henry from side to side, he covered their backs while they mounted, then waited until the drum of their hooves faded to back to the Ovaro and swing into the stirrups.

"Think you're smart, don't you?" Locan snarled. "But you won't get a mile. We'll ride you down and exterminate you."

"Really?" Fargo wagged the Henry at the hitch rail. "Is one of these horses yours?"

"The piebald."

"Get on. You're coming with me." Fargo had to watch all the people in the street and the windows and the doors at the same time.

"Over my dead body!"

Fargo fixed the Henry's sights on the center of Locan's forehead. "That's up to you. But make up your mind quick. And let them know that if I see anyone after us, you'll be the first to eat lead."

Locan was seething. He glanced at the sprawled forms of Vern and Wes, then blistered the air with abuse. Subsiding, he grated through clenched teeth, "You heard this polecat! He's taking me with him. No one is to follow us! And I mean no one, or they answer to me!"

Some of the men grumbled, but no one interfered

as Locan lurched to the piebald, gripped the saddle horn and painfully pulled himself into the saddle. The horse nickered and shied at the scent of the fresh blood, but Locan hauled on the reins and brought it under control. "Ready when you are."

Fargo reined the Ovaro next to Locan's animal and jabbed the Henry against Locan's side. "Nice and slow."

One man, whose face was splotched with dirt, was hunched over with his spindly fingers twitching above his holster. "We've got to do something!" he bawled.

"Don't you dare!" Locan screeched. "You hear me, Isaac? He'll plug me for sure." Beads of sweat sprinkled Locan's brow and neck.

Isaac reluctantly unfurled and thrust his hands out from his sides. "It's a sad day when one hombre can waltz in here and buffalo us like this."

No one else was inclined to dispute Fargo's departure. Twisting in the saddle, he did not relax his vigilance until they had forded the river and were in timber on the other side.

Captain Pendrake and the Landers were anxiously waiting, Pendrake pacing in an excess of nervous energy. "I can't believe it," he remarked as Fargo dismounted. "They were prepared to murder us over a trifle."

"I wouldn't call Claresta that," Fargo said, grinning.

Pendrake was scrutinizing Locan. "In God's name, man, why? There has to be more to it."

"What do you know?" Locan spat. "A fine female like her doesn't come along very often. All pretty and clean and smelling like a rose."

"You would have murdered for *that*?" Pendrake put a hand to his forehead. "What manner of men live in this land? Isn't there a shred of decency among them?"

"Listen to you!" Locan scoffed. "You make it sound like wantin' a woman is unnatural. For some of us, it's what makes life worth livin'." He openly ogled Claresta. "I'd give anything for a night with her. But since I don't have much to give, I take what I want."

"You're obscene," Pendrake said. "What about the other women in Lucifer? Or don't they count?"

"Hell, I've had all of them more times than you have fingers and toes," Locan boasted. "But if all a man eats every day is venison, he gets a powerful hankering for beef. Savvy?"

"What does he mean?" Ruthie asked.

Pendrake turned crimson with embarrassment. Locan leered at her and said, "I'd be happy to explain, little darlin'. In a year or two you'll be ripe yourself, and you should know what you're in—"

Fargo did not let him get any further. Gripping Locan's good leg, he tumbled him into the grass. Locan yipped and started to rise, his wound pumping fresh blood, but he did not make it to his feet. Fargo slammed the Henry's stock against his head and Locan keeled onto his side, unconscious.

"Serves him right," Ruthie said.

Claresta patted her head. "Forget his vile words. For every cur like him, there are decent men like Mr. Fargo and Captain Pendrake."

Fargo could think of a parson or two who would strongly disagree with her assessment of his character. He was as fond of the fairer sex as Locan, if not more so. However, he never took a woman by force, and never would. To him, rape was as low as a man could stoop.

"What now?" Ruthie asked.

"We water our horses and fill our canteens," Fargo said. Then it was off across the arid wasteland. Over a week of burning days and hot nights. Over a week of only a few swallows of water a day unless a spring he knew of was still there.

"And him?" This from Claresta, who bobbed her chin at the mound of disjointed limbs and filthy clothes.

"He'll wake up about sunset with the biggest headache he's ever had," Fargo predicted. "It will take him an hour to reach Lucifer. Another half an hour to have his leg tended. Then more time for all the men to get ready to come after us."

"Do you really think they will?" Ruthie asked nervously.

From time to time Fargo heard others say that things always happened in threes. He wasn't the superstitious sort, but first Aces Malone sent gunnies after him, then Pol Edmunds came after Claresta and now this. "It all depends. Maybe they won't."

Captain Pendrake nudged Locan. "It won't take this vermin an hour to reach that sorry excuse for a town."

"It will on foot." Fargo took hold of the reins to Locan's piebald and gave them to Ruthie. "Here you go. Your very own horse."

The girl was momentarily speechless, then blurted, "For me? But I can't! It would be the same as stealing, and that's wrong." She looked at her mother in a mix of confusion and hope.

"It wouldn't be right," Claresta said, but she didn't sound entirely convinced, especially since Fargo had given her Edmunds' horse.

"The worst stretch of the trail is ahead," Fargo said.

"We can use the extra animal." He placed a hand on her shoulder. She was warm to the touch, and oh so soft. "Think of it as Locan's gift for putting us through hell back in Lucifer."

"It's still stealing," Claresta said. But she smiled at Ruthie and nodded. "Very well. You can keep it for your own."

"Maybe we should take up rustling for a living," Pendrake said drily.

Ordinarily Fargo would never think of taking another man's mount, but he wanted to delay Locan in reaching Lucifer. After what Locan had tried to pull, he felt no guilt whatsoever.

Ruthie was admiring the piebald with unabashed enthusiasm. "It sure is pretty. I've never had a horse of my very own before."

Pendrake clasped his hands behind his back. "Every girl should." Opening a pouch, he palmed a small leather poke and asked Fargo, "How much would you say it's worth?"

Prices of horses varied. A mustang that went for forty dollars in Texas might fetch a hundred in Denver. Good saddle horses, though, were considerably higher everywhere. The average was a hundred and fifty, although Fargo had seen them go for as much as two hundred. "Eighty. A hundred if you include the saddle."

"You're going to pay for it?" Claresta shook her head. "No. Please. If anyone should, it's me."

"Indulge me. Consider it a gift to your charming daughter." Captain Pendrake rolled Locan over and stuffed the bills into one of his pockets. "Besides, with extra horses, we need not worry if one goes lame."

Fargo wasn't fooled. He noticed how Pendrake

beamed when Ruthie giggled and excitedly clapped her hands.

In ten minutes they were under way. They had to traverse a series of low hills. From the top of the last one they stared out across a sea of bleak terrain. Ripples of heat shimmered under the brilliant sun. A few brown spots of vegetation were the only signs of life.

"We have to cross that?" Ruthie sounded scared.

"Don't you fret, little one," Captain Pendrake reassured her. "Mr. Fargo is one of the best scouts alive. He'll see us safely through." But an hour later, as they wound across the parched landscape, he spurred his mount up next to the Ovaro and quietly asked, "You can, can't you? I never imagined it would be like this." He mopped a sleeve across his face.

"I told you before. There are no guarantees."

Pendrake pulled his hat brim low against the glare. "Frankly, I don't see how you have survived as long as you have. The men west of the Mississippi are animals, the animals are worse and even Nature itself is against you."

Fargo thought of all the bad men who had tried to put windows in his skull. He recollected his run-ins with Apaches and Comanches and other hostile tribes. He remembered the many knife fights and gunfights he had been in. He recalled an instance where a grizzly tried to rip him to bits and another where he was nearly trampled in a buffalo stampede, and he said, "You haven't seen anything yet."

Captain Pendrake squinted into the glare of the oven they were crossing and frowned. "That's what I'm afraid of."

11

Three days of sweltering heat had taken their toll. The horses plodded along with their heads drooping. Skye Fargo rose in the stirrups to survey the rocky terrain to the northwest for sign of a certain bluff. He was sure he would remember it even though several years had gone by since he saw it last. Memorizing landmarks was one of the most important skills a scout possessed.

Captain Pendrake and Ruthie were riding side by side, quietly talking. The heat did not have much of an effect on the girl's boundless vitality. She was still a perpetual bundle of questions, and Pendrake soaked up her interest in him and the world around them.

Hooves clattered, and Claresta Landers matched the pace of her chestnut to the Ovaro's. "You haven't said a lot the past few days."

"I'm not a chatterbox like some I could name," Fargo said, with a grin and a glance at the two behind them.

"I pity the poor captain. When Ruth takes a shine to someone, she can be a nuisance."

"You don't hear Pendrake complaining," Fargo remarked. Himself, he was partial to mature company, particularly women as finely shaped as Ruthie's mother, whose dusty dress clung so nicely to her full figure, accenting her charms.

"It's sweet of him to put up with her," Claresta said. She flicked a stray curl from her cheek and squinted at the cloudless sky. "Lord, it's hot."

"That it is," Fargo agreed. She had more on her mind, and he was interested in learning what.

"I've been meaning to thank you properly for all you've done for us. I didn't ask you to protect me from Pol Edmunds, yet you did it anyway. And back there in Lucifer, you stood up for me when you were under no obligation to do so."

Fargo shrugged. "Locan grated on my nerves."

"There was more to it than that." Claresta saw through his false modesty. "You put your life at risk on my account. I'd like to know why."

"I would do the same for most any woman."

"Would you indeed?" Claresta did not believe him. "I've seen how you look at me. I've seen the hunger in your eyes."

Fargo prided himself on his poker face, so it annoyed him to learn he was being so transparent. "Which must make me no better than Locan in your eyes."

"Quite the contrary. He and those others lusted after me like they would a dove in a saloon or a harlot walking the streets," Claresta said. "Your hunger is different. You want me but you're too much of a gentleman to take me unless I want you to."

"I'm just too tired at night after twelve hours in the saddle to think about fooling around."

Claresta's lilting laughter was borne aloft on the hot wind. "I'm not buying it. You're nicer than you're willing to admit."

"You've seen me kill three men and shoot a

fourth," Fargo reminded her. "Nice might be a poor choice of words."

"A person can be nice and tough at the same time. My father was that way. My grandfather before him." Claresta regarded him intently. "It's taken me this long to realize you're more like them than any man I've met, including my dear, beloved husband."

"I do what I have to," Fargo said. He would never stoop to justifying how he lived. He was how he was, and that was that.

"I envy you in a way," Claresta mentioned. "We aren't all as honest with ourselves as you are. I always bend over backwards for others, even when they're in the wrong. You don't. I don't mind admitting that you interest me."

Fargo was more interested in how the swell of her thigh was outlined by her clinging dress. "Just so you know. We'll be parting company eventually."

"Ah. That's your way of saying I shouldn't become as fond of you as Ruth is of Captain Pendrake? Never fear. I'm a grown woman. I make my own bed and lie in it too."

Fargo imagined her lying naked and gorgeous on a white sheet, and felt stirring below his belt.

"I gave up girlish things a long time ago. Life has a way of doing that, of stripping us of our illusions." Claresta sighed, her bosom swelling. "Have you ever wanted to shut the world out for a while? To forget all your cares and woes, if only for an hour or two?" She did not wait for an answer. "I do. There are days when the burden is almost too much, when I look in the mirror and ask myself what I'm trying to prove."

"You're trying to be a good mother to your daughter," Fargo said.

Claresta looked at him strangely, then nodded. "Nothing in this world means more to me than she does. No matter what, I want to go to my grave knowing I tried my best for her. That has to count for something."

A bump appeared on the horizon. As the minutes passed it grew to resemble a hillock, then a hill, then a rounded bluff with three sheer sides that towered hundreds of feet above the blistered flats.

Fargo reined toward it, saying, "There's where we'll make camp tonight."

"Is that where you hope to find water?" Claresta gazed all around. "How did you find it in the middle of so much nothing?"

"I've had a lot of practice." To Fargo it was second nature. His sense of direction was as finely honed as the sharp edge of a saber. It had to be. His life depended on being able to get where he needed to go and back again.

"I wouldn't last a week in the wilds on my own," Claresta said. "If you and the captain hadn't come along, Ruth and I would be dead."

"It took a lot of courage to do what you did," Fargo said. Few people would dare the mountains on foot and unarmed.

"Desperation is a mighty motivator."

After that neither spoke until they were near enough to the bluff to see a sloping mound of talus at the bottom. Vegetation was conspicuous by its absence.

"Maybe the spring dried up," Claresta said. "Can we make it the rest of the way with only the little water we have left?"

"No." Fargo reined toward the north side of the

bluff. It was latticed with cracks. Long ago part of the cliff had collapsed, leaving sections where it appeared as if the stone surface had been scooped out by a giant spoon. Piles of debris littered the base, and dust covered everything up to a quarter of an inch thick.

Scores of animal tracks speckled the dust, deer and raccoon and rabbit. Some of the tracks had been made as recently as the day before.

"The water is there," Fargo informed Claresta. He drew rein before a slab of rock bigger than the Ovaro. Sliding down, he led the pinto to a stone overhang. Under it, in a cavity thirty feet wide and almost as high, lay a quiet pool of welcome water.

"My goodness!" Claresta breathed. "You're amazing."

When Pendrake and Ruthie came up, Fargo took charge of all the horses, and after letting them drink, he sheltered them in the deep shade between the pool and the bluff wall, where it was bearably cool.

Ruthie was laughing and splashing water on herself. "I was so hot, I was roasting alive."

"That makes two of us, little one," Captain Pendrake said. He had removed his hat and bandanna, and was meticulously cleaning his hair and face. "We tend to take life's necessities for granted until we are deprived of them."

Fargo drank last, then sat back. "It's early yet, but we'll stay the night." He was concerned for the horses; the extra rest would do them good.

Squealing in delight, Ruthie gripped her mother's hand and pumped it up and down. "We get to relax and enjoy ourselves! Can we take a bath? Please?"

"Only if Mr. Fargo says it is all right," Claresta said.

Fargo had no objections. He and Pendrake walked

out past the slab and whiled away half an hour until the Landers called for them to come back. Mother and daughter were scrubbed clean, their hair still wet.

They laid out their bedrolls and sat down to relax and chat. Except for Fargo. He hiked to the east end of the bluff and climbed partway up the talus to a flat earthen strip, high enough to verify no one was on their back trail. He still expected Locan's pack of killers to show up, and was surprised they hadn't.

The sun was on its westward descent and the east side of the bluff became shrouded in shadow. Fargo leaned back, in no hurry to return to the others. He enjoyed being by himself for a while. As much as he liked the Landers, he was by nature a loner.

Most scouts and frontiersmen were hewn from the same mold. Their own company was company enough. Not that Fargo disliked people. Far from it. He enjoyed a spell in town as much as the next man. But after a while the perennial urge to wander would come over him, and off he would go, alone again.

Fargo suddenly sat up. Specks had appeared in the distance. For a minute he thought they were riders, but it was soon apparent that they were much too small. Antelope, drifting toward the bluff, probably to slake their thirst. "You'll have to wait a while," he said aloud. They would not come anywhere near the spring until he and the others were gone.

Rocks clattered below him, and Fargo looked down to find Claresta Landers climbing the talus. She had hiked the hem of her dress midway to her knees, and he glimpsed flashes of shapely calves as she hopped from rock to rock with the agility of a mountain goat. Soon she reached the flat nook he had chosen for his lookout.

"So this is where you got to." Claresta gazed eastward and saw the antelope. "I wouldn't mind fresh meat right about now."

"In a few days you'll feast on roast venison," Fargo promised.

"Still no sign of Locan and his bunch?" Claresta roosted next to him, so close their shoulders brushed. Stretching her legs out, she arched her back and her dress molded to her bosom like a second skin, leaving little to the imagination. "Maybe they decided it was smarter not to push their luck."

"Locan wouldn't care. He'll want my hide nailed to a wall." Fargo leaned back, his hands propped behind him.

"After how you humiliated him, that's natural," Claresta said. "But he's no fool. He knows how dangerous you are."

"No more than most," Fargo said.

Claresta arched an eyebrow. "That's like saying a mountain lion is no more dangerous than a house cat. You strike me as being the most dangerous man I've ever met. In more ways than one."

"I would never harm a hair on your or Ruthie's heads."

"I knew that the moment I laid eyes on you," Claresta claimed. "Call it a woman's intuition. It's partly why I let you talk me into coming along. The other part was fear. Fear of what Edmunds would do to me and the future in store for Ruthie if he dragged me back to Elkhorn."

"That's over and done with. You're safe."

"Thanks to you." Leaning toward him, Claresta pecked him on the cheek. "And I still haven't thanked you properly." She gazed into his eyes, then gave a start and looked guiltily away. "You're a remarkable man."

"I put on my pants one leg at a time, the same as everyone else." Fargo moved the Henry so he could lie down with his hands interlocked under his head.

"There you go again," Claresta said. "Pretending you're ordinary when you're not. "Most men would be afraid to do what you do. To roam the wilds on their lonesome, with nothing to rely on but their own wits."

"There are plenty just like me." Fargo could think of a dozen or more who lived exactly the same sort of life. Scouts, mostly, who were more at home in the mountains and deserts than in a city or town.

"Have it your way. But I know better." Claresta shifted so she was facing him, and smoothed her dress over her legs. "Would you consider it too bold of me if I tell you that I find you incredibly handsome?"

"Do you need spectacles?"

Claresta laughed and touched his arm. "My husband had a wonderful sense of humor, too. God, there are days when I miss him so much, all I want to do is cry." She coughed and sobered and said, "I'm sorry. It was awkward of me to bring him up. But you can never forget someone you've loved."

"Who says you have to?" Fargo was growing drowsy, his eyelids leaden. He had not been able to relax in days, and a nap was appealing.

"It's strange how life works out, isn't it?" Claresta droned on. "We think we're settled into what will be the pattern for the rest of our days, and out of the blue everything changes. I never thought I would lose Brad. I always figured the two of us would grow old together and die of old age."

Fargo had learned long ago never to take anything for granted, but he held his tongue and stifled a yawn.

"Now here I am, alone again. No man to share my life with. No man to keep me warm at night. Oh, I'm sure any number of men would leap at the chance, but I'm not that kind of woman."

Fargo closed his eyes. He was on the verge of dozing off.

"But I have yearnings, the same as everyone else. My mother would roll over in her grave if she heard me now, but I can't deny them like she could. She used to say that once a month was enough to do her wifely duty, as she called it."

Sleep nipped at Fargo's mind. Another few moments and he would succumb.

"Brad and I liked to do it a lot more often. Heaven help me, but I enjoy the touch of a man's hands on my body."

Belatedly what she was saying registered, and Fargo struggled to shake off his drowsiness.

"I can't believe I am telling you this. If I've offended you, if you think less of me, just say so and I will go and never bring it up again."

Fargo tried to get his vocal cords to work so he could assure her that he had not been offended in the least. Quite the opposite.

"No answer? I guess that means you don't want to hurt my feelings. Very well. I'm terribly sorry I bothered you." Claresta was distressed. She looked away and started to rise.

"Hold on," Fargo said, clasping her wrist. She did not resist. "Don't rush off on my account. This is just getting interesting."

12

Casting off lingering tendrils of drowsiness, Skye Fargo sat up. "No man in his right mind would be offended by you," he told her, and kissed her lightly on the mouth.

"Oh!" Startled, she pressed her fingertips to her lips. "I thought I was making a fool of myself."

Fargo eased her down beside him and draped his arm around her slender shoulders. Her lustrous hair was soft to the touch, the skin at the nape of her neck as smooth as silk. "I would be the fool if I let you walk off." He parted her hair and kissed her small, delicate ear.

"Oh, my," Claresta said. "I've dreamt about us being together, but now that we're alone, I'm frightened."

"You can walk away if you want. I won't hold it against you." Fargo nipped at her earlobe and rimmed her ear with his thumb. She was sensitive there, and squirmed deliciously.

"You won't think me a hussy?" Claresta asked.

"Like you said, women have yearnings, too." Fargo's own desire brought a warm tingle to his skin.

"I won't think any less of you for doing what I've wanted to do since I met you."

"Really?" Immensely pleased, Claresta giggled girlishly and swiped at her hair. "I should warn you, I've never done anything like this before. I honestly don't know if I can go through with it."

"Fair enough," Fargo said, and kissed her on the mouth again, only this time he let the kiss linger while rimming her lips and her teeth with his tongue. She became a statue, frozen by fear or indecision or a combination of both. When he drew back, he was growing hard.

"Goodness gracious," Claresta breathed. "You're a marvelous kisser. Brad never liked to use his tongue. He said it was sinful."

Fargo glued his lips to hers anew, and she parted hers to admit his tongue in a delectable probe of her velvety mouth. She might not have had much experience, but she learned fast; she sucked on his tongue as if it were honey.

Pulling her against him so they were face to face, chest to bosom and thigh to thigh, Fargo ran his hand down her back and she shivered. When he brazenly cupped her bottom and squeezed, she gasped and drew back.

"My head is spinning. You do things to me no one has ever done."

Fargo was just getting started. Embracing her, he locked mouths in the longest kiss yet, and this time he sucked on her tongue. She wriggled and cooed, her breath growing hotter and hotter. Suddenly she pulled away, groaned loudly and shuddered. "Are you all right?" he asked.

"Yes, oh yes. It's just—" Claresta raised eyes hooded with raw lust. "It's just that I'm scared."

"I won't bite"—Fargo grinned—"unless you want me to."

"It's not you, it's me. When Brad and I were courting, he was so shy he wouldn't kiss me unless I asked him to. And after we were married, he treated me like I was a china doll, as if he thought if he squeezed me too hard, I would break."

"Let's find out," Fargo said, and covering her breasts with both hands, he squeezed hard enough to elicit a sharp cry.

"Ahhhhh!" Claresta closed her eyes and rolled her head from side to side, the pink tip of her tongue poking from her cherry lips.

Fargo found her nipples and pinched them through the fabric. Her reaction was to open her mouth as if to scream. Throwing her arms around him, she sculpted her body to his and kissed him with burning intensity. When she broke for air she was breathing as if she had just run a mile and quaking with unbridled desire. "What about your daughter?" he brought up before they went any further.

"Ruthie? What about her?" Claresta's passion had befuddled her thinking.

"You don't want her showing up, do you?"

"She's helping the captain fix supper. I told her I was going to take a walk and would be back in half an hour."

"That doesn't give us much time," Fargo said. In order not to waste another second, he snuggled against her and licked her neck while his left hand explored the curve of her back. He ran his palm over her bottom and kneaded it as she might knead bread dough.

"Ohhhhhh," Claresta husked, her fingernails biting into his shoulders. "Keep that up and I'm liable to rip your buckskins off."

Fargo kept it up, then did her one better. He slid his hand between her thighs and ran his finger across her womanhood. Even though the dress was bunched up and he couldn't touch her core, she nearly came up off the ground.

"More! I want more!"

So did Fargo. He began undoing her stays and buttons to get at the charms underneath, but there were so many, and the buttons so tiny, that in a fit of annoyance he grabbed her dress, and without thinking was about to wrench it when her palm enclosed his wrist.

"No! Please! It's the only dress I own."

Fargo had to content himself with unfastening the rest, one by monotonous one, until at length her bosom popped free of its restraints. Her undergarments were not nearly as formidable. Then, like a flower unfolding its petals, her breasts were revealed in all their full and rounded glory. Her nipples were as erect as nails. Inhaling one, he rolled it with his tongue, and grunted in pain when she nearly tore his hair out by the roots.

"Yes! Yes! Like that!"

Fargo switched to her other nipple but did not neglect the first. Pinching it between his thumb and forefinger, he doubled her pleasure. He lathered both mounds with his tongue. By now they were heaving with wanton lust. He licked every square inch in shrinking concentric circles until his mouth was once again fastened to a nipple.

For her part, Claresta was emboldened to run a hand from his neck to his waist and back again. The feel of his buckskin shirt, though, did not satisfy her. Soon she pried at it until it was loose enough for her to slide her hand underneath. At the contact of her hand with his skin, she sighed contentedly. Then, ever so slowly, almost timidly, she caressed his chest and his ribs and brought her roving hand to his abdomen. "Mercy me," she whispered. "You have more muscles than Brad."

Fargo hoped she wouldn't go on comparing him to her late husband. He undid more of her stays and peeled her garments down about her waist. She was breathtakingly beautiful. Her ripe globes arched upward in perfect contour, her belly was smooth and flat, her hips flared with the promise below.

Claresta shifted under his gaze and made as if to cover herself. "I'm not much to look at, am I?"

Pushing her hands apart, Fargo kissed one breast and then the other. "You're beautiful," he said, entirely sincere. She could hold her own with any dove, any woman, anywhere.

"You're just saying that," Claresta said, but in gratitude she bestowed a wet, passionate kiss.

Fargo started to slide her dress down, but felt her tense up. Glancing to the north to be sure they were alone, he lavished kisses from her neck to her navel, arousing her by gradual degrees so when he tried to slide her dress down a second time, she lay relaxed, and even smiled in anticipation.

Nature had been generous. Her lower half rivaled her top. Claresta's thighs were marvels of softness, her legs exquisitely formed. The curly thatch that crowned her nether mound crinkled to his touch. The instant his finger brushed her wet slit, she arched her back and bit off a cry of ecstasy.

114

Fargo fused his mouth to hers while slowly sliding his finger into her. She was molten lava inside. A thrust of his hand, and her bottom rose in the rhythm ingrained into men and women since the dawn of time.

"The things you do to me," Claresta mewed into his ear. "I don't know how long I can control myself."

"You're not supposed to," Fargo set her straight, and inserting a second finger, he thrust both in as far as they would go. His thumb found her tiny knob and flicked, with the result he wanted.

"Oh! Oh! Ohhhhhhh!" Claresta gushed and gushed, her inner walls clinging to his fingers even as her hands clung to his shoulders and her teeth sank into his right arm. She bucked like a bronco, her legs spread wide, her body bent like a bow.

The sight was enough to harden Fargo's member to the rigidity of iron, but he did not enter her. Not yet, not until he aroused her to a fever pitch, until she craved him as she had never craved anything.

With a low moan Claresta sank onto her back and was still except for the rise and fall of her breasts. "I have never," she said, but she did not finish her statement. She traced his jaw with a tapered forefinger and lightly tugged on his chin. "You sure know how to please a woman. I can tell I'm not your first."

She had no idea. Fargo bent to her breasts again, and while running his tongue around and around, he moved his fingers around and around inside her. A long, low groan fluttered from her throat and she entwined her fingers in his hair. But only for a few seconds. Abruptly bending, she tugged at his buckskin shirt and with some effort slipped it off over his head.

Fargo was unprepared for what she did next. Her

right hand dipped lower, to his belt buckle, and with newfound urgency she undid it and pushed at his pants until they slid down around his knees.

Once aroused, Claresta was a tigress. Her hand enfolded his manhood and gently stroked. Fargo almost exploded then and there. Gritting his teeth, he focused on the sky, on the bluff, on anything but the sensations she was provoking with the delicate manipulation of her fingers.

Claresta's shoulder dipped and her hand roved lower. Her luscious lips curled in a hungry grin as she cupped him. "Do you like that?" she whispered.

Again she had no idea. A knot formed in Fargo's throat and he had to cough to clear it. Gripping her bottom, he spread her thighs wider. He was about to align his member with her moist slit but she did it for him, rubbing him up and down a few times first.

Now it was Fargo whose skin was on fire. His blood pounded in his veins. He inserted his pole into her satin tunnel, but only an inch or so, enough to tantalize and tease.

"Please," Claresta said. "Please."

Gripping her hips, Fargo thrust into her to the hilt. Her red lips parted and her head bent back and she sank her nails into his biceps deep enough to draw trickles of blood. For a span of heartbeats neither moved, then Fargo rocked on his knees.

In and out, in and out, Fargo paced himself, delaying the inevitable for as long as he could. Claresta matched the tempo he set.

How long they had been at it when he became aware of movement at the north end of the bluff, Fargo couldn't say. One glance, and he froze and put his hand over Claresta's mouth. "Your daughter," he whispered.

Ruthie was scanning the east face of the bluff but had not spotted them. They had several large boulders to thank, and the fact the earthen strip was not visible until someone was right on top of it.

Panic filled Claresta's eyes. "Has she seen us?" she asked when Fargo removed his hand and bent low.

Shaking his head, Fargo mentally crossed his fingers that Ruthie would turn and go back, but to his considerable consternation she skipped toward the talus. Picking up a flat rock, she threw it high into the air.

Claresta raised her head high enough for a peek, and stiffened. "I will never forgive myself if she finds us like this," she whispered.

Fargo debated whether to slide out of her and dress, but before he could, who should come swaggering around the end of the bluff but Captain Edgar Pendrake.

"Oh, God," Claresta said.

Pendrake surveyed the talus, then shouted to Ruth, "Any sign of them, little one?"

"I don't see them anywhere," Ruthie answered. "Where can they have gotten to?"

To Fargo it was obvious. Two sets of tracks led from the bottom of the talus to the shelf. A few more yards and Ruthie was bound to notice them.

"They could be anywhere," Pendrake said. "I think it best we wait at the spring until they return."

Ruthie slowed. "It's not like my mother to be gone this long. Something must have happened."

"If they ran into trouble we would have heard shots. Fargo isn't one to go down without a fight."

"I want to keep looking," Ruthie insisted. "They have to be around here somewhere."

"Your mother told you to stay put, remember? She might not take too kindly to being disobeyed."

"I worry, is all. I've already lost my father, I don't want to lose my mother too."

Pendrake held out a hand. "Come on. She left you in my care and we should do what I think best."

Ruthie came to a halt barely a stone's throw from where Fargo and her mother lay. "I suppose."

Beckoning, Pendrake said, "They might be at the spring waiting for us, for all we know. You'll have some explaining to do."

That settled it. Ruthie hurried back to him and took his hand in hers. "Sorry I snuck off when you weren't looking."

"It's only natural when you love someone." Pendrake ushered her around the bluff and out of sight.

Claresta exhaled loudly and slumped on her back. "For a second there I thought she would find us. I would die of shame." She blinked, then said softly, "My-oh-my. You're still as hard as a rock."

Taking hold of her hips again, Fargo grinned. "Now where were we?"

13

Fort Crittenden was not much of a fort. It was more like a camp, which was why it had been known as Camp Floyd until it had recently been renamed after a U.S. senator. Situated west of Utah Lake, its purpose was to safeguard mail delivery by the Overland Mail Company.

Skye Fargo rode up to the hitch rail in front of the sutler's and dismounted. He was caked with dust and weary from so many long days in the saddle.

The Landers were worse off. Claresta's hair was disheveled and her dress in need of washing. Ruthie was worn to a husk.

As for Pendrake, his uniform was as immaculate as ever and he carried himself with the same ramrod military bearing. But crow's-feet crinkled the corners of his eyes and he could not hide his fatigue.

Removing his hat, Fargo slapped at his buckskins, creating a cloud of dust motes, then placed it back on his head and turned to go inside.

"As I live and breathe! Fargo, is that you?"

A middle-aged officer with gray temples smiled and offered a welcoming calloused hand. "I haven't seen you since Fort Laramie. How have you been?"

"Colonel Seaver," Fargo said, shaking. He had

scouted for Seaver on a campaign against renegades who attacked a wagon train, and respected the officer highly. "Are you in charge here?"

"In a manner of speaking." Seaver had a deep, gravelly voice. "The Army has decided, in its infinite wisdom, that the post is no longer essential, and they sent me to close it down. Another month and only the Overland Mail people will be left."

Captain Pendrake alighted, drew himself up to his full height and executed a snappy salute while introducing himself. "Mr. Fargo and I are on government business with orders direct out of Washington."

"You don't say. What kind of business?" Colonel Seaver inquired.

"I'm afraid that's confidential," Pendrake said. "I'm under strict orders from General Horace Foster not to reveal its nature to anyone."

"I take it you're one of those who live by the book," Seaver remarked, not without a tinge of reproach.

"An officer must always follow his orders," Pendrake stated with absolute conviction. "It's the nature of the military."

"That, and knowing when to bend a little." Colonel Seaver shrugged. "But do as you please. And before I forget, a dispatch came for you over a week ago. I have it somewhere in my office."

Fargo introduced the Landers. Claresta excused herself after asking where they could find a tub and a bar of lye soap and being told the operator of the Overland Mail office charged fifty cents for the use of a large wash basin out behind the building.

"About that dispatch, sir?" Pendrake asked as the mother and child hustled off.

"Patience, Captain, patience," Colonel Seaver advised, and made for the headquarters building.

Fargo fell into step beside the post commander. "We're heading for Seattle. What's the latest on hostile activity between here and there?"

"It's been quiet. A band of Paiutes raided a few farms six weeks ago, but all they did was steal some horses and help themselves to food for their families. There's word the Modocs have killed two white men, but they're well south of the route you'll take."

"Any word on more disappearances from up near Seattle, sir?" Captain Pendrake was eager to learn.

"None that I'm aware of, no," Colonel Seaver answered. "But our updates don't always include the latest reports from that far north."

"The land is to blame, not the army," Pendrake said. "Until I came west I had no idea how vast it is. To think we can be everywhere at once is ridiculous."

"An astute observation, Captain. But try convincing that bunch of desk-bound incompetents in Washington. To them a mountain is a squiggle on a map that should take a man on horseback a day to cross when it can actually take six or seven. They measure distances in inches, while we measure it in hundreds of miles."

"That's a tad harsh, isn't it, sir?"

"Not when you've been on the receiving end of some of their orders," Colonel Seaver said. "Their answer to every difficulty with Indians is force and more force. No wonder most tribes would rather scalp us than befriend us."

"I never thought I would live to see the day where an officer of the United States Army would side with the savages."

Colonel Seaver stopped dead. "Young man, I've served my country with distinction for three decades. When you have been out here that long, then you can judge me. Otherwise, spare us your ignorance and keep your foolish comments to yourself."

"But—" Pendrake began, only to be cut off.

"Indians are not *savages*. Yes, they kill whites on occasion, but you would, too, if invaders came and took your land from you. Or wiped out whole tribes with disease. Or killed off all your game." Colonel Seaver poked the younger officer in the chest. "Always remember, Captain, there are two sides to every issue. Only look at one side and you do yourself and the United State Government a disservice."

Pendrake had snapped to attention, his lips a thin slit. "I intended no disrespect, sir."

"None taken," Seaver rasped, and motioned to Fargo. "Makes you wonder, doesn't it, about the quality of the West Point graduates these days?"

"Edgar learns fast," Fargo sought to mollify him. "I wouldn't stick with him if I didn't think he could cut it."

"It's your life," Colonel Seaver said, "but you always know what you're doing."

Fargo hoped so. Stupidity killed more men than all the arrows and claws in creation. All it took was one mistake.

A corporal rose from behind a desk to greet them. Colonel Seaver ushered them into his office, then closed the door. He hung his hat on a hat stand, and settled with a sigh into his chair. His desk was cluttered with papers and reports. He had to slide a pile aside to make room for his forearms. "Now then. What did I do with that dispatch?"

Pendrake was staring at the clutter as if it would leap up and bite him. "I hope you haven't lost it, sir."

"My duties leave me little time to indulge in petty tidiness, Captain," Colonel Seaver said without looking up. "But I always manage to get my job done, thank you very much."

Pendrake started to respond, but to his credit finally had the good sense to shut up.

"You remind me of the last quisling from the inspector general's office," Colonel Seaver mentioned while rummaging through a stack. "He was horrified to find horse droppings on our parade ground. So in his report he suggested I assign two men to chase our horses around and clean up after them."

Fargo chuckled as he sank into a chair by a large map tacked to a wall. "I would like to see that."

"I bet you would." The colonel grinned. "But I told the inspector that the only horseshit he need worry about was the stuff coming out his ears."

"You didn't!" Captain Pendrake exclaimed.

Fargo knew that many officers lived in fear of poor performance reports. Understandable, since the reports adversely affected their career.

Seaver finished sorting through one stack and switched to another. "Son, an officer has to have his priorities straight. My men have enough regular duties to perform without needlessly adding to their burdens. A soldier's life is hard enough as it is."

Another thing Fargo liked about the colonel was that he genuinely cared about those serving under him. Not all officers shared that trait.

Seaver wasn't done. "When I was your age, Captain Pendrake, I was all spit and polish, just like you. Experience has taught me that a clean uniform or a clean parade ground doesn't amount to a hill of beans when a hostile war party is trying to turn you into a pincushion."

"Regulations have a purpose, sir," Pendrake said.

"That they do. But anything carried to an extreme does more harm than good—a point to bear in mind should you ever have a command of your own." Seaver switched to a third stack. "Ah. Here it is." He held out the packet. "How did HQ know you would stop here?"

Pendrake eagerly snatched the envelope. "I arranged with General Foster beforehand, should he need to contact me." He read the writing on the cover. "If you don't mind, I must read this in private."

Colonel Seaver nodded and Pendrake hurried out. "Hard to believe I had a broom that far up my ass once." Opening a drawer, the colonel displayed a silver flask. "As I recall, you're not one to refuse a nip of the nectar of the gods."

"A nip, hell. Pour me a glass," Fargo said.

From another drawer Colonel Seaver produced one and filled it halfway. "Here you go." He sipped from the flask and thoughtfully regarded the closed door. "I'd be careful of that one, were I you. He might not be what he seems."

Fargo savored a long gulp of the finest whiskey money could buy. "What are you talking about?"

"I've heard of General Foster. He heads a special department. Secret stuff. Things the rest of us aren't supposed to know anything about. Like those disappearances the captain mentioned." Seaver swallowed and smacked his lips. "I happen to have picked up a few tidbits here and there. Tidbits that might interest you."

"I'm listening," Fargo said.

"There's talk of a crisis brewing. Talk that the Canadian government is very unhappy with ours. It has something to do with more than thirty people who have vanished on their side of the border. They blame Indians on our side. We blame Indians on their side for close to forty disappearances."

"Seventy, all told?" Fargo was stunned.

"That's a conservative estimate." Seaver leaned toward him. "You see, it's been going on since the first whites arrived."

Fargo paused with the glass halfway to his mouth. "That long? It has to be one of the local tribes."

"You would think so, yes," Seaver conceded, "except that Indians have been disappearing too. Over a hundred, rumor has it. There isn't a tribe along the north section of coast that hasn't had people vanish into thin air. Warriors included."

Fargo did not know what to make of it. "They must have some idea who is behind it."

"If they do, they're not talking."

"How did you find out?"

"A friend of mine has a son, a lieutenant, who was stationed at Fort Townsend on the Olympic Peninsula for a year. Later he was reassigned to Fort Leavenworth, where I made his acquaintance. He says Indians have been vanishing for as long as the tribes can remember."

"I'm obliged," Fargo said.

"There's more. An Indian scout told the lieutenant that whoever is behind it is not human, but he wouldn't elaborate. The Salish say ghosts are to blame. The Nootkans say it's the hairy men of the woods."

Fargo had heard accounts of hairy men himself. They were supposed to inhabit the deep woods of the Northwest, and sighting one would send an entire tribe into a panic. The Spokane Indians claimed that hairy giants liked to take fish from their nets and rip the nets to shreds, and would steal women and children.

"I've never placed much credence in the reports myself," Colonel Seaver said. "About six years ago I met an old Flathead who told me that he saw a hairy giant when he was a boy of ten or twelve. He was fishing with his father on the shore of Flathead Lake when one of the creatures stepped out of the forest and stared at them awhile, then walked back into the trees. His father was so scared, they left everything they had and fled to their village. When they came back later with friends, the fish they had caught were gone, and the old man swore there were giant footprints everywhere."

In all his travels Fargo had never seen one of the hairy men. Nor, for that matter, had he ever encountered a thunderbird or any of the many lake monsters such as the aquatic beast believed to inhabit the murky depths of Flathead Lake.

"Makes you wonder why General Foster is involved," Colonel Seaver commented. "Hairy men don't sound like something he would take notice of. Not unless they are a threat to our nation's security."

"Strange," Fargo conceded. He polished off the rest of his whiskey and set the glass on the desk. "I think I'll go have a talk with the captain."

"You do that. Just keep in mind what I said. His only loyalty is to Foster, not to you or anyone else."

Pendrake was leaning against a porch post, reading the dispatch. The moment Fargo walked out the door, he quickly folded the message, undid a button and slid it inside his shirt. "Done visiting with your friend?"

"Anything I should know?" Fargo asked, nodding at the bulge.

"It's for my eyes alone." Pendrake stepped off the porch, but Fargo wasn't done.

"I don't like being left in the dark, Edgar. If you don't share all you know, you can go on to Seattle without me."

"That's your decision," Pendrake said, "but after coming all this way, I should think you would want to see it through."

Fargo watched him walk toward the sutler's. He'd had his fill of the secrecy. He would try one more time, and if Pendrake didn't tell him the truth, he was off to San Francisco, where poker was king and doves were willing and wanton.

Just then Claresta and Ruth came around the corner. "There you are," the mother said.

"We've been looking all over for you," Ruthie added.

Claresta nodded. "We've talked it over and come to a decision. I figure Seattle is as good a place as any to start over. So we would like to go with you and Captain Pendrake when you ride out in the morning."

"What do you say?" Ruthie eagerly asked.

Fargo envisioned them on the trail with only the inexperienced young officer to protect them. "It's fine by me."

"Are you sure? You look a trifle upset."

"I was just thinking how much I'm looking forward to seeing Seattle again."

14

The green hills of Seattle overlooked Puget Sound. Barely a decade old, the fledgling town was thriving thanks to its gateway to the Pacific Ocean. Sailing ships from San Francisco and points south routinely put in to take on loads of lumber from the busy saw-mill and to unload trade goods.

Like mushrooms sprouting on tree stumps, homes had sprouted on every hill. Seattle's leading citizens liked to boast that in another ten years Seattle would have a population of more than a thousand hardy souls.

A schooner was at anchor in the harbor. Out on the bay the white canvas sails to an approaching vessel were a stark contrast to the blue of the water.

During the rainy season Seattle's dirt streets turned into mud quagmires, but it had not rained in two months and now puffs of dust rose from the wheels of wagons and buckboards and the hooves of passing horses. Pigs, chickens, dogs and cats were all allowed to run loose.

"So this is Seattle?" Claresta Landers said. "It's not as backwards as I feared it might be."

"It's pretty," was Ruthie's assessment. "Our new home! I can't wait to find a place of our own."

"Let's not get ahead of ourselves," Claresta said. "And don't forget to thank Mr. Fargo and Captain Pendrake for bringing us."

"You did well," Fargo remarked. Without complaint they had endured weeks of blazing heat, little food and less water.

"It was a pleasure to have your company," Pendrake said.

Fargo had expected him to say no when they asked to come along. After all, Pendrake had griped and griped about the Landers slowing them down. Yet when they asked, he happily agreed.

"Where's Fort Townsend?" Claresta asked.

"Across the bay," Pendrake said. "Fargo and I will take the ferry across tomorrow."

"Then we can spend this one last night together, can't we?" Ruthie asked.

"Let's not push them," Claresta cautioned her offspring. "After all these weeks they must be tired of our company."

At that, Fargo twisted in the saddle so no one could see his face and grinned. Twice since that day at the bluff Claresta had contrived to be alone with him and they spent hours in heated lovemaking. He would have liked to do it more often, but she was petrified by the idea of being caught. "I couldn't bear to lose Ruth's respect," was how she summed up her feelings.

"I want a hot meal more than anything," Pendrake said. "I am so tired of my own cooking, I could scream."

"You are a wonderful cook," Ruthie praised him for the hundredth time.

"I thank you, little one. It's nice to know my talent is appreciated."

It did not take a genius to see that the reason Pendrake let the Landers come had to do with his friendship with the child. She and the captain had spent every waking hour talking nonstop. Not once did Fargo see any sign that it was anything other than friendship on Pendrake's part. Yet he could not shake the nagging hunch that there was more to it than met the eye. Nothing sinister, nothing lewd, but something Pendrake did not care to share.

The late-afternoon sun had turned the surface of the bay golden. Graceful as a swan, a brigantine neared the docks, trimming her sails.

"I bet it's fun to be on a ship that big," Ruth said.

Captain Pendrake's features clouded. "It can be. It can also be a nightmare if things go wrong."

"Is that experience speaking?" Claresta asked, but he did not answer.

After so many days and nights in the wilderness, the sights and sounds of Seattle were a tonic for their frayed senses. Ladies in gay dresses paraded past. Lumberjacks strolled shoulder to shoulder with clerks and businessmen. From a saloon came the tinny notes of a piano. Laughter spilled from a second-floor window.

They rode up one hill and down another until a boy hawking newspapers bounded up to Pendrake and waved a copy of the lastest edition.

"Care for a paper, sir?"

"Can't say as I do, no."

"Read all the latest news," the boy persisted. Most hawkers were coached in what to say and he had a litany. "There's talk of Washington Territory becoming a state. The Banner brothers have gone on trial for murder. And Chief Talokma says his tribe will go on the warpath if his missing daughter is not found.

Captain Pendrake reined up. "What was that last one?"

"Talokma," the boy said. "He's chief of the Kwachenie tribe. His daughter vanished."

"I guess I will take one of those papers." Pendrake paid and folded the newspaper in half. "Luck is with us, Mr. Fargo. Perhaps we can employ your tracking skills sooner than I anticipated."

"That poor Indian girl," Ruthie sympathized. "What could have happened to her?"

"That's what Mr. Fargo and I are going to find out," Pendrake vowed. "We will take whomever is responsible into custody or die trying."

"Speak for yourself," Fargo said. He would do his best, but he would be damned if he would be turned into maggot bait if he could help it.

"A perfect illustration," Captain Pendrake intoned, "of the difference between a civilian scout and a professional soldier."

The waters of the sound lapped the bottom of the next hill. Nestled in a wooded grove at the water's edge was a restaurant built of rough-hewn logs. An open-air patio extended out over the water, supported by enormous timbers. A waiter in a green apron ushered them to a table near the rail and provided them with menus.

"Look at that fish!" Ruthie exclaimed as a large one leaped clear and splashed down again.

"Be careful you don't fall in," Claresta warned. "You've never learned to swim."

"I will soon," Ruthie said, gazing across the bay. "I

like Seattle already. I hope we live here the rest of our lives."

"Time will tell, daughter. In the meantime, what would you like to eat?"

Pendrake was reading the newspaper, not his menu. "It says here the chief's daughter was snatched out of their lodge in the middle of the night four days ago. Dozens of Kwachenie were asleep nearby, but no one heard or saw anything." He grinned and smacked the paper. "This fits the pattern. When we get to Fort Townsend, I'll send General Foster word of our imminent success."

"Aren't you getting ahead of yourself?" Fargo had followed spoor older than four days, but a lot depended on how cleverly the maiden's abductors covered their tracks. If whoever took her were even half as good as, say, the Apaches, it would be a daunting challenge.

"I have every confidence in you," Captain Pendrake said.

They ordered their food. Fargo had a two-inch-thick steak smothered in onions and mushrooms, heaping portions of potatoes and asparagus, and three thick slices of bread layered with butter. He washed it all down with five cups of piping hot coffee.

For the first time in weeks Fargo could relax. There were no hostiles or outlaws to worry about, no grizzlies grunting off in the trees, no roaming packs of wolves interested in a meal of horse flesh. He could indulge in whatever he wanted, and the thing he wanted most was a game of cards and a bottle of red-eye.

"What next?" Ruthie asked her mother.

Claresta had been fiddling with her hair. "I think

we should take a room at a hotel, treat ourselves to baths, then go buy new dresses and shoes."

"Oh, can we?" Ruthie squealed. "But what about Captain Pendrake and Mr. Fargo? Aren't we spending one more night together?"

"I'm afraid I must visit the newspaper to see if there are any other recent reports of disappearances," Pendrake told her. "But I'll make it a point to stop and see you before I return to Washington, D.C."

Ruthie made him promise and cross his heart.

For dessert Fargo indulged in a slice of apple pie. His stomach was fit to burst when he slid his chair back and set down his fork. "I can't eat another bite." He caught Claresta's eye. "I reckon I have things to do, too. It's been a pleasure knowing you."

"Same here." She folded her cloth napkin and placed it on her plate. "I hope you will look us up, too, before you leave. It would mean a lot to me."

"We'll see," was the best Fargo would offer her. Clean breaks were sometimes best. He could tell Claresta had grown enormously fond of him, and he would spare her tears if he could.

Pendrake insisted on paying for the meal. As they stood in front of the restaurant watching Claresta and Ruthie walk off, he said more to himself than to Fargo, "God, I'll miss them. Especially the girl. She's as sweet as sweet can be."

"You would make a good father," Fargo mentioned. "You should have a daughter of your own one day."

"I already did," Pendrake revealed. "Her name was Penelope. She and her mother were washed overboard when our vessel was caught in a storm en route from New York City to London. We were going to vacation in Europe." Pendrake's voice nearly broke. "It was to be the time of our lives."

"You were married?" Fargo would never have guessed.

"For five of the best years of my life." Pendrake grew downcast. "I'll never forget that night. The ship tossing and tilting, the waves crashing over the deck. The captain was at the wheel, trying to keep us from capsizing. We were in the wheelhouse with him because Penelope was seasick and couldn't stand being cooped in our cabin. The captain told me to take them below but I wouldn't listen." Pendrake was close to tears.

"Don't talk about it if you don't want to," Fargo said, but the officer did not hear him.

"A huge wave came over the side. The wheelhouse door flew open and we were all knocked off our feet. When I got back up, I saw that the window had been smashed out, and there was no sign of my wife and daughter." Pendrake stopped and shuddered. "A crewman saw them washed overboard. He said my daughter was clinging to my wife, and they both looked terrified."

An awkward silence fell. Pendrake adjusted his hat and his shirt and shammed an interest in several clouds.

"So that's why you took such a shine to Ruthie," Fargo said to take Pendrake's mind off his loss.

"She reminds me of my little Penelope. So inquisitive, such a bundle of energy." Pendrake stared after them. "It was after I lost my family that I went to my father and asked him to help get me into West Point. I needed to do something, needed to take my mind off my loss. I can't tell you how many times I've put a loaded revolver to my head. But I couldn't bring myself to pull the trigger."

Fargo had a disturbing thought. "Does this have anything to do with your working for General Foster?"

Captain Pendrake smiled, his composure restored. "I commend you. That's an astute observation. The general's specialty is solving crises. Those who work for him are constantly placed in harm's way. Four have been lost in the last year alone. Is it any wonder I volunteered?"

"Why didn't you tell me this sooner?"

"Is there a problem?" Pendrake feigned innocence.

"There damn sure is," Fargo snapped. "You didn't volunteer to work for Foster because you're devoted to your uniform. You didn't do it because your family is patriotic. You did it because you're trying to get yourself killed and this seemed the best way."

"That's absurd."

"Like hell it is." Fargo refused to mince words. "You want to join your wife and daughter. You're hoping that someone will do what you can't and put a bullet in your brain. Duty has nothing to do with your working for Foster. It's your clever way of committing suicide. "

"Even if that were true," Pendrake said defensively, "it's no concern of yours. You have no call to be so mad."

"Don't I?" Fargo disputed him. "I was counting on you to back my play if we run into trouble so we make it through alive. But you don't care whether you go on breathing; you would be happier dead."

"Never fear. I will perform my duties to the best of my ability. I won't do anything that might result in your death."

"How nice," Fargo said sarcastically, and he had another thought. "Does General Foster know about your family and your death wish?"

"He's aware I lost them, yes. He's fine with that since he thinks it best that his operatives be unencumbered in that regard. As for the other, let's just say that what he doesn't know is better for me."

Fargo shook his head. "I have half a mind to track the missing Kwachenie girl myself, Edgar. Or better yet, to let the commander of Fort Townsend know what you're up to."

Pendrake gripped his arm. "Please don't. I'm asking you man to man. I won't let you down."

"Damn you." Fargo sighed and walked to the hitch rail. "Take the other horses to the stable. I'll see you in the morning. Eight o'clock at the ferry landing. Don't be late."

"You won't tell anyone?"

"You're asking a lot." Fargo forked leather and lifted the reins. He needed a drink. Better yet, a whole bottle.

"I promise to pick the time and place with care." Pendrake had a panicked look. "I give you my solemn word I won't inconvenience you."

What a strange way to put it, Fargo thought. Wheeling the Ovaro, he headed into the heart of Seattle, where the bars and taverns were most numerous. He was in the mood for a rowdy night on the town. Play a little cards, be friendly with a few doves in tight dresses. Maybe he would get lucky and some loudmouth would pick a fight. He could pretend he was beating Pendrake senseless instead.

15

The Crown and Cork looked promising. Situated on the top of a hill, it was ablaze with light. The hubbub of voices, the clink of poker chips and a cloud of cigar smoke greeted Skye Fargo as he strode inside. He smiled in satisfaction.

The place was packed. Customers lined the bar two deep, and every chair at every table was filled. Everyone was having a fine time, drinking and jesting and playing their favorite games of chance. Buxom women circulated among them, enticing those with empty glasses to refill them and spreading smiles and inviting hints.

This was Fargo's element. The only difference between the Crown and Cork and a saloon in Texas or Dodge City was that the patrons wore caps and derbies and bowlers instead of wide-brimmed hats, and flannel shirts with checkered pants and flat-soled boots or shoes instead of homespun and chaps and high-heeled boots with spurs.

Fargo waded in, and almost immediately a fetching redhead attached herself to his left arm.

"Well, what have we here? It's plain you're not a timberman or a sailor, handsome." She displayed dazzling white teeth. Her eyes were sea-green, her lips full and ripe. "I'm Astoria. Everyone calls me Asty for short."

Fargo told her his name while threading toward the bar.

"If you're after a good time, you've come to the right place," Asty assured him. "Name your poison and we have it."

Running his gaze from her breasts to her thighs, Fargo winked and asked, "Does that include poison in dresses?"

Asty laughed uproariously. "A gent who knows what he wants and isn't shy about saying so. I like that in a man." Now it was her turn to appraise him from head to toe. "You sure are a strapping cuss. And those deep blue eyes you have. A girl could lose herself in them."

"You're welcome to get lost anytime you want." Fargo made his intentions as plain as possible.

"I might just take you up on that, big man," Asty said. "I don't get off until midnight, though, so you have to wait around or come back later."

"I'm not going anywhere." Fargo shouldered past several drinkers and smacked the bar. "A bottle of your best coffin varnish and two glasses." He paid and filled her glass and then his. "To new friends."

Asty clinked her glass against his. "To handsome strangers who look at a woman as if she's as naked as the day she was born."

"You're wearing clothes?" Fargo said, precipitating another round of mirth. "I haven't taken a sip yet and already I must be drunk."

Playfully slapping his arm, Asty emptied her glass in one swallow. "You sure know how to tickle my fancy."

"I'll tickle a lot more later," Fargo said.

"Later, then," Asty said, caressing his cheek with a red fingernail. "And I must say, I haven't looked forward this much to being with a man in more months than I care to remember." She sashayed off, returning his wink over her shoulder.

Faro and poker were the games of choice. Fargo stood beside a poker table until one of the players folded, and quickly claimed the empty chair. "Mind if I sit in, boys?"

"Not at all," said a suave character in an expensive suit, "so long as you don't mind losing your money to us." He was clean-shaven, with bushy eyebrows and curly brown hair. "Clancy is my name. I'm a local. I own a part interest in the sawmill."

"You've lived here a while, then?"

"Longer than most," Clancy admitted. "When I arrived, Seattle was a bunch of shacks on Alki Point. It's grown by leaps and bounds since."

Fargo played a few hands, settling into the rhythm of the game and taking his measure of the other players, before he said to Clancy, "You must know the goings-on around here better than most."

"Is there anything in particular you're referring to?" Clancy asked for two cards and the dealer slid them across the table.

"The disappearances," Fargo said, and did not know what to make of it when the other players paused at whatever they were doing and glanced sharply at him. "Did I say something wrong?"

"It's a touchy subject, friend," answered a lean man in a seaman's cap with an unlit pipe clenched between his teeth. "There ain't one of us but knows someone who has gone missing."

"There have been that many?"

"Sixty-four that I know of from Washington Territory," Clancy said. "Maybe more from across the border."

The total kept growing. Fargo asked the dealer for one card. "Does that include Indians?"

"The ones we know about, yes," Clancy said. "But most of the time they don't tell us. They tend to keep to themselves."

"And good riddance, I say," another player remarked.

Fargo did not say anything. Bitter feelings ran strong in Seattle after the recent Indian wars, brought on when the governor tried to induce all the tribes in the region to sign treaties so the governor could force them on reservations, freeing up more land for whites.

"Now, now," Clancy said. "They're not all as bad as that, Billings. Some are friendly."

"I don't care how friendly they are," Billings groused. "I lost an uncle and two cousins to stinking savages. I'd as soon every last one was rounded up and hung. Squaws and kids, too."

"That's the attitude to have." Clancy oozed disdain. "Kill everyone with different skin than ours."

"Don't put words in my mouth," Billings objected. "I didn't say we should hang the blacks or the Chinese, did I? Just the redskins."

"Sixty-four," Fargo said to end their dispute. "How can there be that many?"

"It's been happening for decades." Clancy confirmed what Colonel Seaver had told him. "I spoke to an old-timer who swore by his sainted mother that the first white to vanish was one of the early Hudson's Bay men."

Fargo was familiar with the history of Washington Territory. The Hudson's Bay Company was a British firm. They established Fort Vancouver nearly forty years ago to exploit the rich fur trade.

Clancy was still talking. "Later, when Americans moved into the area, they started disappearing too. It got so the men wouldn't go anywhere unless it was in pairs, and no one ever went into the woods unarmed."

"The hostiles up to their usual foul tricks," was Billings' opinion. "What else could it be?"

"The thing is," Clancy said, "the Indians all deny it."

"What else would you expect them to do?" Billings asked skeptically. "Come right out and confess?"

"The heathens are always squabbling among themselves. That's nothing new," another player commented. "It has to be the work of one tribe. All we have to do is figure out which."

"Could be," Clancy allowed. "But a lot of people on both sides are spooked. If it keeps up, it wouldn't take much to trigger another war." He added five dollars to the pot.

Fargo wanted to learn more. "What can you tell me about the Kwachenie and Chief Talokma?"

"Not a whole lot. They're a small tribe. Friendly enough, but they're not real happy about the influx of whites. Then again, which tribe is?"

Billings pushed his five dollars to the center of the table, then said, "You sure are asking a lot of questions, stranger. What's all this to you?"

"I've agreed to help the army get to the bottom of it," Fargo revealed.

The old seaman snorted. "The army? I've yet to meet a soldier who could find his ass if it was on fire.

Hell, most of them aren't old enough to shave. Boys in uniforms is all they are."

Fargo agreed. Most came from poor families and enlisted for the paltry pittance the army paid. Few could ride well, even fewer could shoot well and barely one in a hundred possessed enough backwoods savvy to live off the land.

"Strange the army is doing something about it now," Clancy remarked.

"Why do you say that?"

Before the Irishman could answer, the front door opened and in strode a broad-shouldered slab of arrogance who pushed those in his way aside if they did not skip out of his path fast enough. A few curses were voiced in protest, but that was all. He wore a seaman's clothes and had a square, rugged face and piercing black eyes.

"Oh, great. Harkner is back," Clancy said in disgust. "His boat must have docked today. There will be hell to pay."

"Why?" Fargo saw the brawny seaman send a much smaller man stumbling.

"Because Harkner is a bully. He breaks men in half for the fun of it. The last time his vessel put into port, he was in a fistfight and broke the jaw and five ribs of the fellow he was fighting."

"He wasn't thrown in jail?" Fargo had butted heads with more than a few of the world's Harkners, and never liked one of them.

"The other fellow took the first swing," Clancy related, "after being goaded into it, so Harkner couldn't be blamed."

The talk shifted to a rumor that a new sawmill would start up before the year was out. Fargo concentrated on the game. After half an hour he was up forty dollars. After an hour, seventy dollars. The other players were amateurs. They bet too high on hands with long odds. Half the time their expressions gave away whether their hands were good or bad.

For Fargo, it was like taking hard molasses from an infant. He raised whenever he sensed weakness and it paid off handsomely. He was so engrossed in the game that when a woman swore loudly and a *smack* rang out, he did not realize it was Astoria until she squealed, "Don't touch me there again!"

She was steaming mad and shaking a finger in Harkner's face. "Who do you think you are, anyhow, to go around putting your paws where they haven't been invited?"

"I like a gal with spunk," Harkner said. "How about you and me get together later?"

"I already have a date." Asty turned to make her rounds, but he seized her by the wrist and spun her around.

"You *had* a date. You have one with me now."

"Let go!" Astoria twisted her arm back and forth, but she was powerless in his grip.

"You heard the lady!" someone hollered.

"Come over here and say that to my face," Harkner rebutted, and when the challenger stayed where he was, Harkner puckered his lips and pulled Astoria toward him. "Come on, wench. Give us a kiss."

Fargo set down his cards, pushed his chair back and stood. Lifting the chair, he walked up behind the brawny seaman. "Care for a lump, you stupid son of a bitch?"

"What did you say?" Harkner turned just as Fargo swung the chair with all his might. It caught the sea-

143

man full on the head and shoulders, and shattered under the impact. Harkner took a single step back, blood trickling from his scalp, and collapsed.

Stunned silence gripped the tavern. Then someone whooped and laughed and dozens did likewise.

Astoria threw herself at Fargo, grinning in delight. "That was about the nicest thing anyone has ever done for me."

"Just don't forget midnight," Fargo reminded her, and went back to the table. The proprietor brought a replacement chair from a rear room, and the game resumed.

Two husky seamen dragged Harkner out.

By eleven o'clock Fargo had won more than two hundred dollars. On his next hand he was dealt three eights. He asked for two cards and received a pair of jacks. When Clancy bet the limit, he called and won.

"Damn, you're good, boyo," the Irishman said.

A few minutes to midnight a warm hand fell on Fargo's shoulder and soft lips brushed his ear. "I'm ready to leave when you are, handsome." Astoria had thrown a green shawl over her shoulders and brushed her long red hair.

Fargo played out the hand and stood. "Drinks all around," he said, tossing a ten dollar gold piece to Clancy. "Thanks for the game."

The crowd had thinned. Astoria's arm looped in his, Fargo steered her toward the door. Her perfume reminded him of vanilla. "Your place, or do I rent a hotel room for the night?"

"I stay in a boarding house," Astoria said. "The lady who runs it is very strict about male visitors. But my room is at the back, and if you're real quiet, I can sneak you in with no one the wiser."

"I can be a mouse when I have to be." Fargo grinned and received a quick kiss on the cheek.

The breeze off the bay was laced with moisture. Fargo breathed deep as he unwound the Ovaro's reins.

Astoria pulled her shawl tighter. "Brrrrr. It gets chilly this time of night. Good thing I have a stove so I can stoke a fire."

"I'll stoke your fire for you," Fargo said, and swatted her fanny. She squealed, then pressed against him and molded her lips to his.

"Nice," was Astoria's verdict. "You're a good kisser." She leaned her head on his shoulder. "Take a left up ahead."

They walked slowly, the Ovaro's hooves clomping loudly in the nearly deserted street.

Most businesses had long since closed, and Seattle lay quiet under the stars. A third vessel was now at anchor, along with scores of fishing craft.

Fargo couldn't wait to get to the boarding house. Asty's breasts were ripe melons waiting to be plucked, and her hips swayed with a saucy flair that hinted she shared his desire. They came to the intersection and turned up the next street.

To their rear, footsteps pounded. Whirling, Fargo pushed Astoria behind him as three figures rushed out of the shadows. The biggest smacked his right fist against his left palm and sneered.

"You didn't think you had seen the last of me, did you, buckskin?" Harkner asked. "Any last words before I break every bone in your body?"

16

Skye Fargo was feeling good. He had half a bottle of whiskey under his belt and a willing dove on his arm. He was looking forward to the next several hours and did not want anything to mar it. So instead of tearing into Harkner and the other two seamen, he simply said, "Go pester someone else."

Astoria giggled, which only made Harkner madder. "Did you really think you could bust a chair over my head and get away with it?"

"That's nothing compared to what I'll do if you don't make yourself scarce," Fargo vowed.

"Tough man, is that it?" Harkner scoffed. "I don't think you're taking me seriously. Which is why I brought three friends along."

Fargo only saw two. Suddenly Astoria cried out, and he spun to find that she had been grabbed from behind by the third, who had a hand to her throat. His good mood evaporated, replaced by red-hot fury. "You're making a mistake."

"No, you're the one who made it," Harkner growled, rolling up his sleeves. "When they find you in the morning and word gets around, everyone will be more scared of me than ever."

Fargo let go of the Ovaro's reins. "You like that, don't you? People being afraid of you."

"I'm the meanest sea dog alive and damn proud of it," Harkner crowed. "I break jackasses like you like sticks. I grind guts and bust bones and laugh while I'm doing it. Does that answer your question?"

"But you don't wear a gun," Fargo observed.

"Why should I when my fists are all I need?" Harkner's were big as sledges, his knuckles as knobby as walnuts. "I can split a board with one blow. Or bust a man's skull."

Fargo was holding the half-empty whiskey bottle close to his leg. In the dark it was doubtful any of the seamen had noticed it. Shifting, he firmed his hold on the bottle's neck. "I'd like to see you bust mine."

"Would you now? Well, never let it be said I don't aim to please." Wearing a vicious smirk, Harkner lunged.

Fargo did not move until the sea dog was almost on top of him. Sidestepping and ducking under a ponderous swing, he whipped the bottle up and around and smashed it against Harkner's head.

Harkner howled and stopped and ran a sleeve across his whiskey-drenched eyes. "Damn your bones!" he thundered. "This is twice now you've caught me by surprise. There won't be a third time."

"You're right about that," Fargo said, and kicked him in the right knee. At the *crack*, Harkner's leg buckled and he clutched his knee in agony. Fargo closed in, but the other two leaped to confront him. Blades flashed in the night. Cold steel lanced at his throat and he dropped under it, his right hand darting to his right boot and the Arkansas Toothpick nestled in its ankle sheath. So swiftly did he move, he lanced the toothpick up and out before the seaman could set himself. In the toothpick's wake a dark mist spurted from the seaman's wrist. The man's dirk clattered to the ground and he staggered back.

Harkner was trying to rise and reached out to grab Fargo's arm. Dodging, Fargo looped his left fist into Harkner's nose. At the *crunch*, Harkner bellowed and fell.

The second seaman had learned from the mistake of the first and came in low and fast. He was wielding a double-edged dagger, which he sliced from side to side in an effort to rip Fargo open. Skipping left, then right, Fargo speared the toothpick at the seaman's wrist, as he had done with the first one. But his wily adversary was expecting it and sprang to the left, straight into Fargo's real blow. The slash had been a feint. Fargo felt the toothpick sink into the man's side, felt a damp sensation on his fingers.

Once more Harkner was attempting to stand. The lower half of his face was caked with blood, and he could not put his full weight on his broken knee.

Fargo kicked him in the other one.

"Can't any of you do anything right?" snarled the seaman holding Astoria. He flung her aside and leaped into the fray, producing a knife from under his jacket. He was savvy, this one, a seasoned knife fighter who knew enough not to come in too fast.

Fargo crouched, the toothpick held low. The seaman stopped, unsure of where it was, and glanced down. Instantly, Fargo sprang and stabbed upward. Predictably, the seaman countered with his own blade. Steel rang on steel, even as Fargo's other arm darted out and he jabbed a finger into the man's eye.

The man flung himself backward, blinking and swinging his knife in wide arcs to keep Fargo at bay.

Harkner was cursing like a madman and trying to push up off the street. "Kill him!" he raged. "Kill! Kill! Kill!"

"Kill this," Fargo said, and kicked him in the mouth. Teeth cracked and splintered, and Harkner gagged.

The two seamen Fargo had cut were retreating, one holding his ribs, the other with his wrist pressed to his shirt to stem the flow of his life's blood.

As for the man Fargo had jabbed in the eye, he steadied himself and snarled, "I'm going to slice off your oysters and feed them to the fish."

"I'm tired of this," Fargo said. Drawing the Colt, he cocked the hammer. "Run or have your brains blown out. I really don't give a damn which."

The seaman mimicked a street post. "What kind of coward are you that you pull a pistol?"

"You only like it when it's four to one, is that how it goes?" Fargo took a step. "Tell you what. I'll count to four, and if you're still here, you're dead." He crisply barked, "One. Two. Th—"

"What about him?" the seaman asked, with a nod at Harkner.

"Come back in half an hour and take him to a doctor." Fargo sighted down the Colt. "Now where was I? Oh, yes. Three."

"I'm going!" The seaman dropped his knife, spun on his heels and raced after his friends.

Harkner was on his hands and knees, spitting blood and bits of teeth. "I'll hunt you down if it takes the rest of my life. You'll never have a minute's rest. Never stop looking over your shoulder."

"In that case," Fargo said, and brought his boot down hard on top of Harkner's right hand. Bones snapped like dry twigs, and Harkner cried out and fell onto his elbow.

"Bastard! Rotten, miserable bastard! You broke my hand!"

"Only one?" Fargo pivoted and brought his boot down on top of Harkner's other one. More bones snapped and knuckles popped.

Harkner pitched onto his face, swearing savagely. He stared at his bent fingers and thumbs. "Look at what you've done!"

"Maybe the next time you decide to beat someone up for the fun of it, you'll think twice," Fargo said, and taking a quick short step, he kicked him in the groin.

Gurgling and whining and groaning, Harkner convulsed in violent spasms. His hands were misshapen claws, his face a travesty. He looked up at Fargo in rank fear.

"No more," he blubbered. "I've had enough."

"Not quite yet you haven't." Fargo swung a last blow. The Colt caught Harkner above the ear and Harkner went limp.

"Sweet Jesus," Astoria breathed. "I never saw anything like that in all my life. Who *are* you?"

"Someone who is randy as hell." Fargo twirled the Colt into his holster, snatched the Ovaro's reins and took her hand. "Now where exactly is this boarding house of yours?"

No one had witnessed the fight, or if they had, they had run off. The street was empty. So was the next, and the one after that, which was lined with log homes with neatly maintained yards and flower gardens.

"Here we are," Astoria announced, stopping beside a gate in a white picket fence. "Now remember. We do this quietly, or Mrs. Fisher, the biddy, will throw us out."

"As quiet as a mouse," Fargo said. He tied the Ovaro to the fence and followed her up the walk to a porch. A board creaked under his boot but not loud enough to be heard inside.

Astoria felt about in her bag for the key and slowly inserted it. Placing a finger to her lips, she unlocked the door and opened it wide enough to admit them.

The house was as quiet as a cemetery and dark. Astoria tiptoed down a narrow hall to a room at the rear and used a smaller key to unlock it.

"Why didn't we just come in the back way?" Fargo whispered, pointing at a door at the far end of the kitchen.

"Mrs. Fisher keeps a dog out back," Astoria explained. "A schnauzer she treats as if it were her kid. The damn thing barks its fool head off at anything that moves, even butterflies."

Her room was small but nicely furnished. In addition to the stove and a bed, she had a table and chair and a pendulum wall clock that ticked noisily with each stroke of the bob. She threw her handbag on the table and locked and bolted the door. "We don't want to be disturbed."

"No," Fargo said, and pulled her to him. Her neck and ears were fragrant with the vanilla perfume, and her hair gave off a minty scent. "You smell nice." He lightly ran his lips from her earlobe to her throat to her cheek.

"I hope those weren't your idea of kisses," Astoria teased, and planted her mouth full on his.

Her lips were burning hot, her tongue molten velvet. Fargo felt her melt into him, her breasts buoyed against his chest, her thighs tight against his. In a twinkling his manhood was rigid.

Astoria pushed him toward the bed. Her hands explored every part of his body she could reach. His arms, his hair, his shoulders, his back, his butt. She was not shy about her hunger, not inhibited by her needs.

Fargo's own need was soaring by the second. They reached the bed but stood caressing and groping one another. He pulled at the lower half of her dress, raising it high until it was bunched about her waist. Her lacy underthings posed no obstacle. Within moments he had gained access to her innermost sanctuary, but he refrained from touching her there just yet. Placing his hands under her bottom, he lifted her off her feet.

"What are you—?" Astoria began.

Maybe it was the whiskey. Maybe it was the fight. Maybe it was her luscious body and ripe lips and the undisguised desire in her eyes. Maybe it was a combination of everything. But Fargo wanted to be inside her, wanted it right then, without delay. Smiling, he parted her thighs wide and abruptly lowered her, and the deed was done. Her wet walls enfolded him like a sheath.

Astoria gasped and stiffened and arched her back. "Yesssss," she whispered. "Oh, God, yesssssssssss." She wrapped her long legs around him and clung to his broad shoulders.

Fargo stood still, savoring the feel of her. Her inner walls rippled and contracted as she rubbed her nether mound up and down.

"Just so you know, handsome, I'm in no rush," Astoria said huskily.

Neither was Fargo. He ground against her but not too hard, not too fast. She took off his hat and tossed it at the foot of the bed, then pried at his shirt so she could slide her hands under it and knead the layers of muscle on his stomach and chest.

"You must be as strong as a bear," Astoria whispered. "The way you handled those sailors."

Fargo slid a hand between them.

"It made me hot watching you. Half the men in Seattle have wanted to take that big bully down a peg, and you did it without working up a sweat. What manner of man are you?"

"The kind who knows when to gab and when not to," Fargo said, seeking the tiny swollen knob with which he could incite her to new heights. At the contact of his middle finger, she quivered and bit her lower lip. He stroked softly and she moaned, then sank her teeth into his shoulder.

"You have no idea what you are doing to me."

She was wrong there. Fargo knew just what he was doing. Bending his mouth to her bosom, he kissed and licked while continuing to caress her lower down.

Astoria began to pant. Her hips pumped harder and her legs were viselike clamps. Entwining her fingers in his hair, she raised his face to hers and hungrily devoured his mouth.

A thump from somewhere on the second floor caused her to draw back and nervously regard the ceiling.

"Something wrong?" Fargo asked.

"Mrs. Fisher might be up," Astoria whispered. "I

don't want to be caught. She'll throw me out, and good rooms are hard to come by."

"I have something just as hard," Fargo said, and thrust up into her, arching onto the tips of his toes.

Astoria's eyes grew as wide as saucers and her ruby lips formed an *O* of pure pleasure. She kissed him, inhaling him into her. When he flicked her knob, she thrust her bottom up and down with rising urgency. "I want it," she whispered. "I want it bad."

Fargo rocked on his heels. Churning his hips, he slammed up into her. Most women would cry out in ecstasy, but Astoria had to settle for tiny mews and coos and soft fluttery sounds her landlady would not hear. They moved faster and faster, their mutual lust eclipsing all else. Fargo squeezed her buns and rubbed her knob and nuzzled a breast free of its restraints so he could suck on her hard nipple.

Suddenly Astoria spurted. Her body a blur, she gushed and gushed, unable to stop if she had wanted to, and she plainly did not want to. "Oh! Do me, big man! Do me!" she whispered.

Something about the way she said it triggered Fargo's own release. He came in throbbing waves, and for a while there was just the two of them and the room and nothing else in the whole wide world mattered.

17

The ferry was big enough to transport three or four covered wagons and their teams and still have room to spare. Only a handful of travelers was crossing at so early an hour. Fargo and Captain Edgar Pendrake had a corner of the deck all to themselves and their mounts.

"Did you see the way the ferryman looked at me when I mentioned where we were going?" Pendrake asked.

Fargo had not been paying particular attention. He was stiff and sore from his wild night with Astoria. They had made love until almost four, and only stopped because they were both spent. "He must take soldiers across all the time."

Fort Townsend had been built five years ago on the northeast tip of the Olympic Peninsula. As with most posts, its purpose was to protect settlers from hostiles. Fargo had only been there once, and remembered it as small and not well protected.

"Maybe he has a grudge against the military," Pendrake speculated. "You would be surprised how many people I run into who think we do more harm than good."

For some folks the army was a necessary evil. They

needed protection, but they believed the army's presence was enough to incite unfriendly Indians into violent reprisals. So they wanted the army close but not *too* close.

"I wear my uniform with pride," Pendrake said, loud enough so the ferryman would hear.

Small waves lapped the sides. Out over the bay gulls screeched and wheeled, and ospreys dived for fish. A seal broke the surface, stared at the ferry and sank from view.

"My wife and daughter would have loved it here," Pendrake said, and his features darkened. "Susannah and Penelope were everything to me."

"What would your wife say about your death wish?"

"I'm not the same man I was when I was with her. Something inside of me died when they died. I am like an empty bottle waiting to be broken."

"Until Ruthie came along." Fargo saw a fin break the surface for a few fleeting seconds.

"Until Ruthie came along," Pendrake repeated. "I had forgotten what it's like to feel life is worthwhile."

"It's not?"

Pendrake gripped the rail and bowed his head. "What's the purpose of deceiving ourselves? We lose it all sooner or later. Everyone and everything that matters. I refuse to go through such heartbreak ever again. It is the worst loss, the worst pain any man can endure. And I refuse to go through life a shell of the man I once was. What does that leave me, my friend, but to choose the time and the place?"

Fargo had lost his parents and his brother when he was younger than Pendrake, and Pendrake was right, it was a wound that never healed. The only way to deal with it was to not think about it, to shut it from his mind, and when memories of them were rekindled now and again, to suffer in silence.

The crossing took longer than they reckoned. A shift in the wind slowed the ferry to a crawl. When, at long last, they reached the peninsula and the ramp was lowered, they were first in line.

Pendrake was anxious to reach the post and learn all he could about the disappearance of Talokma's daughter. "It's a lucky break for us," he commented as they rode north along a well-marked trail. "We'll find out where to find the Kwachenie and take it from there."

"What if they don't want our help?"

"General Foster was quite explicit. My orders are to find those responsible at all costs."

Even though it had been months since the last skirmishes, the region was still a powder keg. Most whites distrusted the Indians and most Indians distrusted the whites. It would not take much to ignite the two sides. "We don't want another bloodbath," he agreed.

"I'm glad you agree. Then you can appreciate the urgency of our mission."

The trail bore the imprint of a lot of horses and wagons, as it should, since it was the main link to the fort. But as Fargo rode along, he noticed that most of the tracks and wagon ruts were at least a couple of weeks old, if not older. He made mention of it to Pendrake.

"That can't be. Patrols come and go all the time. Supplies are ferried in once a week, then there are civilian visitors and the like." Pendrake's brow puckered. "I hope you're as good as they say you are and I haven't gone to all this trouble for nothing."

Fargo let the implied insult go unchallenged. He had no need to prove himself.

A cluster of buildings appeared in the distance, and the captain pointed. "There's Fort Townsend. I have a letter of introduction for Colonel Chandler. General Foster has instructed him to cooperate fully."

They cantered another forty feet and Pendrake rose in the stirrups and squinted into the morning haze. "That's odd. The flag isn't flying from the flagpole."

The American flag was proudly flown at every military post in the country. Fargo had witnessed the raising and lowering ceremonies at dawn and dusk more times than he could count.

A quarter of a mile more and they were close enough for Captain Pendrake to quizzically ask, "Why haven't sentries been posted?"

Fargo's eyes were sharper. He did not see a single living soul. "It looks to me as if Fort Townsend is deserted."

"Impossible," Pendrake scoffed. "General Foster would have told me if that were the case."

"Maybe word hadn't reached him yet." Fargo had dealt with the government enough to know that often the right hand did not know what the left hand was doing. The army's chain of command was efficient, but delays in communications routinely posed problems. "Did you know that Fort Crittenden was closing in a month?"

"No," Pendrake admitted. "There have been a lot of post closures and reshuffling of personnel of late."

So Fargo had heard. The increasingly fiery war of words between the North and the South was to blame. Both sides were preparing for a conflict neither said they really wanted.

Fort Townsend had indeed been abandoned. The buildings were silent, several of the doors ajar, windows left partway open. Pendrake rode to the hitch rail in front of the headquarters and dismounted. "Just when things were going so well." He went inside.

Fargo stayed in the saddle. He figured they might as well head right back. If they hurried, they could catch the ferry before it cast off for its return trip to Seattle.

From a long, low barracks came a metallic clang. A few seconds later there was a muffled thud. Sliding down, Fargo approached the open door with his hand on his Colt.

Someone muttered something, and out of the barracks ambled a stout oldster in shabby buckskins. He had a salt-and-pepper beard and wore a floppy hat with holes in it. Bundled in his arms were a pot, a blanket and a pair of army boots.

"Hey, there," Fargo said.

The man nearly jumped out of his skin. "Thunderation!" he declared, backing up in alarm. "Where in blazes did you come from, pilgrim?"

"I'm here with an officer—" Fargo began to explain, and was puzzled when the man dropped the pot, the blanket and the old army boots as if they were red-hot coals. The pot struck with a loud *clang*.

"There's an officer here? I thought they were done with this place." The man wiped a hand on his pants and came over, smiling. Two of his upper front teeth were missing and one of his bottom front teeth was a vivid yellow. "I'm Clevis Bickett. I'm a scout."

Fargo had met many of the more well-known scouts and had never heard Bickett's name. "Is that a fact?"

"Yep. The army hired me because I've lived here

nigh on thirty years and no one knows this part of the country like I do."

"Interesting," Fargo said. If true, the man's knowledge could come in handy.

"What do you do for a living?" Bickett looked him up and down. "You're sure not a boy in blue."

"I'm a tracker," Fargo allowed. "I came to help Captain Pendrake find out why so many people have gone missing."

"To do what?" Bickett was startled. "Mister, you're asking for grief. The soldiers here tried for years and couldn't make head nor tails of it."

"Maybe we'll have better luck."

Bickett glanced past Fargo and asked, "Is that him?" Then he hurried toward Pendrake, who had emerged scowling. "Captain? Captain Pendrake, is it? I'm right pleased to meet you." He introduced himself.

Pendrake shook hands, then gestured. "What happened here? Where the hell is everyone?"

"You don't know?" Bickett rejoined. "The army closed the post. Ordered most of the troopers back East."

Sizzling mad by now, Pendrake smacked his leg. "This is most inconvenient. I was counting on the support and help of the fort's personnel."

"It's probably just as well," Bickett said, rubbing his beard. "Your friend told me why you're here, and you're on a wild goose chase. The folks who go missing are never seen again. Leave it go at that and you'll live longer."

"I have my orders," Pendrake said stiffly. "Now suppose you explain exactly what you're doing here."

"Colonel Chandler hired me to do scouting for him

for ten dollars a month," Bickett revealed. He pointed at a shack across the compound. "He also let me live there for free."

"An unusual arrangement," said Pendrake.

Most scouts, Fargo included, were paid considerably more. He had to wonder if the pittance Bickett earned was a reflection on his ability.

"I don't see what's so strange about it," the local was saying. "The colonel wanted me handy when patrols went out. That's all."

Pendrake sniffed a few times. "Is it me, or do you reek of alcohol? Could it be there was more to your arrangement than you've told me? That perhaps the colonel kept you close to keep you from overindulging?"

Fargo had noticed the reek but had not said anything. He was hardly the one to go around criticizing others for drinking too much.

"Danged smart of you," Bickett told Pendrake. "Yes, I'm a mite too fond of the hard stuff. And yes, the colonel got tired of me showing up half drunk, and wanted to keep an eye on me."

"How is it you're still here after everyone else has gone?"

Bickett's shoulders drooped and he poked at the dirt with a badly scuffed boot. "I didn't have anywhere else to go. It's not like I'm doing anything wrong, am I? I mean, sure, I've scrounged a few things they left behind, but where's the harm in that?"

"Do as you want." Pendrake had lost interest. "It's of no concern to me." He turned to Fargo. "Staying longer is pointless. We might as well mount up and go find Chief Talokma." He turned toward their horses.

Clevis Bickett snatched at his sleeve. "Hold on

there, boy! What's this about Talokma? I know him real well."

"His daughter has vanished." Pendrake pulled free and resumed walking, but Bickett snagged his arm a second time.

"I can help, youngster. I know Kwachenie territory. I've been to Talokma's village three or four times."

Frowning, Pendrake peeled Bickett's fingers off. "Thank you, but we can manage on our own."

"You don't believe me, do you?" Bickett made a clucking sound. "Go right ahead, then. But keep in mind the woods hereabouts are awful thick and the mountains are awful steep. It can take forever to get somewhere unless you know all the shortcuts like I do. I know every trail there is between here and Vancouver, and that's no lie."

"I'm sure it isn't," Pendrake said, reaching for the reins to his horse, "but Mr. Fargo is perfectly capable of guiding me wherever I need to go."

"Maybe he is." Bickett refused to give up. "But is he on good terms with Talokma? The chief has never been all that fond of whites, and usually wants nothing to do with our kind. White men caught in his territory are escorted out and warned never to return."

Pendrake paused in the act of raising his leg to the stirrup. "You can guarantee an audience with him?"

"I'll do my best. But it depends on his frame of mind. He's powerful fond of that gal of his, and if she's vanished, he'll be out for blood."

"You've met her?"

"Once. About as pretty a filly as you're ever likely to see, white or red. Sweet as can be, that one. Always smiling and polite. She is Talokma's pride and joy."

Pendrake lowered his leg. "Perhaps you can be of

some use. What do you think, Fargo? Should we take him along?"

"It might smooth things over with the Kwachenie," Fargo said.

"Very well. Mr. Bickett, I will pay you twenty dollars to serve as our guide for the duration of our stay."

The old man whooped and spun in a circle.

"Keep in mind you are under my orders at all times, and if your performance is not to my liking, I will dismiss you just like that." Pendrake snapped his fingers.

"You won't regret it, youngster. No, sir," Bickett happily assured him.

"Tell me something," Pendrake said. "You've lived here all this time. You must know a lot about the disappearances."

"No more than anyone else."

"But who do you think is to blame?"

Bickett grew somber and shifted his weight from one foot to the other. "I've heard lots of rumors. Some say it's this tribe or that tribe or some other tribe. Some say it's the hairy men of the woods. Others whisper it's the work of ghosts and such."

"I don't believe in childish nonsense," Pendrake said.

"Me neither," Bickett agreed, "but someone, or something, is sure as hell behind it, and hunting them might get you killed."

Captain Pendrake smiled. "Really?"

18

The deep woods of the Pacific Northwest were a darkling domain of lush greens and inky blacks. The heavy rains for which the region was notorious resulted in verdant vegetation. Trees so tall, they dwarfed those of the Rockies and the Appalachian forests. Undergrowth so thick, it made the tangled thickets of the South and the timberland of the Rocky Mountains seem paltry by comparison.

The Pacific Northwest was home to the redwoods, the greatest trees on the continent. Some were so high, when Fargo stood at their base and peered upward, he would swear they brushed the clouds. Some were so wide, tunnels were carved out of them for wagons to pass through.

Ferns found nowhere else grew to giant size. Creepers as thick as a man's arm formed impassable barriers. Madrones with their bizarrely smooth bark were everywhere. Plants of all kinds thrived in a riot of profusion.

Fargo had seen it all before. Even so, the woods inspired a wonder that could not be denied.

More so in Captain Edgar Pendrake, who had never set foot in them before. "I had no idea," he marveled as they filed between moss-covered patriarchs. "It's beautiful beyond compare."

"So folks keep saying." Clevis Bickett was leading their two pack animals. He had an old Walker Colt in a holster draped over his saddle horn, and an old Sharps rifle slung over his back. "As far as I'm concerned, it's just woods."

"Have you no sense of grandeur in your soul?" Pendrake asked.

"Hell, I don't even know if I have a soul, sonny," Bickett responded. "When I look at a tree, I see a tree. When I look at a rock, I see a rock. There's nothing grand about any of it. It's just how things are."

They had been riding northeast for five and a half days. Kwachenie country was not along the coast but inland, in the Cascade Range. The tribe laid claim to a broad watershed with access to the sea. Fiercely protective of their territory, they traded far and wide with the coast tribes. They also regularly sent trading parties to Seattle to obtain goods they could not find anywhere else.

"A missionary went to live among them not long ago," Bickett mentioned the seventh evening around the fire. "He tried to get them to give up their heathen ways and turn to the Lord. But it was a trick."

"A trick?" Pendrake said between sips of coffee.

"Not on his part, on theirs. Talokma played him for a fool. It was Talokma himself who invited the Bible-thumper. But Talokma wasn't interested in the white man's religion, he wanted to learn the white man's tongue. When he could speak passable English, he escorted the missionary back to Seattle and gave him a blanket for his trouble."

"Why a blanket?"

Fargo knew the answer to that one. In the old days it was common for the Hudson's Bay Company and others to pay for prime pelts with trade blankets. While some of the blankets were well made, the Indians invariably got the worse of the bargain.

"So this Talokma is shrewd and not to be trusted," Pendrake concluded after Fargo explained. "I would expect as much. I wouldn't trust a savage as far as I could throw him."

Fargo mentally counted to ten. He couldn't stand bigots, whether white or red. But he didn't place Pendrake in that ilk: Pendrake was guilty of ignorance more than anything else, and with time and experience might learn better.

At night they always took turns keeping watch. Pendrake until midnight, Fargo from midnight until three, Bickett from three until daylight.

Out of long habit, Fargo always woke up when the first faint tinge of light banded the eastern horizon. Today was no exception. He rolled onto his back and stretched, then slowly sat up, groping for his hat. He saw Clevis Bickett seated by the fire, which had dwindled to embers, with his arms held at an odd angle out from his sides. About to ask what Bickett was doing, Fargo froze.

The clearing was ringed by warriors. Arrows nocked to strings were centered on him and the others. Lances were poised to be thrown. War clubs were brandished.

Fargo's hand was near his Colt. He could draw and drop five or six of them, but the rest would rip him apart. Left with no recourse, he raised his arms. "Are these Kwachenies?"

"Yep. Sorry they took me by surprise. One second they weren't there, the next they were. I couldn't yell to warn you."

"Have they let you know what they want?"

"Not yet. They've just been standing here waiting for you two to wake up. Danged polite of them."

All the warriors wore headbands, plain shirts and leggings. Most were stocky and swarthy-complected, with high cheekbones and dark eyes. Fargo read no hatred in their expressions, only curiosity.

Suddenly a tall warrior with a splash of blue paint on his face came up close to him. The man had a barbed shaft notched to a sinew string, and trained the tip on Fargo's chest. The warrior's eyes bored into Fargo's as if he were trying to plumb the depths of Fargo's being. Then the warrior grunted, lowered the bow and said in a clipped accent, "Kwachenie land. White men go."

"We want to talk to your chief about his missing daughter," Fargo said. "We would like to help find her."

The tall warrior motioned sharply. "White men go. Kwachenie not want help. Kwachenie not like."

Clevis Bickett coughed to get the warrior's attention. "Remember me, Nonihnak? I've visited your village. I was a guest in Talokma's lodge."

"Nonihnak remember, old one," the warrior said with little warmth.

"Take us to him," Bickett said. He pointed at Pendrake, who still snored lightly. "This officer came from far away, from the Great Father himself, to put a stop to folks' disappearing."

Nonihnak walked over to Pendrake and poked him

with the bow. Muttering and snorting, Pendrake pulled his blanket up to his chin but did not wake up. Nonihnak jabbed him again.

"What the devil?" Pendrake snapped, blinking and rising on an elbow. At the sight of the Kwachenies he came out from under the blanket as if fired from a cannon, but had the presence of mind not to try and draw his revolver. "Who are they? Where did they come from?"

It was Bickett who filled him in, and Bickett who advised, "Let's not any of us do anything rash. They're not liable to use us for target practice if we behave. Talokma likes me, and they won't care to rile him."

"How is it you're on such good terms with him?" Pendrake voiced a question Fargo had wondered about.

"I bring Talokma things he has a hard time getting," Bickett said. "Ammunition for his shotgun, whiskey, that sort of stuff."

"Selling liquor to the Indians is against the law," Pendrake rightly noted. "You could be thrown in jail."

"I don't sell it," Bickett said. "I *trade* it."

"For what?"

"Favors."

"What kind of favors?"

"Oh, you know, this and that." Bickett proved evasive. "It's not anything the army would be interested in."

"Let me be the judge of that," Pendrake said. Before he could delve deeper, Nonihnak barked orders in his own tongue and the ring tightened.

"We take you chief," he announced.

Under the wary scrutiny of the warriors, Fargo saddled the Ovaro while Pendrake and Bickett prepared their mounts, and they were soon ready to ride. But the Kwachenies did not let them mount. Instead, they had to lead their animals by the reins, with warriors on both sides and behind so they dared not try to escape.

In a short while they came to a trail that saw frequent use. It wound along the base of a mountain capped by a rocky crag that vaguely resembled the silhouette of a bird's head.

"Hawk Mountain, the Kwachenies call it," Bickett revealed. "It's sacred to their people. They've lived in its shadow as long as any of them can remember. When they dance they wear wooden masks with long beaks."

Beyond Hawk Mountain lay a shimmering lake, the water so pure and clear that as Fargo followed the shoreline he could see fish dart about in its depths. The Kwachenie village was situated along the north shore. Nine cedar-plank lodges were arranged in a semicircle, in effect forming a protective wall between the forest and the lake.

Plank lodges were common among the tribes of the Northwest. Some tribes were renowned for their craftsmanship. The Kwachenies evidently took great pride in their dwellings, which were as soundly built as any frame house ever constructed by whites. The only difference was that, in typical fashion, the Kwachenie lodges lacked windows.

Several totem poles had been erected in the semicircle, another common practice. Atop the highest of the Kwachenie totems was a face carved in the distinct likeness of a hawk. Another bore the head of what might be an ape with a conical forehead. Other visages Fargo could not begin to identify.

A warrior had gone ahead to forewarn the village.

Every last man, woman and child had turned out. Some of the men wore buckskins, others trade shirts. Elaborate patterns had been woven into them from bits of bone, beads or, in rare instances, mother-of-pearl, according to the tastes and wealth of the wearer. The women were partial to finely treated doeskin trimmed with fur. One woman, and only one, wore a dress sewn from the hide of a caribou. She stood near the center of the open space, slightly behind a broad-chested man who wore a conical cap fringed with strips of ermine and decorated with quills. Two large hawk feathers crowned the cap at right angles.

Fargo did not need Bickett to tell him that the stern-faced figure in the cap was Talokma. Piercing brown eyes studied Captain Pendrake and him intently.

The captain surprised all of them by walking up to the chief and crisply saluting. "You are Talokma, I presume? I am honored to meet you, sir. Captain Edgar Pendrake, at your service. I have come many miles to put an end to the disappearances of red man and white man alike. The Great White Father is concerned for your welfare."

Fargo nearly laughed out loud when Talokma asked, "Do whites call their President the Great White Father, or do they only use that term when speaking to ignorant Indians like us?"

Pendrake was taken aback. "I was told you knew our tongue, but I was not told how well."

"Yes, I speak English," Talokma said. "Some French, too, and the dialects of eleven of the neighboring tribes. How many languages do you speak, soldier?"

Pendrake squirmed like a worm on a hook. "One."

"Then perhaps we Indians are not as ignorant as you whites would believe." Talokma turned to Clevis Bickett. "I am not pleased you have brought these men to our land."

Bickett nervously licked his lips. "I figured you wouldn't mind, what with Mikahwon missing and all. These two are here to get to the bottom of things."

"We cannot do it on our own?" Talokma's face became sterner as he shifted toward Fargo. "And you, tall one. What do you have to say for yourself that these others have not?"

"I speak for myself and myself alone," Fargo said. "Whoever took your daughter should be chopped into bits and pieces and fed to the fish in your lake."

The chief was inscrutable. "Why should you care? Mikahwon means nothing to you. She is one of many who have vanished."

"The important thing is that she means something to you. All the more reason to stop whoever is behind it."

The chief was silent awhile, then said, "Your words are wisest, white man." Talokma held out his hand. "I believe this is the custom among your kind."

Fargo had shaken hands with scores of men, but few were as strong as the leader of the Kwachenies. "I'm surprised your people are not out beating the brush."

"Sometimes a man can do more by doing nothing than by doing everything," was Talokma's reply. "Twenty of our best trackers are out searching for signs. Tomorrow by noon they are to report what they have found. I will take it from there."

"Will you permit us to lend a hand?" Fargo asked.

"I will think on your request tonight and give you

my answer in the morning." Talokma clapped his hands and his people began moving about. "For now you are my guests. Tonight there will be a meal in your honor in my lodge." He walked off, but stopped when Captain Pendrake called his name.

"I want to hear more about your daughter's disappearance. All the details. There might be clues you have overlooked."

Talokma glanced at Fargo. "Teach the soldier manners," he said, and left them.

"Well, that was rude," Pendrake remarked.

"So was calling him stupid." Fargo led the Ovaro toward the lake. Many of the Kwachenies had dispersed, but a dozen or so children and some adults remained, overcome by curiosity. A small boy ran up to him and touched his leg, then ran off, giggling hysterically.

Pendrake was following him. "Can we trust these people?" The officer's immaturity reared yet again.

"They've never harmed me," Bickett brought up. "Never harmed any whites that I've heard about."

"But don't let that stop you from worrying," Fargo said.

"Why do I have the distinct impression that there are times when you look down your nose at me?" Pendrake asked.

Fargo sighed and let the Ovaro dip its muzzle to the water. He happened to be gazing toward the trail that brought them to the village and spied a solitary warrior jogging toward it. The warrior was stripped to the waist and glistening with sweat. Weaving erratically, he was on the verge of collapse from exhaustion. Several Kwachenies spotted him and yelled to alert the rest.

The warrior staggered between two lodges and collapsed on his hands and knees. Talokma was one of the first to reach him. Whatever the warrior said caused a flurry of excitement. Under Talokma's direction, men began dashing every which way.

"Have you any idea what's going on?" Captain Pendrake asked Bickett.

"I sure do. That there is one of the trackers the chief sent out. He's found sign. Now Talokma is organizing a war party to go after his daughter." Bickett paused. "Damn. I was looking forward to that feast tonight."

19

Forty Kwachenie warriors cat-footed along a deep stream with Talokma and the weary tracker at their head. Skye Fargo and his two companions were at the rear, where the chief had made it plain they were to stay. Fargo did not like it, but for the time being he would go along with Talokma's wishes.

The stream they were following did not have a name. Not one bestowed by whites, anyway. The Kwachenie called it Broken Woman Stream, according to Clevis Bickett, but he did not know why.

Approximately seven miles from Hawk Mountain and the village, at a bend in the stream, was a broad gravel bar. It was here the tracker had found tracks, and something more. Abuzz with excitement, the Kwachenie warriors pointed at the ground and talked in low tones.

Dismounting, Fargo shouldered through them to see for himself. Furrows showed where two canoes had been hauled out of the stream onto the gravel bar. The furrows were narrow and deep, unlike those typical canoes would make. Fargo had seen their like before, and it set him to thinking. They were the type of drag marks a seaworthy canoe would make, and

Bickett had told him the stream eventually flowed into the Pacific Ocean.

The footprints were a mystery and a wonderment. Roughly human in shape, they bore the imprint of what appeared to be *scales* on the soles. Squatting, Fargo examined one closely. The outline of the scales, or something that resembled scales, was unmistakable. In all his travels he had never come across anything like it.

Talokma was at the water's edge, staring forlornly westward. He did not look at Fargo when Fargo came over beside him, but said, "The legends are true, then. The Salish, the Makah, the Quileute, they have all been saying it is so and I did not believe them."

The chief stopped and Fargo waited for him to go on.

"For as long as the sun has been in the sky, for as long as my people can remember, there have been stories about them. About how they come in the night to steal people. They prefer women, but men and children have been taken."

"Who does this?" Fargo prompted.

Talokma did not answer right away. Then he said, "In English they would be called Island Devils."

Fargo had never heard of them, and mentioned as much.

"They are from the old time. From long before the coming of the white man. From before my people and the Salish and other tribes claimed this land as our own. Little is known about them other than what the elders remember." Talokma bowed his head. "And now they have my daughter."

"We will find her and bring her back."

"It is not so easy. The Island Devils are not human, like us. They do not think like we do. They do not die as ordinary men die. The legends say that their life spans are as ten of ours."

"Legends can exaggerate," Fargo remarked. Some of the Plains tribes believed that at one time giant birds known as Thunderbirds shook the sky with the beating of their wings and carried off buffalo in their talons.

"Some legends, yes," Talokma conceded, "but some do not." He indicated a footprint in the soft earth, the many tiny indentations as clear as crystal. "The elders say that the Island Devils are part snake, that the reason they live so long is that they spend years at a time asleep in a giant cave that goes down to the center of the world, and only come out when hunger moves them to search for humans to eat."

"And you believe this?" Fargo sought to gauge the chief's personal view.

"I am not sure what I believe," Talokma said frankly. "But I know Mikahwon has been taken. I know that those who took her came in sea canoes, and that they have scales on their feet. The Island Devils steal women, they come from the sea and they are part snake."

"You must have canoes of your own," Fargo said, although, now that he mentioned it, he did not recollect seeing any back at the village.

"A few, for fishing on Hawk Lake. But we are not a water people, we are land people. We never travel far in our canoes."

"We must travel far now," Fargo said. It was fifty to sixty miles to the Pacific Ocean.

"We?" Talokma said. "You and the soldier and Bickett?"

"And however many of your warriors you bring." Fargo figured a force of twenty would be large enough.

"There will only be me."

"Why? Surely your people want to help?" Only then did Fargo notice that the other warriors had moved from the gravel bar to the bank and were huddled in small groups, whispering, with many a sidelong glance at their chief.

"The Island Devils are bad medicine. Very bad medicine. Everyone who has ever gone against them has died." Talokma wearily rubbed his eyes. It was apparent he had not enjoyed a good night's sleep since his daughter's disappearance. "There is a story about a coast tribe from long ago. No one remembers their name, but they were a strong people. Until one night the Island Devils came and took one of their women, so they decided to destroy the Island Devils. All the men set out in canoes, and after many moons and many hardships, they found the island where the Island Devils live. They found the great cave that goes down to the center of the world. And when the Island Devils rushed out, the warriors shot them with arrows. But the Island Devils would not die, and in the end the Island Devils killed all the warriors except one, who made it back to his people and told them all before he died."

"So you won't ask your people for help?"

"I cannot. I will not bring the wrath of the Island Devils down on my tribe. Mikahwon is my daughter. I must do this myself."

Fargo knew better than to argue. Indians were as firm in their beliefs about good and bad medicine as the white man was about good and bad luck, if not more so.

"I will have canoes brought. We will be under way in four hours, as you whites measure the day." His broad shoulders slumped, Talokma walked toward the bank.

Captain Pendrake and Bickett had kept to one side, but now they came over and Pendrake asked, "What were you two talking about?"

Fargo filled him in, then said, "It will just be the four of us. We'll have to leave our horses with the Kwachenie"—a notion, he inwardly admitted, he did not particularly like, not because he distrusted them, but because he did not like being separated from the Ovaro for long lengths of time.

"Hold on a second, friend," Bickett said. "I agreed to guide you to the Kwachenie village. That's it. I don't know anything about these Island Devils, and I don't care to make their acquaintance."

"We can use your help," Pendrake said.

"There's nothing I can do that all of you can't do a hell of a lot better," Bickett rebutted, and vigorously shook his head. "I'm sorry. I'll take my twenty dollars and be on my way."

"What if I increased your pay to fifty dollars?"

"No," Bickett said.

"One hundred dollars, and you can keep one of our pack horses for your own. I'll even pay half now and the other half when this is over. That's generous, isn't it?"

Too generous, Fargo thought, given that Bickett could wind up dead. But Bickett was a grown man and could speak for himself.

"Damn your bones, sonny. That's more money than I've had at one time since I was your age. Lord help me, I know I'm making the mistake of my life, but you have yourself a deal. Shake on it."

They did, and Pendrake smiled smugly and walked toward the horses.

"I shouldn't have done that," Bickett lamented. "But it will buy enough liquor to keep me booze-blind for a year." He chewed on his lip. "Or maybe to take a trip back East and visit my kin in Illinois. That's where I'm from. It's where my brothers and sisters are."

"You miss them," Fargo gathered.

"Of course. I haven't been back in nigh on twenty years. Most of them must reckon I'm long dead." Bickett frowned. "My folks tried to talk me out of coming West. They said nothing would ever come of it, and they were right. Look at me. I don't amount to a hill of beans."

"You did what you thought was best for you."

"You're right there. I had a powerful hankering to gallivant all over creation and see what there was to see. I thought I would strike it rich somewhere or somehow and go home a success. Instead, I've had to scrabble to make ends meet. I've swept saloons and worked in stables and done just about every low, dirty job you can think of. Now here I am. Pushing sixty, and I'll never be more than I am right now."

Fargo was reminded of his own wanderlust. But to him money was a means to enjoy whiskey, women and cards, not an end unto itself. "There's no predicting the future."

"What a kind thing to say," Bickett replied. "There comes a point, though, when all the wishes in the world won't make us better than we are."

179

For Fargo that day was far off, if it ever came. He was happy as he was, with no desire to change.

"It's funny how life works," Bickett prattled. "When we're young we think we have all the answers but we don't really know a thing. We grow old and find the answers but by then we're too close to the grave to put what we've learned to much use. Seems sort of backwards to me."

"You do realize what we are in for?" Fargo asked. "None of us might come back alive."

"I'm not stupid," Bickett said. "I'm gambling with my life, I know. Taking a chance for a hundred paltry dollars. But, hell: Every day is a roll of the dice."

Fargo couldn't fault him there. Even so, he said, "If we run into trouble, light a shuck. Leave the fighting, if there is any, to the rest of us."

"No worries there," Bickett grinned. "I've never been much of a scrapper. I'd rather run than throw a punch or chuck lead."

Captain Pendrake had the fifty dollars. "Here you go, Mr. Bickett. Try not to lose it on our journey."

"Are you kidding?" Bickett dipped a hand under his belt and down his pants and pulled out an old leather poke. A cord had been wound around the top, then knotted and tied to his belt. "I'd have to lose my britches for that to happen."

The Kwachenie were settling down to wait. Talokma had sent twenty warriors back, and there was nothing anyone could do until the canoes arrived. The chief was perched on the bank a few yards upstream from the rest, deep in thought.

Fargo joined him. "I hope you don't mind the company." Since their lives depended on how well they worked together, Fargo was interested in getting to know him better.

Talokma was no fool. "Can you count on me if you must? Is that the question in your eyes?" He answered it with, "I have no great love for your kind. White men are too proud, too arrogant. They think they are better than everyone else, and that the world is theirs for the taking."

"My kind call it 'manifest destiny.'"

"So Father McCallum told me," Talokma said. "Strange ideas, you whites have. My people would never think to want all the land there is to be ours." He stared across the stream at the dense woodland. "When I was a boy, no one had ever heard of white men. Then a few came seeking furs, and after them came the traders, who built a trading post on what your people call Vancouver Island. Since then more and more whites have come until now they have much of the land for themselves, and talk of moving all Indians onto reservations so they can take that land, too."

The same thing had been done to the Cherokees and scores of other tribes in the East, Fargo reflected, and one day, if the politicians and the newspapers were to be believed, the same fate awaited the plains and mountain tribes, and yes, even those of the remote Northwest. He hoped to God he did not live long enough to see that day come to pass.

"But while I have no great love for your kind," Talokma was saying, "I do not hate whites because they are whites, as many of my tribe do. A few whites, very few, are my friends. Father McCallum is one. He is a missionary. I invited him to live among my people so I could learn more about your ways. He tried to get them to believe in his white god and was upset when they would not."

Fargo did not mention he had heard the story. "What was the most important thing you learned?"

Talokma looked at him. "That for all your pride and your numbers and the great cities you build, you are children. You do not see the world as a mature person does."

"Some do, some don't," Fargo said. The same could be said of more than a few Indians he had met. Maturity came from experience, not from the color of one's skin.

"I do not know you or these others. I cannot trust you until I do. But I promise that if someone tries to shed our blood, I will do all I can to see that their blood is spilled and not ours. I can do no more."

Fargo admired the chief's honesty. "You watch my back and I'll watch yours."

They talked then of mutual interests, of wildlife and hunting and the tribes along the coast, and the four hours seemed like forty minutes. An additional ten warriors returned with the twenty who had gone for canoes, bearing them on their shoulders.

They had brought someone with them. A white man. A scarecrow in a flowing black robe, his thin face framed by a sparse beard. "Talokma!" he exclaimed, and embracing the chief, clapped him on the back. "When I heard about Mikahwon, I came as soon as I could. I am sorry, my brother."

"She is not lost to us yet, Father McCallum," Talokma said. "These other whites and I soon leave to find her. You and I will visit another day."

"Nonsense," the missionary said, with a friendly

nod at Fargo. "Am I any less a man than Daniel, who fearlessly braved a den of lions?"

"I do not understand," Talokma said.

Fargo did, and frowned.

"You will not venture into the valley of the shadow alone," Father McCallum declared. "As proof of my devotion to you and to your people, I am going with you."

20

It was called the Stillaguamish River. From where Broken Woman Stream flowed into the Stillaguamish, Fargo estimated they had forty miles to go to reach the sea. For hours they paddled, taking turns so whoever wasn't paddling could catch up on their rest.

At the moment, Fargo, Pendrake and the missionary were in the first canoe, Clevis Bickett and Talokma in the second. Pendrake was in the stern, paddling. Fargo had just been relieved and was in the bow, his head resting on his arm, trying without success to doze off.

Father McCallum was smiling. But then, he nearly always smiled. "It's a fine thing you're doing," he said to the officer, "helping the Indians like this."

"They're a means to an end," Pendrake said. "I was sent to ensure no more whites go missing. If they do, this territory might shrivel and die."

"How so?" Father McCallum asked.

"Word has spread. Accounts from the Seattle newspaper have been reprinted in papers in the States. Our government wants to put an end to it before people start to think Washington Territory is too dangerous."

This was the first Fargo had heard of the Eastern

newspapers. He shifted to make himself more comfortable, but it was simply too cramped for his liking.

"Ah. Then you are not motivated by brotherly love?" Father McCallum's smile faded. "What was I thinking? Yes, I can understand why those in authority wouldn't want the number of emigrants to dwindle to a trickle. Washington Territory's existence would be in jeopardy."

"There you have it," Pendrake said. "But you make it sound as if protecting our vested interests is a bad thing."

"Those interests are only worthwhile if they are in the best interests of everyone, red and white."

"And you're saying they aren't in this case?"

"Your words, not mine," Father McCallum hedged. "All I know is that if more and more whites pour into the territory, more and more Indians will be driven out or forced onto reservations."

"An odd sentiment coming from someone who tried to convert the Kwachenie," Pendrake observed.

The priest touched the silver cross on a silver chain around his neck. "Converting them to the one true faith and destroying their way of life are two different things."

"Are they?" Pendrake countered. "Taking away their religion and replacing it with a version of ours will destroy their culture just the same."

"I'm not asking that they adopt all our ways," Father McCallum said. "Only that they forsake their idolatry for the divine words of our Lord." From under his robe he drew a leather-bound Bible. "I am a voice crying in the wilderness, and they are my flock."

"Did you like the blanket Talokma gave you for all your effort?" Captain Pendrake asked testily.

The missionary grinned. "Heard about that, did you? Yes, for a while I was a laughingstock. But I haven't let it dissuade me from my work. I consider it a fair exchange. I taught him English, he gave me a fine blanket his wife made with her own hands. A high honor according to Kwachenie custom."

"Do you still think there is a chance you can convert them?" Pendrake scoffed.

"With God all things are possible," Father McCallum said. "I am but his humble servant. His will is my will."

"I doubt it was the Almighty's will that you come with us," Pendrake said. "You don't have a weapon. You won't kill. What use will you be?"

"One never knows until one is put to the test." The missionary cupped his hands and raised his gaze to the heavens. "I only pray I will prove worthy."

"I wish you had taken my advice and stayed at their village," Pendrake grumped. "This is work for soldiers and warriors, not someone who believes in turning the other cheek."

Fargo was tired of their petty bickering and was about to tell them so when the priest posed an interesting question.

"Is it me you despise, Captain Pendrake, or do you despise religion in general?"

"Let's just say I have good reason to doubt the good Lord is as concerned about us as you priests and ministers claim, and let it go at that."

"Whenever I hear someone say that, it usually means that person has lost someone close to them."

"Two someones," Pendrake said coldly, "and I'll thank you not to bring it up again. Nothing you say or do will ever change my mind."

At that, Father McCallum fell silent, and Fargo

dozed off. When he awoke to a hand on his arm, twilight had fallen and the wind had picked up, bringing with it a new scent. "We're near the sea."

"The captain's shoulders are about to give out," Father McCallum said. "Can you relieve him?"

Nodding, Fargo sat up. The second canoe was twenty yards behind them, Bickett stroking the paddle while Talokma sat in the bow with a blanket over his shoulders. Fargo started to slide past the missionary to change places with Pendrake when Father McCallum suddenly pointed.

"We have company!"

Four canoes had pushed off from the north shore and were hastening to intercept them. Each canoe was twice as long as theirs and bristled with well-armed warriors.

Fargo reached for the Henry but did not pick it up. He recognized the other Indians. They were Salish, and friendly to whites, the last he knew. "Bring us to a stop," he told Pendrake.

"None of them have guns. We can blast our way through them."

"They're friendly. And you're to do as I say, remember?" Fargo was trying to recall the Salish word for friend when Father McCallum stood up and addressed them in the Salish tongue. Their leader smiled and responded in kind, and after a flurry of words, McCallum glanced down and said, "You didn't think the Kwachenie was the only tribe I've visited, did you?"

Bickett brought the other canoe alongside. On seeing Talokma, the Salishs' warm welcome evaporated. War clubs were raised and the Salish leader spoke harshly to the priest.

"There is bad blood between my people and theirs," Talokma explained to Fargo. "They might not let me pass."

Warfare between the coast tribes, while not as widespread as between the plains and mountains tribes, existed long before the coming of the white man. Bitter enmities had been made. Hatreds were usually held in check by trade: A thriving commerce in furs, pearls, shells and beads did what no amount of peace talks could ever do. The tribes would rather swap goods than spill blood, for the most part.

Father McCallum went on at some length, and now the Salish were whispering among themselves. "I told them about Mikahwon. They have lost loved ones to the Island Devils, too."

"Ask them to join us," Fargo suggested. If they could enlist help from every tribe they passed along the way, they would have a small army.

Another exchange ended with the missionary saying, "They say to oppose the Island Devils is to invite death. They wish us well but they will not accompany us."

"And Talokma?"

Father McCallum spoke to the Salish leader. "Talokma is free to go. But I would not dally or they might change their minds."

"One more thing," Fargo gambled. "Do they have any idea where to find the Island Devils?"

"We must go north," the priest translated. "Toward the land of ice and white bears. But how far, they cannot say."

Several minutes of hard paddling brought them to the mouth of the Stillaguamish. Hugging the coastline, they bore north. Toward midnight they passed between two large islands and heard waves crashing on breakers.

Fargo tried not to dwell on how easily their fragile canoes could be dashed to bits on the rocks. Once in the clear, they bore northwest toward Vancouver Island. When one tired, another took over. When the sea was choppy, two men paddled. The priest insisted on helping and proved to be adept. Apparently McCallum had ranged up and down the coast in his quest to convert the local tribes, including several visits to Vancouver Island, where he was warmly greeted when they arrived.

Initially named Fort Camosack and then Fort Albert, the post was later called Fort Victoria for the longest while. Now known simply as Victoria, a town had sprung up around it, and there was talk of incorporating Victoria as a full-fledged city within the next year or so. The Fraser Gold Rush was largely responsible for the boom, and more and more settlers were arriving every year. The natural harbor had proven a boon to business, and Victoria was the busiest port north of San Francisco.

It was also the last great outpost of civilization for a thousand miles. Beyond lay the largely unexplored coast and the many islands fringing it.

"Why did we put in here?" Clevis Bickett asked as he turned from helping pull a canoe onto the beach.

"We need information," Captain Pendrake said, smoothing his uniform, "anything and everything we can learn about these so-called Island Devils. I will visit the post and speak to the commander." He glanced at Father McCallum. "Didn't you say Victoria has its own newspaper?"

"The British Colonist," the priest confirmed.

"I'll stop there, too," Pendrake said. "We can meet back here in, say, four hours."

Father McCallum also strode off. "Should anyone need me, I will be at the church. Perhaps Father Jacobs or Father Laurence knows something."

"Talokma and me will ask around too," Clevis Bickett offered.

That left Fargo. He had only been to Vancouver Island a few times, but he did know someone who might be of help. Accordingly, he made his way into the shantytown of brothels and bars for which Victoria was notorious and asked at each place about Iron Mike Adams. Adams had lived there since the first sawmill opened at Mill Stream. Fargo met him over a game of cards, and they struck up an acquaintance based on their mutual fondness for whiskey and Adams's love of telling tales about the early days.

Old-timers like Adams were invaluable fonts of information. No one knew an area better than those who had been there the longest, no one knew more about local happenings.

Fargo spent nearly an hour tracking Adams down, and eventually found him in a bar, seated at a table at the rear, nursing a bottle.

"Can it be? Are my eyes playing tricks? Skye Fargo!" Adams came out of his chair and pumped Fargo's hand as if he were trying to break it. "I was beginning to think you would never make it back this way ever again. How have you been, youngster?"

After Fargo made small talk for a few minutes, he had the bartender bring a glass of whiskey. He sipped the red-eye, smacked his lips and said, "The reason I'm here is to find out if you have ever heard of the Island Devils."

Adams paused with his glass halfway to his mouth. He was a great bear of a man, with a bushy gray beard and gray eyes that abruptly mirrored unease. "Sure. Anyone who has been here any length of time has heard of them. They're bogeymen. Demons. Beasts in human form. Take your pick."

"Where can I find them?"

"Why would you want to?" Adams rejoined, and after Fargo explained, he shook his head and leaned forward. "Take my advice and forget the whole business."

"I can't. I have it to do." Fargo lowered his voice. "Is it true they take Canadians too?"

"All the time. There's a pattern to it. Once a month someone disappears either on this side of the border or your side. Now and then it's two in one month, but always about the same time."

"No one has tried to stop them?"

"What do you take us for?" Adams retorted. "On two occasions soldiers were sent after them. Both times the soldiers failed to come back."

"And your government let it drop?" Fargo asked in surprise.

Adams shrugged. "Short of sending out the whole army, what else could they do? I don't need to tell you how much territory there is between here and Alaska. Waterways and forests no white man has ever set foot in. Finding them would be like finding a very small toothpick in the world's biggest hayloft." He scanned the neighboring tables, then whispered, "The Indians are no help. They're too damn scared. There isn't a tribe from the Columbia River to Anchorage that hasn't heard of the Island Devils and doesn't live in fear of them."

191

"So you have no idea where their lair is?" Keen disappointment knifed through Fargo.

"I didn't say that. If you're intent on pushing up moss, who am I to stand in your way?" A crooked grin twisted Adams' mouth. "As a matter of fact, a few years ago I became interested in them myself. The niece of a friend of mine vanished, and the Indians claimed the Island Devils were to blame. So I asked around. The best I could narrow it down, the Island Devils live on an island."

Fargo waited, and when Adams sat there grinning, he asked, "That's it?"

Adams laughed heartily, then sobered. "Not quite. The Tlingit Indians believe the island is shaped like a snake. The Haida Indians say the Island Devils call themselves the Snake People. The Tsimshian think they worship a giant snake." He drummed his fingers on the table. "Notice a trend there?"

"The snake." Fargo was thinking of the vaguely human tracks he had seen on the gravel bar, tracks that seemed to show the soles had been covered with scales.

"Exactly. What it all means is anyone's guess."

Fargo plied Adams with more questions and soon learned an intriguing tidbit.

"Some years ago there was a story making the rounds that a Nishga woman had been taken by the Island Devils and somehow escaped. If true, she's the only person to ever see them and live to tell about it. I never met her, mind you, but the locals swear the story is true. Just as they swear that a month after she came back, she vanished again. But before she did, she told them that the Island Devils were closer than any of them imagined."

Half an hour later Fargo strolled through the shantytown mired in thought. The Tlingit, Haida, Tsimshian and Nishga all lived well to the north, and all fairly close to one another. It stood to reason, then, that they must live nearest to the Island Devils or Snake People or whatever they were. Which narrowed the area to be searched from a thousand miles to several hundred. Still more than enough to take until Armageddon.

Maybe, as Adams told him in parting, he was on a wild-goose chase. And maybe Adams had been right about something else: "No one puts their head in the mouth of a hungry griz or jumps headfirst into quicksand. But that's exactly what you're doing, friend. It was nice knowing you."

21

Mile after mile, inlet after inlet, island after island, the coastline a spine of land bisecting the heart of darkness. The days stretched into a week, the week into half a month.

From records at the post, Captain Pendrake had learned that more people had vanished from the Canadian side of the border than anyone south of it suspected. Fifty-seven souls over the past several decades, not counting the soldiers who had gone out and never returned.

From records at the church, Father McCallum learned that the very first priest to land on Vancouver Island, Father Jean Baptiste Bolduc, had left a journal in which the Island Devils were briefly mentioned. According to Bolduc, local Indians had been vanishing for centuries.

From a man he met at a general store, Clevis Bickett learned that a French-Canadian by the name of Henri LeBeau was the latest to go missing. Since LeBeau was a trapper by trade and was often gone from Victoria for long spells, no one thought much of his extended absence until the decomposed remains of his naked body were found on rocks at the high-tide mark by gold-seekers on their way to Alaska who stumbled on it by merest chance. It was their opinion that the body had washed ashore from one of the many islands.

And from a wizened, almost toothless Nootkan, Talokma learned of an interesting Nootka legend. It seemed that in the early days the tribe occasionally encountered a type of snake so fierce, so formidable, they held it in more dread than any other creature. They said it could live both on land and in the sea, and killed its prey by wrapping its mighty coils around its victim and squeezing. The serpents were believed to have died out long before the arrival of the white man, although the old Nootkan said that one had been killed not ten winters ago by his people after it became ensnared in their fishing nets.

The pieces of the puzzle were slowly coming together. But Fargo and his companions had yet to find sign of their quarry.

Then, on a hazy morning, with the sea as tranquil as the sea ever became, they rounded a headland and in the distance were a cluster of islands. On their right, tangled woodland choked the shore. To their left, the Pacific Ocean stretched for as far as the eye could see.

Fargo was paddling. Father McCallum was reading his Bible. Captain Pendrake was curled up in the bow and wearily rubbed his eyes when the priest mentioned the islands ahead.

"I don't see any that resemble a snake."

"That could be a myth," McCallum said. "Indians delight in their tall tales of yesteryear as much as we do. Ever heard of Jason and the Golden Fleece? Or King Arthur and the Round Table?" He closed his Bible. "In any event, I doubt we're far enough north. It could be another month before we find them. If we ever do."

Fargo wasn't so sure it would take that long. He could not see the Island Devils or Snake People or whatever they called themselves traveling clear from the North Pole to abduct victims. He had a hunch the Nishga woman had been telling the truth: They were a lot closer than anyone suspected.

By late afternoon their canoes were near islands, making slow but persistent headway against a strong wind. Captain Pendrake was doing the paddling when he remarked, "If neither of you object, I propose we make camp early tonight and rest up so we can get an early start."

"Fine by me," Father McCallum said. "I could go for a night on land."

Fargo hollered back to Clevis Bickett and motioned toward shore. In a small cove sheltered by tall pines they drew their canoes onto shore. The woods were uncommonly quiet except for the rustling of leaves and limbs in the strong wind.

While Clevis and Talokma went in search of firewood, Fargo went hunting for game. They could use fresh meat. He was as tired as everyone else of the jerked venison Pendrake procured in Victoria.

Fargo set each foot down with care, avoiding dry twigs and brush. Once he spied a patch of brown but it was gone before he could bring the Henry to bear. Another time, a doe bounded from a thicket and fled, but again he did not have a decent shot.

Fargo never squeezed the trigger unless he was certain it was a kill shot. He did not like to wound an animal. Often they had enough vitality left to go off and die in lingering agony.

Now, moving as silently as a specter through the shadow-dappled realm of the north woods, Fargo paused often to listen and sniff the air. The pungent scent of deer urine drew him to a fresh bed in high grass, used the previous night by a buck and vacated early that morning.

Soon the woods thinned and Fargo came to the edge of a broad meadow. A robin hopped about in search of worms. A rabbit nibbled tender shoots. Fargo fixed a bead on it but promptly changed his mind when movement alerted him to a large animal on the other side of the meadow. It was a buck, maybe the same buck from the bed of grass, bigger than any he had ever shot. Again he went to fix a bead, only to have the buck melt into the greenery.

Reluctant to wander too far from camp, Fargo decided to stalk it until sunset, at which point, if he hadn't brought it down, he would settle for rabbit stew. Circling the meadow so as not to give himself away, he entered the trees. Its tracks were plain in the soft soil. It was in no great hurry to get where it was going, and meandered at random.

Fargo stalked it with the tireless patience of an Apache. He was about five hundred yards behind it when he entered the trees; an hour later he was only a hundred yards behind it, and glimpsed it now and again off through the pines. He had to be careful: The slightest sound would send it flying. So far it had not caught his scent, but if the wind changed it would.

The buck unwittingly cooperated by stopping in a clearing to graze. By then Fargo was seventy yards away. He wedged the Henry to his shoulder, took steady aim, held his breath to steady the rifle, and when the buck raised its head and looked directly at him, he fired.

Now came the hard part. Fargo rigged a travois

using downed branches he trimmed with the Arkansas Toothpick and whangs from his buckskins. On it he placed as much of the meat as he could drag; the rest would lie there until the smell brought in every scavenger around.

The ends of the support poles under each arm, Fargo trudged westward. It was damned difficult. Soon he was caked with sweat and wishing he had shot a rabbit instead.

Another hour went by. The sun perched on the rim of the world and then slowly relinquished the firmament to a multitude of stars. Fargo kept looking for the glow of their campfire but did not see it. He was beginning to think he had drifted north of the cove when a low groan brought him to an instant halt. A groan of pain, from a thicket that hove out of the dark.

Quietly lowering the travois, Fargo glided forward. He peered into the tangle of limbs but did not detect anything out of the ordinary. The groan was repeated. Stepping to the right, Fargo saw part of an arm and a hand and the sleeve of a black robe.

Dropping to his knees, Fargo placed his hand on the man's wrist. "Father McCallum?" he whispered. Whoever had done this might still be around.

The priest slowly raised his head. A vicious gash on his forehead was bleeding profusely. "Fargo?" he croaked.

A quick survey assured Fargo they were alone. Setting the Henry down, he slipped his hands under McCallum's shoulders and eased him from the thicket. The head wound wasn't the only one. McCallum's robe was rent in several places, and his chest and thigh were bleeding.

"Who did this?" Fargo whispered.

McCallum tried to speak. Blinking blood from his eyes, he groped for Fargo's hand and started to pull himself to his feet, but suddenly collapsed, unconscious.

Fargo lowered him to the ground and picked up the Henry. He listened intently but heard only the hoot of an owl and the far-off howl of a wolf. Wrapping an arm around the priest, Fargo hoisted him erect and hiked west. He did not like leaving the travois and the meat, but it could not be helped. Whenever he heard a sound, however faint, he stopped and probed the night.

The rhythmic lapping of surf quickened Fargo's pace. He was close to the ocean, close to the cove. Presently he stepped from the forest onto a pebble-strewn beach. The canoes were close by. Depositing Father McCallum beside them, Fargo looked for the others. He found a pile of firewood. He found where their campfire had been, but someone had kicked dirt and sand on it, putting it out. He found Pendrake's haversack and Bickett's bedroll. He found their water skins. But he did not find Pendrake, Bickett or Talokma.

Hunkering, Fargo cut a strip from Bickett's blanket and moistened it using water from the water skin. The bleeding had slowed, and after wiping off most of the blood, he cut another strip, moistened it as well and bandaged the wound. As he was tying a last knot, Father McCallum's eyes fluttered open.

"I'm still alive, I take it?"

"Afraid so," Fargo said. "But you won't be doing somersaults for a while." He aligned the bandage, and nodded. "That will have to do. How do you feel?"

"As if I've been kicked by a moose," the priest answered. He grinned, then winced and clutched his side. "I think a few of my ribs are broken."

The two lowest were. Fargo tightly wrapped McCallum's middle, then checked McCallum's thigh. The cut wasn't deep or life-threatening but it required bandaging, too. "Any I've missed?"

"Only a few bumps and bruises." The priest propped himself against a canoe, and grunted. "If not for Captain Pendrake I might well be dead."

"What happened?" Fargo asked. The cove was empty, the beach deserted, the night deceptively still.

"They came out of the sea. How many, I couldn't say. My back was to them and I was reading my Bible when Mr. Bickett yelled a warning. I turned and one of them struck me with a war club. Pendrake rushed to my aid and knocked the man down, then he and Bickett and Talokma were fighting for their lives. The last I remember is staggering into the trees. "

Fargo had to ask. "Did you get a good look at them? Were they Island Devils?"

"I saw the one who hit me quite clearly," Father McCallum replied. "He wore a mask made of snakeskin and shaped to look like the head of snake, and his arms and legs were covered with the most amazing mutilations."

"How do you mean?"

"Scar tissue in the most intricate patterns. Tattoos, I guess, but different from any I've ever seen. The effect was unsettling." McCallum moistened his lips with his tongue. "I would imagine they hold some special significance, but what it would be escapes me."

"Anything else?"

"He wore some sort of armor. Not metal armor like our knights of old, but made of wood."

Fargo once came across a tribe that wore something similar. It was more widespread in the old days when arrows and lances were all warriors had to worry about. With the advent of guns, everything changed.

Father McCallum tried to say more but he could not keep his eyes open. "I feel tired. So very tired."

"Get some rest," Fargo advised. He went on a quick sweep of the cove but there were no bodies and no blood. Drag marks hinted at the fate of Pendrake and the others. The waves lapping at his boots, Fargo stared off across the benighted sea. He had no idea which direction the Island Devils had taken.

A dilemma loomed. Should he go after them in the dark or wait until first light? Fargo returned to the canoes. He carried the haversack and the bedroll into the trees, then he lifted Father McCallum, who stirred and muttered.

"Rest easy, padre. It's only me."

Risking a small fire on the landward side of a log so the flames were not visible from the open ocean, Fargo put water on to boil. When it was bubbling, he added pieces of pemmican, and stirred. He was slicing the blanket into additional strips when the priest rolled onto his side.

"Any trace of the others?"

"Go back to sleep," Fargo said. "You need your rest."

"I would if I could, but my head is throbbing. Did you happen to see my Bible anywhere? I would hate to lose it. It was given to me by a cardinal on a pilgrimage I made to Rome."

"Sorry," Fargo said. He would look for it in the morning with the few minutes he could spare.

Father McCallum touched the bandage on his head. "I must confess to the sin of pride. In my visits to all kinds of tribes, never once was I harmed. I thought I was immune, that the Lord would personally protect me." McCallum made a tepee of his hands. "It's true that pride goes before a fall."

"Let's change that bandage," Fargo suggested. He removed the blood-soaked strip and replaced it with not one but two clean ones, partially covering the priest's right eye.

"I have never been so close to death before," Father McCallum mentioned as Fargo worked. "It's not an experience I recommend."

"I made soup. Help yourself when you're hungry." Fargo opened the haversack. To the best of his recollection, the item he was after should still be in it.

"Have you ever been close to death's embrace, my son?"

"Every damn day and twice on Sundays." Fargo's fingers closed on the smooth metal surface of Pendrake's spyglass. Rising, he walked to a pine, wedged the spyglass under his belt and began climbing.

"What on earth?" Father McCallum exclaimed.

Some of the limbs were sticky with sap. Fargo went as high as his weight allowed, then unfolded the telescope. He swept it from north to south and back again, and swore.

The tree rose another twenty feet, but the limbs were precariously thin. Gingerly testing each one before applying his full weight, Fargo climbed to within six feet of the top. The tree was swaying in the wind and might snap at any moment.

Again Fargo raised the telescope to his right eye. To the south lay blackness as inky as the bottom of a well. To the north was more of the same until he trained the telescope on the islands and was rewarded with a reddish-orange tongue of light.

"Got you," Fargo said.

22

In the black hour before dawn, a sleek canoe cleaved the sea as smoothly as a swordfish. Fargo was bent low to minimize his silhouette. He stroked the paddle lightly so as not to splash, his gaze glued to the shadowy vegetation that rose from the island. He had swung wide to approach it from the north and not the south as the Island Devils might expect. There was no sign of life, but the fire he had spotted belied its absence.

When the canoe was fifty feet from shore, Fargo stopped paddling and let the current carry him the rest of the way. Quietly placing the paddle down, he exchanged it for the Henry. The moment the bow crunched onto solid ground he vaulted over the side and dragged the canoe in under the trees.

Crouching, Fargo waited for an outcry. When there was none, he warily stalked into the vegetation. Unease gripped him. Every nerve was taut, every muscle tense. He had the feeling unseen eyes were on him, but mentally shook it off. He was letting the old tales spook him. The Island Devils were men. Human beings, not devils, and as such, they could be brought low by a bullet or a blade.

Still, Fargo's unease grew. Men they might be, but

they had held sway over a thousand miles of western coastland since the dawn of antiquity. They raided every tribe in their domain with impunity. They wiped out anyone who opposed them. They were formidable, these Island Devils, and he must not make the mistake of taking them lightly.

The squawk of a startled bird caused Fargo to drop into a crouch. Had he spooked it or had someone else? He strained his eyes but could not penetrate the green mantle.

Trees blotted out the sky. It was so dark, Fargo could not see his hand at arm's length. Alert for logs or boulders, he crept along with a silent ease born of long practice.

Suddenly there was a trail. Hunkering, Fargo ran his fingers over the ground. The dirt was churned by regular use but he could not read the tracks. Not until sunrise, unless he was willing to risk a torch, which was certain suicide.

Right or left? Fargo asked himself, and moments later was answered by the low beat of a drum. Not the hide drum of a plains Indian but the hollow boom of a wood drum, the kind favored by woodland tribes.

Paralleling the trail, Fargo went west. He was mildly surprised he had not stumbled on sentries. But maybe that wasn't so strange when he considered the raw terror the Island Devils instilled in the mainland tribes. Enemy war parties would not dare set foot on their island.

A rustling in the tall grass reminded Fargo of another aspect of the legends; that they worshipped a giant snake. Most legends contained a kernel of truth, so it could be the island was indeed home to the kind of snake the Nootka Indian had described. And Fargo did not care to run into one.

The rustling stopped. Nothing appeared, and Fargo was about to go on when he heard the gurgle of running water. Veering off the trail, he came on a stream. He gingerly slid a leg over the bank until his foot came to rest on the bottom. The water only rose as high as his waist, but he had the impression that further out it was a lot deeper. Easing down, he waded westward, careful to hold the Henry out of the water.

Ahead was a bend. Fargo had started around it when a sharp cough froze him stock still. Rising onto the tips of his toes, he peered over a bush.

On the bank stood a sentry. Details were difficult to distinguish in the gloom. The man was short and stocky. His chest and back appeared to be covered with large scales, but that was not nearly as unnerving as his face. For while his skin was the typical swarthy hue of coast peoples, his face was black as pitch and had a reptilian sheen. Worse, the features seemed to be more serpent than man, an effect heightened when the sentry's tongue flicked out and he licked his thin lips.

Fargo had never seen the like. He imagined a hideous hybrid, a mix of man and snake, spawned by means unknown. But that was ridiculous. He told himself there had to be a logical explanation.

The drum was louder. Fargo was near their village. To reach it, he had to slip past the sentry, who was pacing back and forth, and occasionally yawned. Tucking at the knees, Fargo ducked under the water clear to his shoulders, and with the Henry clasped in front of him, he edged around the bend.

The sentry abruptly stopped pacing. For a few harrowing moments Fargo thought he been seen, but the sentry was gazing in the other direction. The man impatiently stamped a foot. Maybe he was waiting for his relief and his turn as sentry to be over. It was a typically human gesture, not that of a demon.

Then the man muttered something in a tongue Fargo had never heard, sibilant speech, more akin to the hiss of a serpent than the work of human vocal cords.

Fargo dipped lower, to his chin. Moving his legs slowly to avoid creating ripples, he hugged the bank until he was safe. But safe was relative, as the next bend revealed.

The stream widened, and there, lining both banks, squatted the dwellings of the Island Devils. Circular structures, constructed in tiers. Or so Fargo assumed, until he saw a carved snake head atop each one. The dwellings weren't built in tiers; they were made to resemble *coils*.

Fargo glanced over his shoulder. The sentry had resumed pacing. He moved to a long row of large canoes drawn up on the north side of the stream. They were five times as long as the one that brought him, their sides twice as high. The bows sloped up to a point, and the sterns were similarly raised, although not to the same degree. These were craft-built to ply the open seas.

Fargo slid past the first one. Like the rest, it had been hollowed from a single tree. Paddles lay inside, paddles that tapered to points so they could double as weapons. All the canoes had been painted a bright bloodred and bore the likeness of a giant black snake. The snake's head was at the bow, the mouth agape to reveal a long forked tongue and fangs. Its body consisted of long, looping coils that ran the length of the canoe and ended in its blunt tail to the stern.

Fargo counted ten canoes on his side, eight canoes on the other. Each could hold eight to ten warriors. It tallied with his suspicion that the Island Devils were a small tribe. Or maybe he should start thinking of them as the Snake People, as they were supposed to call themselves. It certainly fit.

He moved from canoe to canoe, alert for signs of where they were keeping their captives. The sky to the east had brightened, not a lot, but enough for Fargo to see that the dwellings, like the canoes, were painted red and bore the same images of fearsome snakes. The carved snake heads on top of the dwellings were incredibly lifelike, the pupils a vivid yellow, the fangs a brilliant white.

A buckskin flap parted and out strode a warrior. Short and stocky, he had scales on his chest and back, and a black snakelike face. He carried a war club shaped like the paddles in the canoes. Facing east, he raised his arms to the new dawn.

Fargo saw that the scales were a trick of the light spawned by overlapping slats of polished wood, the armor described by Father McCallum. The man's arms and legs were covered with tattoos formed from hard ridges of scar tissue, in the shape of giant snakes.

The warrior turned and walked to another dwelling. In the pale but growing light, his reptilian face was revealed to be nothing more than a mask. He came to the flap and smacked it, and presently two more similarly attired warriors emerged.

Fargo had to hurry. The whole village would soon be up and about. He had to find Pendrake, Bickett and Tolakma and spirit them out of there. Talokma's daughter, too, if she was still alive.

But warriors were stepping from dwellings on the other side of the stream, too. Fargo rounded the stern of one canoe and moved on to the next. So long as only his head was showing, he might escape detection.

Beyond the village lay a small lake, the stream's source. The lake, in turn, lay at the base of a rock cliff. Footpaths ran around the lake to a circular opening in the cliff: It was the entrance to a cave.

A golden glow bathed the eastern sky and soon would spread. With each minute the danger of being seen rose. Fargo was almost to the end of the canoes and still had no inkling where to find the others.

A warrior stepped from a lodge on the south side of the stream. He was leading a captive by a leash, as a white man would his dog. The captive was white and female, a young woman in her twenties whose clothes had been reduced to tatters and who walked stiffly, her face as blank as a wiped slate, in a state of perpetual shock. Her wrists were bound behind her back. Black and blue marks on her cheeks, neck and shoulders bore mute testament to her treatment at the brutal hands of her captors.

A different warrior came from another snake dwelling leading a second captive by a leash. It was a comely Indian maiden, her buckskin dress in good shape. Her long raven hair was disheveled and she bore bruises of her own, but she walked with her chin tilted in proud defiance.

Mikahwon, Fargo suspected, Talokma's missing daughter.

The two warriors conversed in their strange sibilant

tongue. The one leading Mikahwon jerked on the leash and she nearly tripped. He laughed as if it were funny and said something that brought lusty mirth from the other warrior.

By now the sky was bright with the promise of sunrise. Slipping between the last two canoes, Fargo bided his time. His luck had deserted him. He was trapped there.

More and more Snake People were moving about, women and children as well as men. The children pranced about naked, as playful and happy as young ones everywhere. The women were not nearly as carefree. They huddled in small groups, talking in hushed tones. Bare from the waist up, they wore red buckskin skirts that fell to their ankles. On the front of each skirt was the painted likeness of their serpent god.

Fargo knew it was only a matter of time before someone spotted him. Removing his hat, he hooked an arm over the canoe on his left and slid up and over the side. He did it so quickly, no shouts shattered the morning chill. Rising on an elbow, he peeked over the gunwale.

Indians on both sides of the stream were straggling toward the footpaths that led to the cave. Out of a dwelling near the north path filed three more warriors leading three more captives.

Clevis Bickett was swearing a vicious streak. Captain Pendrake had his shoulders squared and his face set in grim lines of resignation. Talokma had severe wounds on his face and chest but bore them stoically.

Talokma glanced across the stream and saw the Indian maiden. "Mikahwon!" he shouted, and tried to run to her, but the warrior holding the other end of the deer-hide leash brought him up short with a strong jerk. Whirling, Talokma lowered his head like an angry bull elk, and charged. The warrior avoided his angry charge, and an outstretched leg sent him pitching to his face in the dirt.

Many of the Snake People laughed. A pair of husky warriors hauled Talokma to his feet and one struck him, open-handed, across the face. Talokma did not appear to feel it. He had eyes only for his daughter, who was jerking on her leash in a vain bid to go to him.

Suddenly the Snake People stopped whatever they were doing. From out of the stream where it joined the lake had risen a fiendish apparition, a tall figure covered in black wooden scales, his black mask the largest and most hideous of all. His tongue darted in and out as he strode out of the water onto the north shore by the footpath.

Fargo had lived among enough Indians to suspect that this was the tribe's medicine man, as most whites would call him, or shaman. The gaping maw of their snake god had been painted on the front of the wooden slats on his chest.

"That's their chief," Bickett said to Pendrake, "or I'm a jackass."

The tall figure swung toward them.

"Do you speak English?" Captain Pendrake asked. "I am an officer in the United States Army, and unless you release us, unharmed, my government will not rest until every last one of you has been brought to justice."

"He does not understand you," Talokma said. "His tongue is not yours or mine. It is older than both, and known only to his kind."

"Try speaking to him anyway," Pendrake urged. "What have we got to lose?"

Talokma did as he had been bid, but as he predicted, the tall figure did not respond. "I told you," he said.

"What about sign language?" Pendrake brought up. "According to Fargo, a lot of plains and mountain tribes use it."

"I have heard of Indians who talk with their fingers, but my people do not," Talokma enlightened him.

"Wonderful," Pendrake said. "Then I guess we have no choice but to make a break for it when they let down their guard."

"*If* they do," Clevis Bickett amended. "But from what I've seen, this bunch doesn't make many mistakes."

"What do you suppose they have in store for us?" Pendrake wondered.

"Whatever it is," Bickett answered, "I'll bet we won't like it." He gestured at the figure in the black scales. "Cut me loose, you bastard, and give me a fighting chance. Or are you too much of a coward?"

The medicine man or chief or whatever he was made a sharp gesture of his own, and the warrior holding the other end of Bickett's leash turned and struck Bickett on the temple with the flat of his war club. Bickett buckled at the knees and would have fallen, but the warrior savagely jerked him upright again and jabbed him in the ribs.

"There was no call to do that," Captain Pendrake protested. "What will it take to convince you that you cannot hope to prevail against the might of the United States Government?"

"You waste your breath, soldier," Talokma said. "To them we are as animals are to us, to do with as they will."

"I am not an ani—" Pendrake began, then stopped.

The tall figure in the large snake mask was moving swiftly toward them. Toward Pendrake. His intent was unclear until he snatched a long-handled war ax from a warrior. Hefting it, he stopped in front of Pendrake and raised it over his head to strike. Pendrake bravely stood his ground. Just when the blow was about to descend, a shout of alarm rose from the sentry down the stream.

Everyone turned at the outcry, Snake People and captives alike.

All Fargo had to do was twist his head. Disbelief changed to astonishment and then to anger.

Paddling serenely toward the village was Father McCallum.

23

Skye Fargo could do nothing but lie there and watch as the priest paddled past the red canoes and over to the shore near where Pendrake, Bickett and Talokma were transfixed with amazement.

Fargo tried to get Father McCallum's attention as he went past by moving his hand without raising it above the side of the canoe, but McCallum didn't notice.

"Greetings, my friend," the priest said to Talokma as he climbed out. His bandages were stained scarlet and dry blood caked his chin, but he smiled warmly and embraced the Kwachenie chief, perhaps to show the Snake People that he regarded Indians as his brothers.

"Get back in your canoe and leave before it is too late," Talokma advised. "The old ones do not want to hear about your god. They have a god of their own."

"Nonsense," Father McCallum said. "Enlightening primitive souls is what I do. I cannot shirk my duty to my Maker." He smiled at the Snake man wearing the black scales. "Is this their chief? He's dressed differently from all the rest." Spreading his arms wide, Father McCallum embraced him.

Captain Pendrake gasped.

Bickett recoiled and blurted, "What in hell are you doing?"

The Snake People were as shocked as their new captives. All eyes were on their leader, who stood as rigid as a statue, his mask hiding his reaction.

"In the name of the Father and the Son and the holy Catholic church, I offer you my hand in friendship," McCallum said, and did exactly that, extending his right arm.

The tall figure did not move.

"See?" Father McCallum said to Talokma. "Deep down all men are brothers at heart whether they are willing to admit it or not. I'll have you untied in a moment."

Hardly were the words out of his mouth than the leader of the Snake People took a step back and swung. The honed edge of the war ax caught Father McCallum across the wrist, nearly severing it, and Father McCallum fell to his knees, blood spurting everywhere.

"No!" Captain Pendrake cried, and sprang to help him, but was met in mid-leap by a fist to the jaw.

Talokma, too, bounded to the priest's aid, only to be tripped from behind and have the tip of a knife pressed to his throat.

Father McCallum was white as paper. His wrist pressed to his robe, he grit his teeth and smiled up at the hideous mask of his attacker. "I forgive you, my son, for you know not what you do."

The leader raised the war axe for a killing stroke. Why he never followed through, Fargo didn't know. But instead of finishing the priest off, the man slowly lowered the ax, tossed it to the warrior he had taken it from and wrenched off his mask.

To the Snake People the face under the big mask was as familiar as their own. To Fargo it was a grotesque abomination. Nearly every square inch was covered by scar tissue in a pattern that mimicked the scales of a snake. But that wasn't all. To make him even more serpentine, the man's ears had been cut off and his eyes tampered with so they were mere slits. His nose had been removed and the skin sewn shut, leaving a pair of tiny holes much like those of a real snake. And as if that were not enough, his chin had been scraped to the bone to conform to the shape of a snake and his hair had been shaved.

Clevis Bickett was thunderstruck. "That there is the ugliest son of bitch who ever lived!"

The unmasked leader bent over Father McCallum and hissed angrily in the Snake People tongue. Then he placed his mask back on and wheeled.

Warriors seized McCallum. A leash was fastened to his neck. Weak from loss of blood, the priest could not resist. They forced him to stand and prodded him with their axes and lances toward the footpath. Stumbling and weaving, he became part of the procession he had so boldly, and recklessly, interrupted.

Fargo thought about shooting a few and covering his companions while they ran to the canoes. But he only had so many shots in the Henry, and the Snake People would be on him before he could reload. He would be slain or fall into their clutches. So as much as it galled him, the wise thing for him to do was to do nothing.

The warriors were filing around both sides of the lake toward the dark mouth of the cave. They moved in single file in slow cadence. Each would take a step, then pause, take a step, then pause.

Next came the women and children, in pairs, their chins bowed, their arms uplifted.

Fargo was about to climb out of the canoe and follow them when rapid footfalls approached. The sentry was hurrying to catch up. Instantly, Fargo was over the side and sliding the Arkansas Toothpick from its ankle sheath. He timed it perfectly. As the sentry came abreast of the gap between the canoes, he rose and lunged, burying the slender blade in the sentry's throat even as he clamped his other hand over the man's mouth to stifle an outcry.

The man thrashed wildly, but in a few moments his struggles weakened and he went as limp as a wet rag.

Fargo quickly placed the body in the canoe. He removed the mask and discovered the same scarring as the leader's, only nowhere near as detailed. The mask was not made of wood, as he had supposed, but from the skin of snake; a large black one, if the size of the scales was any indication.

Fargo bent to retrieve the Henry and noticed the sentry's wooden sandals. The bottoms were carved to resemble scales, which explained the bizarre tracks.

Everything these people did, every aspect of their lives, was related to the creature they worshipped. In a way, Fargo reflected, it was not that different from the plains tribes, whose lives revolved around the buffalo. Only the plains Indians didn't venerate the buffalo to the degree the old ones did snakes.

By now most of the tribe were in the cave. Only a dozen or more to go. None were looking back, and Fargo felt safe in sprinting to the nearest snake lodge and parting the buckskin flap. The interior was windowless and dim, and smelled of food and sweat and other odors. On the walls hung weapons and armor made of the wood-plate scales. In the center was a fire pit ringed by wood cooking utensils, giving off smoke.

Fargo ran to the pit. A wooden spoon was just what he needed to uncover the embers. Puffing on them until a few glowed red hot, he dashed to a corner where grass mats had been spread out for bedding. The grass was dry and caught instantly.

Racing outside, Fargo went to the next lodge, and the next. In each he started a fire. He wanted to burn them all down but he did not have the time.

Worn by centuries of use, the path around the lake was as smooth as glass. Fargo flew along it until he heard the murmur of voices. From the dark maw in the rock came a stench so vile he covered his mouth and nose and breathed shallow to keep from gagging. Once inside, he paused to let his eyes adjust, then slunk toward a tunnel leading down into the bowels of the earth.

Fargo never liked caves. They were too cramped, too confined. He was a child of the wide-open spaces, of the sky and the sun and wind.

Somewhere, water was dripping. The tunnel appeared empty. His back to the left-hand wall, Fargo slowly moved down it.

The rank stench became worse. Fargo did not know how anyone could stand it. The source was a mystery until he came to a bend. Past it was a large cavern, and a scene of nightmare and madness.

The Snake People were ranged along a broad rock shelf that overlooked a gigantic bowl. Fully half held torches. They were chanting and raising and lowering their arms.

The captives had been lined up at the bowl's brink. In addition to Pendrake and Bickett and the two Kwachenie, there was the white girl Fargo had seen earlier and five others. Three were white, including another, slightly older woman. The last two were Indians.

Below them was a sheer twenty-foot drop to the bottom. The bowl was empty save for a wide hole at the rear. It was on this hole that the Snake People were raptly focused. They began chanting louder and swinging their arms faster, and now they were stamping their sandaled feet.

The purpose for the ceremony was self-explanatory.

Pendrake and Talokma were tugging at their bindings in a bid to slip free. Bickett was quaking in fear. Mikahwon had closed her eyes and bowed her head. The other captives were either paralyzed with fright or blubbering hysterically.

Fargo was not near enough to be of any help. Scanning the cavern, he saw another shelf barely wide enough to walk along. It led from near the end of the tunnel to a rock spur that overlooked the spectacle from midway up the cavern wall.

Hunkering, Fargo dashed down. He had to stretch his arms to either side or lose his footing. The Snake People had their backs to him, and he reached the rock spur without mishap. Lying prone, he tucked the Henry to his shoulder.

Suddenly something moved in the hole at the bottom of the bowl, something blacker than the hole itself. An obscenely long forked tongue whipped out and back, testing the air, and then the tongue's owner slithered into view. A great triangular head rose half a dozen feet into the air and swayed on a scaled neck as thick as a grizzly's. Eyes the size of pie pans regarded the humans above with cold reptilian dispassion.

A cry went up, a cry of joy and elation. Their god had deigned to answer their summons and the Snake People were ecstatic.

"Nooooooooooo!" Clevis Bickett wailed, and tried to turn and flee, but several husky warriors shoved him back to the edge.

The snake slowly slithered into the bowl. Yard after yard of rippling steely might, its black scales glistening brightly in the dancing torchlight. Coiling in on itself, it came to rest with its enormous head scarcely ten feet below the terror-struck captives.

The medicine man motioned, and quiet fell. He stepped to the brink, elevated his arms and did the last thing Fargo expected. He began to sing. A slow, low ululating song. And as he sang, he swayed in imitation of the movements of the great snake.

Fargo thumbed back the Henry's hammer. He disliked shooting from ambush, but it was either that or rush in among them and be slain before he reached the bowl.

The snake's tongue never stopped flicking in and out again. With cold-blooded slowness, the head rose from the coils and the pie-plate yellow eyes roved the row of flesh-and-blood offerings awaiting it.

Talokma moved toward Mikahwon and was beaten about the neck and shoulders until he took his required place.

The medicine man or chief stepped behind Captain Pendrake, raised his arms on high and sang at the top of his lungs.

The great head rose higher. It cleared the rim and went on rising until it was curled above Pendrake. The next flick of its tongue nearly brushed his face. To the young officer's credit, he met its horrid gaze without flinching. When nothing else happened, the medicine man stepped behind Talokma and repeated his loud chant. The snake moved when he did. Its head now above the Kwachenie, it flicked its hideous tongue.

Clevis Bickett was next. He squealed in panic and started to back away, only to be jabbed by a warrior holding a lance. "Oh, God, oh, God, oh, God," he blubbered.

Again the snake merely stared.

The medicine man moved behind Father McCallum, who was so weak from loss of blood, he was on his knees. Dripping sweat, his body shaking from the torment, the priest yelled, "Get thee behind me, Satan!"

Fargo centered the Henry's sights on the snake's left eye. He had a clear shot, his best yet. Lightly curling his forefinger around the trigger, he was a fraction of a second from firing when Father McCallum lurched to his feet and screamed, "Away with you, you vile beast! Back to the pits of hell that spawned you!"

The snake rose higher and its mouth yawned wide, revealing that it did not, in fact, possess the fangs depicted on the carved heads and the paintings.

Fargo raised the Henry to compensate but the very instant he lined up the left eye in his sights, the head dropped again, to within a few inches of Father McCallum, who, instead of shrinking back, struck the serpent on the end of its snout.

The snake did nothing. The medicine man, however, flew into a violent rage, and beat the priest on the back of the head.

"You damned coward!" Clevis Bickett railed. "Hitting a man when he's near dead!"

Once again Fargo centered a bead on the snake's

eye. Its scales were so big and thick, no bullet would penetrate. It had to be an eye. Once again he touched his finger to the trigger, and once again fate intervened.

The snake suddenly coiled in on itself with only part of its snout showing.

The Snake People were as surprised as Fargo. Whispering broke out, and they looked at one another in confusion.

Motioning for quiet, the tall figure in the black scales stepped to the rim and sang the ululating song, but the snake did not move.

Fargo kept his cheek to the Henry. He was waiting for the snake to raise its head. The second it did, he would snap off a shot.

The Snake People craned forward for a better view of their god. Mothers held children in their arms so they could see better.

Warriors moved forward too, including the one who held the other end of the leash around Pendrake's neck. Pendrake was now behind him, and seizing the opportunity, the young officer suddenly kicked the warrior in the back. The warrior shrieked as he went over the side. Fortunately for Pendrake, the man let go of the leash, or Pendrake would have gone over with him.

Flailing empty air, the man hit on his head and shoulder with a sharp *crack*. At the sound, the snake raised its head from out of its coils and swung toward the fallen form.

Stunned silence gripped the Snake People. The medicine man shouted and jabbed a finger at the serpent as if commanding it not to harm the warrior.

Twisting, the snake looked up at him.

Fargo's moment came. He had the rear sight lined up with the front sight and the front sight lined up with the eye, and he stroked the trigger. Although he was fifty feet from the bowl and even more from the giant serpent, he saw its eye erupt in a spray of gore.

Then all hell broke loose.

24

Fargo had not known if a single shot would kill the giant reptile. He found out it wouldn't when in a twinkling the snake uncoiled almost to its full length and reared up out of the bowl. A tremendous hiss drowned out the screams and shouts of the Snake People, and then it was among them, snapping and whipping its great body in a paroxysm of pain and primal rage.

Suddenly the Indians wanted to get as far from their god as they could. In blind panic some rushed toward the tunnel while others sought the dubious haven of the cavern walls.

Fargo fired again but thought he missed.

A wail lifted to the ceiling as the snake rose above the horrified old ones with one of their own in its mouth.

Pendrake and Bickett had sprung to the priest's side and were trying to help him to his feet, but with their hands bound behind their backs, they could not raise him high enough.

Tolokma had reached his daughter and they were making for the tunnel.

Above the bedlam rose the shrieks of the medicine man. He was railing at his people and at their god, but neither paid him any mind. Beside himself, he ran up to the snake and punched it and gestured at the bowl.

The snake let its victim drop and spun with the speed of living lightning. A scream tore from the medicine man's throat as the maw he had fed so many times now closed around him and he was lifted, kicking furiously, into the air. The snake gave a convulsive bob of its head, and the medicine man vanished as had countless others over the years.

Fargo fired again, and a third time, going for the other eye. His hope was that the slugs would penetrate to the reptile's brain, but if they did, the only effect they had was to drive the creature into a frenzy. Its coils whipping from side to side, the snake struck madly at those who had worshipped it.

The Snake People were bowled over like stalks of corn in the path of a tornado. Here a warrior was crushed under a looping coil, there a woman was sent crashing against the wall by the serpent's battering head. A toddler stood crying for her mother, and the next moment was swallowed whole, as a man might swallow a tasty piece of pie.

Some of the warriors were rallying. Some had torn their gaze from the carnage being wrought and swarmed toward the narrow shelf to the rock spur to slay the one they held responsible. Voicing war whoops, each thirsted to be the first to spill his blood.

Fargo had other ideas. He shot the foremost, worked the Henry's lever and shot the second man. Then, drawing the Colt, he dropped three more in swift succession. The rest faltered, unwilling to take the lead.

Captain Pendrake had Father McCallum off the

ground, and the captives were trying to reach the tunnel. Between them and safety loomed the serpent, as well as dozens of panic-struck Snake People. They could not do it on their own, and Fargo could not help them where he was.

Swiftly replacing the spent rounds in the Colt and the Henry, Fargo stepped to the rim and leaped. He landed in madness. Men, women and children were running blindly about and colliding with one another, getting nowhere. Again and again Fargo would start toward the captives only to have his way blocked.

Clevis Bickett appeared out of the mad throng. He had become separated from the others and was trying to reach the tunnel on his own. He caught sight of Fargo and yelled, but whatever he said was lost in the din. He smiled and took a step, and without warning the writhing coils of the giant snake caught him across the shoulders and smashed him to the cavern floor. He tried to rise, but the snake slithered over him, hundreds and hundreds of crushing pounds, leaving Bickett a pulverized smear of shattered bones and ruptured flesh.

Fargo shot the snake in the neck. He was levering a new cartridge into the chamber when a howling warrior streaked at him holding a war club. The warrior's snake mask was so close to the muzzle when Fargo fired that the lower half of the man's jaw was blown off.

Talokma had taken a knife from a dead warrior and freed himself, and now was working to free the others. He slashed the cord binding Captain Pendrake, who immediately bent to lift Father McCallum. The priest was slumped over, his complexion chalky. His partially severed hand flopped when he moved.

A woman holding a child to her bosom ran past Fargo, her fear rendering her heedless of her peril. The snake's coils slammed into her and she was flung over the rim of the bowl.

Fargo ran past warriors struggling to restore some semblance of order. One spun, raising an ax to cleave his skull, and Fargo shot him between the eyes. A woman careened into him. A girl of ten or twelve clutched at his leg, then bolted when she realized he was not of her people.

Pendrake was slowly but persistently forcing his way toward the tunnel. Talokma had freed all the captives and they were hard on Pendrake's heels. A burly warrior leaped at the Kwachenie chief with his arm cocked to hurl a lance, and Fargo shot him through the heart.

The snake was rolling over and over in what might be its death throes. Those caught in its path were either crushed to a pulp or sent flying.

Fargo overtook Pendrake. "The canoes!" he shouted. "They're our only hope!" They had to reach them before the Snake People divined their intention or it would all be for nothing.

Pendrake nodded. "Lead the way! We'll be right behind you!"

Into the thick of things they ran. The tunnel was only twenty yards away but it might as well have been twenty million. Milling Snake People and the bodies of the slain barred their way.

A warrior with a war club rushed Fargo. He ducked under the blow and slammed the Henry's stock against the warrior's forehead and the man toppled. A screeching woman nearly ran into him. Then he heard Pendrake shout his name.

The snake god was rolling toward them, mowing down old ones in droves. Talokma and Mikahwon narrowly sprang clear, but two other captives, an Indian and an emaciated white man, were not as quick. Their broken bodies were added to those already littering the cavern.

The coils swept toward Fargo. He couldn't dodge them, couldn't do anything other than leap straight into the air and hope to heaven he leaped high enough. The snake rolled under him and continued to roll in a circle until it fell into the bowl.

"Move it!" Pendrake bawled at the others. "Move it! Move it! Move it!"

Move they did. Shoulder to shoulder the captives fought their way to the tunnel. They had helped themselves to the weapons of those who had fallen, and the few warriors who tried to stop them paid a fatal price.

Fargo was right behind them, watching their backs. The screams and shrieks had dwindled, replaced by the moans and groans and wails of those hurt and those dying. He started up the incline.

With a loud hiss, the snake's massive head reared up out of the bowl. It was still alive!

Snake People jammed the tunnel. Many were hurt, some were dying. Those who had been spared were helping those who had not. No one tried to stop the captives.

Fargo had seldom been so grateful for fresh air as he was when they emerged from the foul, dank depths into the bright light of the new day. The north footpath was choked with fleeing old ones, but only a few were using the south footpath.

Springing past Pendrake, Fargo assumed the lead. A warrior glanced back and saw them and turned, but when Fargo jammed the Henry to his shoulder, the man wisely lowered his war club and continued running.

Pendrake was huffing and puffing and red in the face. "How did you find us?" he asked. "I was never so glad to see anyone in my life."

"Later," Fargo said. When they were out of danger.

Talokma was now bringing up the rear. He had acquired a war club and his daughter had a lance. Several of the white captives were so overjoyed at their deliverance that they had tears in their eyes, and one was giggling in delight. The Indian captives were more subdued.

Cries of dismay arose. The Snake People had discovered that lodges on the north side of the stream were on fire. Flames crackled high into the sky and were spreading from dwelling to dwelling thanks to the stiff wind.

"Is that your doing?" Pendrake wanted to know.

Fargo nodded.

A high-pitched screech from the north shore was but a prelude to more. Warriors and women were looking back and pointing.

Their snake god was framed in the cliff opening. From its right eye oozed greenish pus, and its head continually twitched as it crawled out of the earth and into the surface world.

Fargo wondered how long it had been since the serpent last saw the sun, if ever. It was gazing about uncertainly, unsure of itself in this new element. Then, like an ebony arrow shot from a bow, it suddenly sped along the north footpath in pursuit of those who had nurtured it for so long.

Fargo was relieved the serpent had taken the other

path, but once it finished with the Snake People on that side of the lake, it might turn its attention to those elsewhere. They must be gone by then. Long gone.

"They caught us unawares," Captain Pendrake was saying between puffs. "Came up out of the sea and jumped us while we were sipping coffee and talking. We resisted but there were too many."

"Save your breath for running," Fargo advised, but as usual, the young officer didn't listen.

"We thought the priest was dead. I told him to run but four of them went after him and later returned alone. They tied us and threw us in their canoe and brought us here."

Screams and yells mixed in strident chorus. The snake had caught up to the old ones and was wreaking havoc. It was almost as if the giant reptile was determined to exterminate them to the last man, woman and child.

The lodges on the south side of the stream were as yet untouched by the growing conflagration. Drawn up along the bank were the eight red canoes, paddles resting on the bottom.

Fargo came to the first and put his shoulder to the stern to push it into the stream. Talokma and Mikahwon bounded to his side to help. The white captives imitated their example with the second canoe.

"Hurry," Fargo urged Pendrake, who had halted and was placing Father McCallum down. "Here. I'll lend a hand." He bent and slid an arm under the priest's, but Pendrake sadly shook his head.

"There's no need."

Father McCallum's eyes were wide open but the spark of life that once animated them was gone.

Fargo felt for a pulse anyway. There was none. He folded McCallum's arms across his chest and straightened. "He shouldn't have followed me."

"We'll take the body with us and give it a proper burial when we can," Pendrake proposed.

"Dead is dead," Fargo disagreed. "We don't have the time, and the priest is past caring."

"I refuse to leave him here. I wasn't of his flock, but I respect him for his courage, and I will do right by him with or without your help."

Fargo never ceased to be amazed at how pigheaded some people could be. Here they were, enemies on all sides, a giant snake gone amok, half the village on fire and Pendrake wanted to ruin what little chance they had of escaping by this needless delay. "Get in the canoe."

"I beg your pardon. Who are you to tell me what to do?"

"I'm in charge, remember?" Fargo reminded him, and seizing Pendrake by the front of his shirt, he pushed him toward the first craft.

"How dare you?" Pendrake stumbled but regained his balance and pugnaciously thrust out his chin. "Try that again and you'll regret it."

"Damn it!" Fargo fumed, and might have said more but just then a lance streaked from across the stream and imbedded itself in the bank inches from Pendrake's foot.

Warriors were moving to stop them.

"In the canoe," Fargo repeated, and waded into the water. The warriors would have to get past him to get at the others. He aimed at a heavily tattooed apparition splashing into the stream, and when the man didn't stop, blew off the top of his head.

Snake People came spilling along the north footpath, some hobbling, some reeling, some covered with blood. On their heels came the great snake, slaying everyone that came within reach.

The second canoe glided into the stream. In the middle were the two white women. They weren't alone. The other white captives and the rest of the Indian captives were with them.

That left Talokma and his daughter, Pendrake and Fargo to handle the first canoe. Talokma and Mikahwon almost had it in the stream. Pendrake added his weight to theirs, and Talokma had to grab the canoe to keep it from floating off empty.

"Climb in," Fargo commanded, and once they had, he gripped the side and hauled himself up and over, into the stern.

"We did it!" Pendrake crowed.

His outcry was premature. Mikahwon pointed at the north bank, and Fargo twisted to see the giant snake slithering toward the stream.

"We must paddle for our lives!" Talokma shouted. "Their god is after us!"

That it was. Without slowing, the snake hurled itself into the water, throwing spray in all directions, and bore down on them.

Their canoe could not gain speed fast enough to outdistance it, and before they knew it, the snake overtook them and its head rose above the stern.

Directly above Skye Fargo.

25

Skye Fargo snapped the Henry to his shoulder even though he doubted he could stop the snake. Its underside was as thickly scaled as the upper half. But he had to try. It was not in his nature to go down without a struggle.

The snake god's remaining eye was a glittering pool of fiery yellow. Its tongue flicked out once, twice, three times, and its great body tensed for the downward thrust of its huge head.

It was then that a warrior ran close to the water on the north side of the stream and hurled a lance with all the strength in his squat body. His wooden scales were spattered with blood and he had torn off his snake mask, revealing a scarred face contorted in outrage that the creature his people venerated had turned on them.

The lance struck the reptile low in its side at a point where two scales met. It sank in a good half a foot, and a misty spray of snake blood dappled the stream.

Hissing like a steam engine, the snake whipped around and flashed toward the source of its pain.

"Paddle!" Fargo shouted to the others, and handed paddles to Talokma and his daughter. Captain Pendrake already had one in hand and was perched in the bow. "Paddle for your lives!"

The other canoe was already well away and rapidly pulling ahead. Everyone in it was paddling with a vigor born of desperation. The Indian in the bow knew to keep to the center of the stream where the channel was deepest, and yelled when they veered too near to either bank.

Fargo stroked with all his might. The snake had momentarily forgotten about them but might decide to take up where it had left off.

The village was a riot of confusion. Most of the lodges on the north side were ablaze. Red-hot embers, borne by the wind, had alighted on two of the dwellings on the south side, and now they, too, were being rapidly engulfed in flames. Thick clouds of smoke spread like fog.

Wounded and the dying littered the ground. Women and children were scurrying about in terror. Several warriors were trying to put out the fires, but most had thrown themselves into the pitched battle with their god.

The giant serpent was at the center of a whirlwind of flashing war axes, clubs and lances. Suddenly its great head streaked down and a warrior was gripped and shaken as a terrier might shake a rat. But the snake did not swallow him. It released the broken body and reared to strike again.

A bend in the stream appeared. Fargo hoped they would make it around without the snake spotting them. If so, they stood a good chance of reaching the ocean, and once there, their canoes would soon leave the hellish lair of the Snake People far behind.

Three warriors were down but the rest fought on in a frenzy of revenge for those who had been slain.

Fargo put his shoulders into each stroke. Mikahwon was in front of him, her father in front of her, then Pendrake. The canoe was designed to be handled by eight, but they were managing. He smiled when the bend was behind them.

Mikahwon looked back and grinned, then surprised him by saying in flawless English, "Thank you for saving us. My father says we could not have escaped without your help."

"He's too modest," Fargo said. "He did as much as I did." Despite her captivity and the abuse she had suffered, she was remarkably lovely.

"When this is over, I hope you will let me thank you with a meal or a gift."

Fargo had an idea of his own what he would like, but now was hardly the right time or place to suggest it. "That would be nice," he settled for saying.

In the light of day the dense woodland was not nearly as unnerving. Birds flew in the trees and a butterfly flitted among wildflowers on the bank.

"The power of the old ones has been broken," Mikahwon said. "Never again will they raid villages and farms in the dark of night to steal people to feed to their god."

"Some are bound to survive," Fargo noted.

"My people will spread word to the other tribes, and the few old ones who do will be hunted down and made an end of. You should be proud of what you have done this day."

It had never been Fargo's aim to wipe them out. Their god was to blame. He wondered how the warriors were faring, and swiveled to check for sign of pursuit. In midstroke he froze.

A sinuous black shape was a hundred yards back, plying the water with streamlined ease.

"It's after us!" Fargo hollered, and redoubled his efforts.

The others bent to their paddles with renewed urgency, and Captain Pendrake shouted, "Shoot it! Maybe you can stop the thing!"

"I've already tried," Fargo said. Besides, four could paddle a lot faster than three. If he were to stop, it would slow them down and enable the monstrosity to catch them that much sooner. As it inevitably would anyway: Their combined sinews were no match for the reptilian Goliath's.

The gap between their canoe and the one ahead had widened. The captives in it were stroking with grim intensity. One of the white women saw the snake and pointed, and their arms fairly flew.

Fargo glanced back. The snake had not gained. It was swimming at the same speed. Fargo was sure it could swim a lot faster if it wanted, leading him to surmise that its many wounds might be slowing it down. Or maybe that was just wishful thinking on his part.

"I was sure this was my day to die," Mikahwon said without breaking her rhythm. "Twice before the old ones took us into the cave for their god to choose, but each time it chose someone else. This time I thought would be my time."

"You were lucky."

"Father McCallum would call it Providence," Mikahwon said. "I will miss him. He was a good man.

He taught my father and me your tongue, and was always kind to my people."

"He had grit, I'll give him that."

"What I liked most about him was that he never watched me with the hungry look most white men do."

Fargo absently responded, "You can't blame them."

She threw him a harsh look. "Are you one of them, then? Do you eat me with your eyes when my back is turned?"

"I would eat you any time."

The young maiden blinked, then laughed and concentrated on paddling. "You say what you think. I like that in a man. We will talk more if we live long enough."

A big if, Fargo reflected. The snake was still back there. Only its eye and part of its head and back were visible.

The ground sloped slightly near where the stream met the ocean, and the current was flowing faster. But once they were out to sea, the wind and the waves would hamper them and they would be taxed to maintain their lead.

Another minute, and excited yells from the other canoe heralded their arrival. Fargo heard waves break on the island's shore and saw gulls wheel in the sky. "Head east!" he shouted, and Captain Pendrake nodded. If they could reach the mainland before the snake reached them, they could hide in the forest until it lost interest and wandered off.

But as soon as their craft cleared the stream's mouth, the wind hit them, buffeting their canoe. The sea had been churned to choppy froth, and for them to make headway, they had to exert themselves as never before.

The only factor in their favor was that the wind was coming out of the northwest, so that it pushed as much as it buffeted, increasing their speed by a slight margin.

"Look there!" Captain Pendrake cried, stabbing an arm out. "What do they think they're doing?"

The other canoe had turned south. The seven captives were paddling with heightened vigor but they were making no headway at all. To the contrary: Their canoe was now almost broadside to the wind and some of the larger waves were breaking over the side, drenching them.

Pendrake cried out again. "It's after them!"

Fargo twisted. The snake had reached the sea. Instead of pursuing their canoe, it was making for easier prey: the floundering craft and the terrified captives pitting their puny strength against the wind and the waves.

Rising on his knees, Fargo cupped his hands to his mouth. "Go east!" he shouted, and pointed at the distant shoreline. But they did not seem to hear him.

"We should help them!" Pendrake proposed, and turned his paddle so the bow would swing south.

"No!" Talokma cried. "We would only die. There is nothing we can do."

Fargo hated to admit it, but he agreed. By the time they reached the other canoe it would be over, and the snake would turn on them. Already it was within a few yards of its quarry. An Indian at the stern rose and swung his paddle, striking the snake across the snout. Instantly, it submerged, and the other captives raised a cheer.

"The fools," Talokma said.

It was harsh but it was true. Suddenly the other canoe bucked and rocked. The captives had to grip the sides or they would have been tossed into the sea. One of the women screamed. Then the bow heaved out of the water until the canoe was almost vertical, and a white man fell out. The canoe slammed back down, narrowly missing him. Several hands were stretched out to pull him in.

From up out of the sea surged a giant triangular head. The man swung his fists as the mouth descended, but he might as well have been punching a tree. He disappeared under the waves.

The other captives did not care to share his fate. They resumed paddling, only now they had learned from their mistake and turned their canoe east.

Fargo was still stroking but he was mesmerized by the unfolding tableau. *Faster!* he wanted to shout. *Paddle faster!*

A black coil mushroomed under the other canoe. The force splintered it, and as it crashed back down, half the captives were pitched into the cold sea. One of the women screamed as she went under and did not reappear. The snake appeared, though, its head high above the hapless forms fighting to stay afloat.

Snatching up the Henry, Fargo banged off a shot. He aimed for the neck. When there was no reaction, he fired again.

The snake's head speared down. A captive shrieked as she was lifted in its iron jaws. But it soon faded to a plaintive whine and her legs dangled limp and lifeless.

Once again the snake did not swallow its victim. It simply dropped the body into the sea and swooped toward another.

It was not commonly known that animals sometimes killed for the sheer sake of killing. Fargo had seen a sheep pen where a mountain lion had slaughtered more than forty sheep and not eaten one. A farmer once showed him a rabbit hutch were a coyote had broken in and killed every last rabbit. Ravens would invade the nests of other birds and destroy their hatchlings. But he had never heard of a snake going amok.

Another scream, another life extinguished. A white woman still clinging to the canoe was sobbing and pleading for God to save her. She looked up as a shadow fell across her, and then the snake's huge weight came crashing down.

"It will be after us next," Pendrake said.

Their canoe was smoothly cleaving the sea, but they were still much too far from the mainland. For the longest while no one spoke. Their oars dipped and rose, dipped and rose.

Finally Talokma glanced back. His brow crinkled and he asked, "Where is it? I do not see it anywhere."

The sea was empty. The other canoe and its occupants were gone. So was their destroyer. Fargo looked and looked, but the serpent had vanished. Legend had it that the snake god thrived in the sea as well as on land, so it could be after them *underwater*. "Don't stop," he said.

Fargo suited his own actions to his admonition. The wind whipped the whangs on his buckskin shirt. Salty spray sprinkled his face and neck. He envied the gulls their wings, and sorely missed the Ovaro.

Captain Pendrake chuckled. "No one would ever believe my report. They'll think I'm insane. Even General Foster."

"You can always take him a snake mask as proof," Fargo ventured.

"I might just do that," Pendrake said. "I'll ask the general to contact the Canadian government and request that a contingent of soldiers be put at my disposal." He paused. "Of course, then I would have to explain to the Canadians why we are operating on their soil without their permission."

"We are?" This was news to Fargo. He had taken it for granted Pendrake would not do anything illegal while on an official U.S. Government mission. "I thought you talked to the post commander at Victoria?"

"I did. But I never told him I was here in a formal capacity. General Foster thought it best to keep our presence a secret."

"Good for him." Fargo made a mental note that if he ever ran into the good general, he would punch him in the mouth.

"General Foster prefers to avoid stirring up ill will after the recent boundary flap," Pendrake explained.

Fargo grunted. For years the United States and Canadian governments had wrangled over where to establish the boundary between the two countries, eventually settling on the Forty-ninth Parallel.

Craning his neck, Pendrake announced, "Another five minutes and we'll reach the beach. Then we can relax."

"No, we can not," Talokma said gravely. He was staring west, in the direction of the island.

Fargo turned, expecting to see the snake god. But it was worse. Much worse. Two bloodred canoes bristling with warriors had swept out of the mouth of the stream and given chase. They were a quarter of a mile back and closing fast.

"They will show us no mercy," Mikahwon predicted.

"When it rains, it pours," Captain Pendrake said, and for some strange reason, he laughed.

26

Sand rasped under the canoe as the four of them hauled it out of the surf. Fargo grabbed the Henry and turned. Their pursuers were only a few hundred yards out, a phalanx of paddles dipping in unison.

"How can they move so fast?" Pendrake marveled. Winded from their final push, he sucked breath into his lungs in deep gulps.

"There are eight of them in each canoe," Talokma said. Neither the Kwachenie chief nor his daughter showed fatigue. Talokma hefted a lance and motioned at the forest. "We must find a place to make a stand."

"Hell, they'll never catch us," Pendrake confidently declared. "We'll cover our tracks as we go."

Mikahwon shook her head. "It would not work. They are good trackers, the old ones. The best. They will find us and they will kill us unless we kill them first."

"They crave revenge for their god and for their people," Talokma noted. "Such men never give up."

Fargo jogged into the trees. They were wasting precious seconds. In the distance were hills he was anxious to reach. He had gone a short way when Pendrake paced him at his elbow.

"Can you slow down a bit? We need to talk."

"Whatever it is, it can wait." Fargo skirted a log and had to sidestep quickly when Pendrake nearly bumped into him.

"I want your word that when this is over, you won't tell anyone. It's best this whole incident remain secret."

"That's all you can think at a time like this?" Fargo tended to forget how by-the-book the young officer could be.

"My duty to my country is always first and foremost," Pendrake said. "So indulge me and give me your word and I can die a happy man."

"Don't worry, Captain. Like you said. Who the hell would believe me?" Fargo had heard enough tall tales to know how people would take it.

Pendrake was quiet awhile except for his labored breathing. Then he remarked, "Those poor white women in the other canoe. I would give anything for a chance to put an end to that snake once and for all."

"There were Indians in that canoe, too," Fargo mentioned.

"That was uncalled for. I don't hate Indians. I just wouldn't marry one, is all." Pendrake glanced back in sudden concern, but Talokma and Mikahwon had not overheard him.

Fargo concentrated on their plight. Sixteen to four were lopsided odds. He must whittle the Island Devils down. He had enough ammunition. All he needed was the right spot to start the bullets flying.

About then a shimmering sunbeam pierced the canopy and bathed a clearing. Fargo crossed it, then halted and told the others to keep going. "I'll catch up when I can."

"What are you up to?" Pendrake asked. "We should stick together."

Talokma was not a chief for nothing. He gazed toward the sea and said, "I will stay and help you."

"The more who wait, the more we might lose," Fargo countered. "And you have your daughter to think of."

"I will stay too," Mikahwon declared.

Fargo backed toward a pine with a broad bole. "What are you waiting for? They'll be here soon. Head for those hills and don't stop for anything." To Pendrake he said, "If I don't make it, sell my horse and my belongings and give the money to Claresta and Ruthie."

"I don't like this," Pendrake said. But he ran on. Talokma and Mikahwon hesitated, then followed. Soon all three blended into the vegetation.

A sparrow chirped nearby as Fargo hunkered behind the pine and rested the Henry's barrel on a low limb. He had been right. He did not have very long to wait.

Like a pack of bloodhounds hot on the scent of a bear, the warriors materialized out of the undergrowth. They loped along in single file, the warrior in the lead with his nose and eyes to the ground, reading the sign.

Fargo thought of all the people who had gone missing, of all the lives lost, the homes and lodges thrown into mourning and turmoil. He thought of *how* the victims had died, of how loathsome it would be to be swallowed alive, of the terror they must have felt, and he pressed his cheek to the Henry and put a slug through the lead warrior's sternum.

At the *crack*, the rest of the warriors scattered.

Fargo whirled and ran. He was playing a deadly game of cat and mouse, only he was the mouse and there were fifteen cats left who were eager to end his life however they could.

The gun smoke pinpointed his position and the warriors quickly converged on the pine. But by then Fargo was eighty yards off in a clump of weeds. The choice of which warrior to shoot was made easy; one was issuing commands to the others, having them fan out. Fargo shot him through the temple.

Now there were fourteen.

Again Fargo whirled and sped into the brush. Angry whoops and yells warned him they were after him. They came on swiftly, hot for his blood, spread out in a long line. He dropped behind a hummock and squeezed off another shot.

This time the warriors didn't scatter. They didn't seek cover. Incensed, they howled in fury and bounded forward for the kill.

All Fargo had to do was stay ahead of them, but that proved harder than he anticipated. Several were fleet of foot, and soon the pad of their wooden sandals spurred him into reaching deep inside himself to tap into the reservoir of stamina that had served him in good stead on more than one occasion. His arms and legs pumping, he came to a cluster of boulders and plunged into a gap between two of the biggest.

With a start Fargo came to a stop. Closely spaced boulders prevented him from going farther. Backpedaling, he burst from the gap as two warriors leapt from the trees. Instantly, one hurled a lance, and the only thing that saved Fargo from being transfixed was that the warrior threw in haste. The lance passed harmlessly over his shoulder. He banged off a shot, dropping the man, then had to raise the Henry to block the sweep of the other warrior's war club.

As broad as a barrel and as strong as a bull, the man unleashed a flurry of blows that came close to battering Fargo to his knees. The Henry in his left hand, he drew his Colt and shot the man twice in the gut.

More crackling of brush and sibilant shouts fell on his ear as Fargo dashed around the boulders. The remaining warriors would be madder than ever. It was now a footrace to see if Fargo could reach the hills before they exacted their vengeance. He was sweating profusely and his legs ached. He would love to stop and rest, but he willed his limbs to move, move, move.

The warriors had spotted him. Strung out from fastest to slowest, they howled and screeched in fierce abandon.

Fargo's lungs began to ache. His temples were pounding and his feet felt leaden. His endurance was better than most, but even he had his limits. A stand of fir trees blotted out the sun and he raced into temporary shadow.

Past the firs were the hills. Fargo looked for Pendrake and the two Kwachenie but did not see them.

Wooden sandals smacked the earth with alarming loudness. The swiftest warrior was almost on top of him, his snake mask bobbing as he ran.

His chest a pit of torment, Fargo palmed the Colt. He would take as many with him as he could. Slowing, he turned, but the warrior was on him before he could fire, and a war ax swished past his ear. The handle caught him across the shoulder with enough force to stagger him. The warrior slashed at his throat, and he jerked back and fired. He was not consciously aiming, he simply pointed the Colt.

The slug cored the warrior's forehead, and the top of his head spouted in a geyser of hair, bone and gore.

Spinning, Fargo sprinted for the hills. When next he looked back, he was surprised to find that the warriors had stopped and were huddled over the body of the last one he slew. Soon he was sufficiently far ahead that he felt safe slowing to a jog. His legs hurt abominably and his chest was a welter of pain, but he made it to the bottom of the first hill and wearily jogged up the virtually treeless slope.

Three figures rose to greet him at the top. Captain Pendrake clapped him on the arm and said, "Well done. But you sure look like hell."

Fargo doubled over and placed his hands on his knees. He needed to catch his breath. Mikahwon smiled and he repaid the favor. Her father was scouring the countryside below.

"They are nowhere to be seen. They must be up to something. I do not believe the old ones will give up until we are dead."

Neither did Fargo. "They can't get at us here without us seeing them. Not in broad daylight, anyway."

"So you think they might wait until dark to attack?" Pendrake asked.

Fargo shrugged. "Who can say? But they know I can kill from a distance with my rifle, so they'll want to get in close." He sucked in a deep breath. "We're just lucky they don't have bows."

"You should rest," Mikahwon said, and taking his hand, drew him to a flat spot. "Here is good. We will keep watch."

"Thanks," Fargo said. He did not mind admitting he was tuckered out. Plopping onto his back, he closed his eyes and waited for his blood to stop racing and his breathing to return to normal.

Pendrake knelt beside him. "What do you think our chances are?"

"Better than before," Fargo said. He had reduced the odds but they were still almost three to one.

"I'd like to borrow one of your guns when they come at us next. They took mine at the village."

Fargo slid the Colt from his holster, reloaded it, and handed it over. "Make every shot count."

"I will. I promise." Pendrake patted it, then tucked it under his belt. "What next? Surely you don't intend to stay here?"

"Why not?" Fargo rejoined. "Can you think of a better spot?"

"But there isn't any water and we don't have any food. When night falls they can sneak up and slit our throats."

Talokma had been listening. Coming over, he said, "We need weapons for when they do. I will take my daughter into the trees to the south and make lances and clubs."

"Too risky," Fargo said. The warriors were bound to surround the hill to prevent them from getting away, if they hadn't already.

"Mikahwon needs weapons," Talokma insisted, "and I only have this one lance. Without more it will be easy for them to slay us."

The chief had another good point but Fargo was still reluctant. "Don't go far and yell if they jump you." He slid the Arkansas Toothpick from its sheath. "Use this to trim and sharpen the limbs."

"We will not be long," Talokma promised, and with his daughter beside him, he sprinted down the hill.

"Keep an eye on them," Fargo directed Pendrake, then placed his right forearm over his eyes and rested until he felt like his old self. When he sat up, an hour had gone by, judging by the sun.

Pendrake was at the south slope, watching.

"How are they doing?" Fargo asked.

"Beats me. I haven't seen them since they went into the woods."

"I told them to say close." Fargo squatted to wait. The minutes dragged by and the only signs of life were a pair of jays.

Out of the blue, Pendrake asked, "Do you ever wonder why some Indians like whites and some want to kill us?"

"The ones who like us don't know us that well," Fargo joked, but it did not spark so much as a grin.

"I'm serious. Why do you suppose some Indians hate us so much?"

"Because we take their land. Because we force them on reservations. Because we make them give up their way of life and live like us. You know all that as well as I do."

"But you make it sound like we're the ones in the wrong. Look at the Island Devils. They hate us and kill us for no other reason than we're white."

"They do the same thing to other Indians." Fargo did not see what Pendrake was leading up to.

"I'd like to take a few of them with me before I cash in my chips. It would be fitting."

"If you say so," Fargo said. In a crouch he started down the hill. "Stay put. Talokma and Mikahwon have been gone too long. I'm going to check on them."

"Be careful. There's no telling where those savages got to."

Fargo wondered if he was referring to the Snake People or the Kwachenie. Flattening, he crawled the rest of the way. Talokma and Mikahwon wouldn't go that far; Talokma was no fool. Yet try as he might, Fargo couldn't locate them.

An awful worry came over him. Fargo rose partway and zigzagged into the pines. Halting, he braced for a rush of sandaled feet but none came. Nearby were saplings that could be fashioned into lances, and it was toward them that he slowly crept.

A moccasin print told Fargo he had guessed right. Several thin saplings had been cut down and trimmed. But the father and daughter were nowhere around. Fargo roved in a small circle, searching for more sign, and had his worst dread realized.

Four Island Devils had snuck up on Talokma and Mikahwon and jumped them when their backs were turned. Flattened weeds, torn grass and drops of blood testified to the ferocity of the struggle the pair put up, but they had been overpowered and dragged off.

Fargo was puzzled as to why the chief or his daughter hadn't cried out for help. Maybe because it would have brought Pendrake and him on the run, straight into an ambush.

Scowling, Fargo broke into a run. The warriors had not made any effort to hide their tracks, which might be a trick in itself. Several times he stopped to study the lay of the land, and that was what he was doing when the north woods were pierced by a scream.

27

Fargo bounded forward before the scream died. It had to be Mikahwon. Since she had proven her courage back on the island, it would take a lot to make a strong woman like her give rein to fear. It would take something terrible. Something that would wrench her emotions to the breaking point.

He came to a dry wash and leaped to the bottom and up the other side. The scream was repeated, much closer, and he checked the next stretch of woods before committing himself. He almost missed spotting a knot of figures in among a group of pines.

Fargo crabbed on his hands and knees until he could see them better. Mikahwon was there, held firm in the grip of a husky warrior wearing wooden scales and a black snake mask. She was kicking and clawing and trying to break free, but he was unfazed. Tears streamed down her cheeks as she called out her father's name.

Talokma was on his knees. Two warriors had him by the arms and would not let him rise. A fourth stood in front of him holding a knife that dripped scarlet in one hand and one of Talokma's fingers in the other. Chortling, he wagged it in front of Talokma's face and traced a blood circle on Talokma's cheek. Another finger—or was it a thumb?—lay on the ground.

Fargo circled for a better shot at the warrior with the knife. His stomach churned when he saw Talokma's face. The chief's nose had been cut off and both cheeks slit down the middle. One eye was bleeding and the other was missing the eyelid.

The warriors chattered in their sibilant tongue and laughed at their grisly handiwork.

Talokma did not utter a sound. He held his head high and glared at his captors. When the warrior torturing him suddenly grabbed him by the hair and sliced off part of his scalp, he grit his teeth and did not give them the perverse satisfaction of hearing him cry out.

Fargo cursed himself for waiting too long. He shot the warrior holding the knife in the head, shifted and aimed at the warrior holding Mikahwon. But quick as thought the man spun her around and held her in front of him as a living shield. Fargo dared not fire for fear of hitting her.

The shot had galvanized Talokma into wresting an arm free and striking the warrior on the left in the groin. The man crumpled, and Talokma turned on the other one just as the warrior was about to cleave his skull with a war ax. Locked together, they grappled for possession.

Fargo trained the Henry on the man the chief was fighting, but he could not get a good shot. Thwarted twice now, he saw Mikahwon jab the warrior holding her in the face but his mask protected him.

The warrior started backing off, his hand locked on the back of her neck.

Fargo shot him in the foot.

Blood spurted from the stumps of two toes and a howl rose from the warrior's throat. Forgetting himself, he let go of Mikahwon and hopped toward a tree.

All Fargo had to do was feed in another cartridge and fire. But just as he did, the warrior tripped, and the slug intended for his skull merely clipped his hair. In a mad scramble the warrior reached the trunk and darted behind it.

Mikahwon sprang to her father's aid. Talokma had been knocked to the ground, and the warrior he had been grappling with turned on her and raised his ax.

Fargo was a shade faster. The Henry boomed and a hole blossomed in the warrior's side. The warrior teetered, pressed his hand to his ribs and spun toward Fargo. Animated by hate, he launched himself through the air. Fargo had his sights on the man's chest, but suddenly Talokma heaved to his feet directly between them. The Kwachenie chief had laid claim to a knife belonging to a dead warrior and buried it to the hilt in his foe. That should have ended it. But in a display of raw animal will, the warrior swung his war ax in a flashing arc that ended splitting Talokma's skull from the crown to the bridge of the nose.

Mikahwon wailed and caught her father as he fell.

The warrior who had struck the fatal blow was dead on his feet, the hilt of the knife sticking from his abdomen. He melted without a sound and quivered a few times.

Fargo ran to the tree the surviving warrior had ducked behind, but the man wasn't there. He was tempted to go after him, but Mikahwon was clasping her father to her bosom and venting her grief in loud, racking sobs. The other warriors had to be around somewhere, and she was in no shape to defend herself. Placing his hand on her shoulder, he said her name several times, but she was sobbing too loud to hear him.

"Mikahwon!" Fargo repeated sternly to jar her out of her misery. "We can't stay here. There are still seven of them left."

"My father!" she cried. "They have killed my father!" Reverting to her own tongue, she lavished words and kisses on Talokma's bloody brow.

"Didn't you hear me?" Fargo shook her. "We must go." He pulled on her arm, but she stayed where she was.

"We take him with us." Mikahwon tried to stand, but the weight was too much for her. She fell back down, Talokma's head leaving a crimson smear on her dress.

"Please," Fargo said. His back was to the woods and his skin was prickling as if he had a heat rash.

Mikahwon looked up, her face wet with tears, blood on her chin. "Help me carry him."

It was loco, Fargo thought, but he did as she requested. Together they lifted him and headed for the hill where they had left Pendrake.

Fargo did not stop scanning the woods. He figured Pendrake would spot them and come down to help, but they came to the bottom of the hill and the young officer had not shown himself. "Edgar!" Fargo called up, and was mystified when he did not receive a reply.

Mikahwon had stopped crying and was moving in a stunned daze.

"Hurry," Fargo urged, and climbed faster. He had to do most of the carrying, plus watch their backs. They gained the summit and he stopped in consternation. Pendrake wasn't there. Setting Talokma down, he made a swift sweep of the hill.

"Where in the hell?" Fargo fumed. His second circuit turned up boot tracks leading down into the woods to the north.

At a loss to explain why Pendrake had left, Fargo hunkered and debated whether to go after him. Two facts convinced him not to. First, so long as they stayed on top of the hill, the warriors could not get at them without being seen. Second, he refused to leave Mikahwon alone until she came to her senses. In her emotional state she was a literal sitting duck.

"Pendrake!" Fargo yelled, and punched the grass in frustration.

Mikahwon was bent over her father, hugging him, her wide eyes fixed on the empty sky.

Ever so slowly the sun reached its zenith. Fargo patrolled the rim every few minutes, but the Snake People were lying low. Mikahwon never moved, never spoke, and he did not intrude on her sorrow.

It was pushing four in the afternoon and Fargo was on his hundredth check of the slopes when she coughed to clear her throat.

"I am sorry for behaving as I have, for being so weak. I loved him with all my heart."

"No need to apologize," Fargo said, glad he could count on her again. "For what it's worth, I respected him."

Mikahwon dabbed at her eyes with a blood-flecked sleeve. "I have been sitting here thinking of the wonderful times we shared. How he would carry me on his shoulder when I was little. How he traded a pile of mink furs once for some beads I wanted. How he always thought of my mother and me before he thought of himself."

"Do you want to bury him?" Fargo asked. They could do it there on top of the hill if one kept watch while the other dug.

"We will take him back with us. My people will wrap him in a blanket and burn him on a pyre as is our custom."

"Be sensible," Fargo cautioned. "By the time we get there his flesh will be rotting and the stink will be awful."

"I can endure it," Mikahwon declared. "I can endure anything after what he endured because of me."

Fargo bit off a sharp reply. Arguing was pointless. In her frame of mind she would never listen to reason.

Suddenly there was a fierce whoop from the bottom of the hill. Fargo turned as something came sailing over the crest. It took a few seconds for him to recognize the rolling object for what it was, and when he did, he ran to it and turned it over with his boot. "Damn."

It was Edgar Pendrake's head. Whatever they had used to saw it off had left ragged strips of skin hanging from the neck. Part of his shirt had been wadded in his mouth, and both eyes had been gouged out.

Mikahwon shuffled over. "The poor captain. How did they get hold of him? Why did he go down there?"

"Your guess is as good as mine," Fargo said. Had Pendrake seen a warrior and gone down the hill to kill him, only to be jumped and taken prisoner? Or had Pendrake finally indulged in his death wish and gone to be with his wife and daughter? If so, the captain had picked a particularly terrible way to die.

"We must end this," Mikahwon said. "The two of us. Me, to avenge my father. You, to avenge your friends."

"We'll wait until sunset," Fargo proposed. Under cover of darkness they could reach the trees unseen.

"I need the lance my father had, or a knife from one of the old ones."

Fargo caught hold of her wrist as she turned. "Don't even think it. You wouldn't make it back." He didn't trust her to listen, so for the next hour he kept a watchful eye on her. The whole time she sat by her father, her head hung low.

Then rustling brought Fargo to the northwest rim. The bushes were moving, far too loudly for it to be one of the Island Devils. He leveled the Henry anyway and had to lower it again when two does emerged. Sighing, he said over his shoulder to Mikahwon, "Another couple of hours and it will be dark enough." Only she wasn't there.

Fargo dashed to the south slope in time to see her dart into the forest. Her craving for revenge had made her careless. He bounded down the hill after her, and a lance streaked out of the foliage and missed him by a hair. His answering shot into the limbs of a tree resulted in a squawk and the crash of a body.

From two sides warriors rushed to intercept him. Fargo shot one in the heart and shifted to confront the second one, but he did not have the lever all the way back when the warrior's club smashed against the Henry's barrel and the rifle was torn from his grasp.

The warrior roared and leaped in close to deliver a death stroke, straight into Fargo's uppercut. Fargo clutched the club but the warrior held on and they spun first one way and then another, tugging and straining, until Fargo kicked the warrior in the knee. Pain weakened the warrior's hold, and with a powerful wrench Fargo had the club in his hands. The warrior clawed for a knife but did not quite have it out when Fargo swung, smashing the snake mask and the scarred face under it.

Casting the club down, Fargo reclaimed the Henry and sped after Mikahwon. Afraid of what he would find, he plowed through the underbrush on a beeline for where her father had been slain. He was still an arrow's flight off when he saw her on her back, slashing and stabbing as the rest of the warriors tried to pin her and do to her as they had done to her father.

Fargo shot the first one to look up. He was among them before they could set themselves. He shot another and drove the butt of the Henry into the face of third, then turned to help Mikahwon. She was locked in a death grip with the last of them, her knife buried in his chest and his knife buried in hers. Her eyes found Fargo's and she smiled as she died.

Fargo dropped onto a knee and felt for a heartbeat, but it was hopeless and he knew it. He swore as he had not sworn in ages: at her, at the sky, at fate, at life, at the unjustness of it all. Then he bowed his head and did not move.

Spreading shadows roused Fargo to life. He checked the Island Devils for life and shot those still breathing. Then he carried Mikahwon up the hill, and using a lance and a war club as digging implements, buried father and daughter side by side.

Finding Pendrake took a while. Pieces of him were scattered over a twenty yard area. Fargo collected all those he could find and buried them. In the process he found his Colt partly covered by leaves. He placed

Pendrake's hat on the mound of fresh earth and offered the only eulogy he could think of: "He was a good soldier, a good husband and a good father."

The hike to the beach took until dark. Fargo kindled a fire and spent the night staring into the flames.

At first light he pushed one of the red canoes into the sea, hopped into the stern and paddled toward the island. The craft took all his skill to handle alone. He could never manage the hundreds of miles to Victoria, so he brought it around to the north shore, and the canoe he had left there the day before.

Fargo was about to shove it into the water when he straightened and gazed toward the village. He had to know. He would always wonder if he did not go and see for himself. Cocking the Henry, he glided through the woods until he reached the lake.

Most of the lodges had been destroyed or heavily damaged by the fire. Bodies were everywhere, a feast for a cloud of vultures and a few gulls. Several canoes were still drawn up on the banks of the stream. But there was no sign of the old ones. The Snake People had abandoned their island. Their god was gone, their day was over.

The reign of terror had ended.

Fargo stared across the lake at the cliff and the cave. He considered going to see if the snake had returned, but decided not to press his luck.

He did not breathe easy until the island was lost in the haze. On the long journey south he had a lot to think about. About the nature of duty and devotion and the sacrifices people made. About the Ovaro, and how it would be a cold day in hell before he traded his saddle in for a canoe again. About a certain lovely woman and her rambunctious daughter, and how he would like to spend a couple of days in Seattle before heading for San Francisco and a week or two of whiskey and cards.

But most of all, how good it felt to be alive.

No other series has this much historical action!

THE TRAILSMAN

Available wherever books are sold or at
www.penguin.com

Signet Historical Fiction

Ralph Cotton

The Big Iron Series

Jurisdiction

0-451-20547-2

Young Arizona Ranger Sam Burrack has vowed to bring
down a posse of murderous outlaws—and save the
impressionable young boy they've befriended.

Vengeance Is a Bullet

0-451-20799-8

Arizona Ranger Sam Burrack must hunt down a lethal
killer whose mind is bent by revenge and won't stop killing
until the desert is piled high with the bodies of those
who wronged him.

Hell's Riders

0-451-21186-3

While escorting a prisoner to the county seat, Arizona Ranger
Sam Burrack comes across the victims of a scalp-hunting
party. Once he learns that the brutal outlaws have
kidnapped a young girl, he joins the local sheriff in the
pursuit—dragging along his reluctant captive.

**Available wherever books are sold or at
www.penguin.com**

"A writer in the tradition of Louis L'Amour and
Zane Grey!" —*Huntsville Times*

National Bestselling Author

RALPH COMPTON

Available wherever books are sold or at
www.penguin.com

S543